Y0-BDI-269

INDIAN RIVER CO. MAIN LIBRARY
3 2901 00565 0792

The Flying Hound

Joseph Rooney

The Flying Hound

A Novel

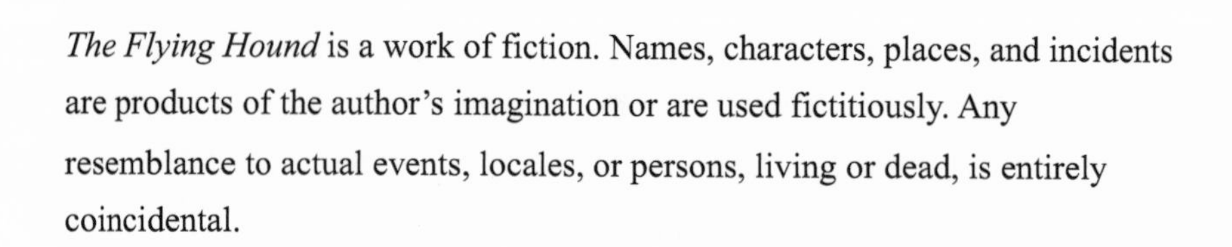
The Flying Hound is a work of fiction. Names, characters, places, and incidents are products of the author's imagination or are used fictitiously. Any resemblance to actual events, locales, or persons, living or dead, is entirely coincidental.

Published in the United States.

ISBN 978-1469981567

Printed in the United States of America
www.joerooneybooks.com
www.facebook.com/theflyinghound

For Kelly, you're my inspiration.
And to my kids, Joe, Lawrence and Melissa, remember to always follow your dreams.

"Uno, dos, tres... catorce"

-U2

Chapter 1

John was in his basement office looking intently at his computer screen. He was running the Flying Hound's numbers like he did every morning. Having been a decent high school athlete and avid sports fan, John reviewed each meal period's performance like a sports score. How did we do compared to yesterday, to last week, last month, or even last year? It was all about competition and performance. If business was up, or down, the theories would start just like in sports when a heavily favored team is upset. It's the rain. Was it the cold? Maybe a new restaurant that opened across town, or crime, or the economy and on and on. There are always reasons or theories on why business may be up or down or in any way different, and to John, figuring out what affects his business is an important exercise. Unfortunately, there isn't always a real explanation.

A knock on his doorframe jolted him from his analysis. He didn't even hear Mack walking down the creaky old steps that led to his office/storage room/liquor room/keg room/basement.

"What are you doing in these parts?" John asked, happy to see his father.

"Just stopped by. I thought you might be interested in a new project I heard about."

He knew instantly that they were heading into well-charted waters. Every so often, Mack would stop in, or call, to tell him about some new opportunity that would be perfect for John. His dad didn't see much of a future running an old saloon. Mack was against his own father's plan to leave John the bar that had been in the family since 1919. He had run the place himself once upon a time, but quickly grew restless and turned the place back to his dad in order to pursue his ambitions in the legal profession.

Mack, an affable pleasant man with a wry sense of humor thought of the bar as a hobby but not much more. His goal was to move his son into a more professional entity in the hospitality industry. John, on the other hand, was surer than ever that his future belonged in the Hound. His summer in Ireland a few years ago cemented that conviction. There was little Mack could do to change his son's mind.

"John, you have to know that this is a tricky business. If this place fails, you have nothing to fall back on. We sent you to Cornell to get your degree in this field but so far you've only applied it here. You could do so much more. Hire a manager to run the Hound and get a real job before you're too old to be considered. I have a good connection with the group that's opening the new Hilton downtown. They need a professional restaurant manager and I think you would be great for the job. I mean, the Hilton for Christ's sake. Great training, benefits…" Mack trailed off sensing John was tuning out. Mack was a maverick himself and knew deep down that his son had inherited his independent nature.

"Look Dad, I'm committed to this place. I've been here for three years now, and I know we're not going out of business. I promised Old Joe I would look after the bar and that's what I intend to do." Mack's father, Old Joe, inherited the Hound from his own father and made it his life's work.

"You can keep your promise, just do it through a manager. We can hire someone to work for you while you get your career going. I am telling you, if you are still here at forty, your Cornell degree will be glorified artwork on your wall."

Chapter 2

Mack was a good father. He wanted what was best for his three kids, but often gave advice that contradicted his own path to financial success. He was a self-made man much like his father and grandfather. None of the Frawley men were traditional in their career choices. John's great-grandfather, Tom, emigrated from Ireland when he was twelve. By the time he was sixteen, he amassed a small fortune "running numbers" in the old neighborhood. He bought his first saloon not far from the Flying Hound when he was nineteen while continuing his "side" business of book making. Eventually, he married and had two daughters and one son, Joe. Old Joe, as most people knew him, inherited Tom's pride and joy, the Flying Hound. Tom built this bar himself with the money he made as a bookie. By the time Joe took over, that part of the business had ceased while the bar thrived. Over the years, Old Joe made many improvements. He added eight guest rooms out of the living quarters above the bar and started taking overnight guests. Old Joe also put in the first kitchen and established the Hound as a good place for basic home-style food.

Joe's wife, Sheilagh, added her own touches to the place adding fancy fixtures to the bar and putting Victorian furnishings in the public areas. Together, they transformed Tom's Flying Hound, a rustic local watering hole, into a real show bar that people would come for miles to see. Old Joe and Sheilagh felt that a saloon was the average man's country club; a place where you could enjoy a beautiful environment, yet still be yourself. To their credit, the bar was now much the same as when they built it. John has made it his business to keep the place as original as possible. While some needed improvements had been made, if Old Joe and Sheilagh walked into the place today, they would feel right at home.

Mack did not share his ancestor's enthusiasm for the bar business. Sure, he spent his childhood working every position in the place, but it never really grabbed hold of him. Thanks to his mother's insistence, Mack was the first Frawley to go to college. He graduated at the top of his class and went on to law school.

By the time he was thirty, Mack had his own very successful law firm and quickly became one of the pillars of the community, yet never turned into a stiff or snob. On the contrary, he is always characterized by the people who know him best as a regular guy. He's a drinker, although less as he gets older, smokes cigars, and socializes with guys he went to high school with. He does live in one of the biggest houses outside of town and drives expensive cars but he never lost touch with the common man. Perhaps growing up in a bar kept him grounded. At any rate, he, like his forefathers, found his success and would desperately like his youngest son to do the same.

Mack decided not to press John further on the issue of the future. Instead, he changed the subject. "Are you coming to the club for dinner on Sunday? Everyone is planning on being there."

John knew everyone meant his mother Mary, his older brother Mack Jr. and his wife Joanne, his younger sister Erin and her boyfriend Shane. John used to like these Sunday get-togethers, but since lately he's had no one to bring, the dinners have become ponderous. "I don't know Dad, Sundays have really become busy. It's Clem's night off and I don't trust leaving the place entirely to Rose yet."

"Well what the hell did you hire her for if she can't cover one shift?"

"Look, I'll try to make it, but I can't come at 6. You people eat so early that I am hungry again by 9. Anyway, I need to spend a little time with Rose to make sure she is set for the night."

"Great, I'll tell your mother to make the reservation for 6:30."

"Make it 7" John insisted.

"Fine" his dad agreed and with a quick wave was back up the cellar steps.

John wasn't actually worried about Rose, his new recruit for floor manager and he also knew Clem; his cranky chef from the mean streets of North Dublin, would come in to cover if he really needed him to. That wasn't really the point. The point was, the Hound was his passion and, despite his love for his family, he winced at the idea of being away from the place, even for one night.

Chapter 3

John was not looking at the figures from lunch anymore. His Dad's visit distracted him and had him thinking of a million different things. First he considered his Dad's opinion. Was he getting too old to go "corporate" and get a real job? What would it be like if he stayed put and ran the Hound for the rest of his life? John often ran through these scenarios. When he was alone, he felt confident that he was making the right decision by honoring his grandfather's wishes to run the bar, but whenever his father began to try to redirect him he would become unsure. Mack wasn't exactly manipulative with his kids, but he always had a great deal of influence. John has always respected his dad's opinion and like most sons, was anxious to win his approval. At the same time, he knew he was not like his dad or either of his siblings. He was always finding his own way and doing his own thing. John wasn't exactly a rebel, but he sure was an individual. He was also fairly confident, especially for a young man that had only graduated from college a few years prior. Still, Mack was his dad and carried a lot of influence.

John may have mulled over his dad's visit a while longer if not for a sudden and somewhat rude interruption.

"If you're not too busy playing video games or looking at porn, I could use a little help up here?" a voice with a heavy Irish accent hollered down the steps.

John smiled a little before responding. "Feck off Mick, fix your own problems." John joked as he got up to see what Clem needed.

Clem had been part of the Hound's staff since he moved here from Boston a little over three years ago. John hired Clem originally as a day barman and waiter, but eventually moved him into the kitchen for two good reasons. First, Clem was a gifted cook. He had a real feel for comfort food, which consistently made people happy. Second, Clem was opinionated, cantankerous, argumentative and generally surly and John felt the less exposure he had to the paying customers, the better. In all of his experience with the Irish, John had often commented that he had never met one with less of a sense of humor.

Clem spent his entire life working in the hotel and restaurant business in Ireland and, later, in the big cities in the Northeastern part of the U.S. It would be an understatement to call Clem old school. The term prehistoric might be a better description. John was not sure exactly how old Clem was but his emigration documents had him at 58. John thought they were shy by at least ten years. Of course, a regular diet of bourbon Presbyterians and pints of Guinness do have a tendency to age one a bit.

Interestingly, John and Clem hit it off from the beginning. John, an inherently friendly gregarious soul was the perfect foil for Clem. Clem's arrogance and bravado appealed to John for reasons that were hard to explain. Many other staff members and even some customers did not see why John put up with him but John knew that deep down, Clem was a good man and, more importantly, a good cook. After only a few months on the job, Clem became a fixture at the Hound and an integral part of its popularity. John was happy to have him on board and put up with his otherwise difficult demeanor.

Chapter 4

Old Joe encouraged all of his grandkids to work at the Hound as often as possible. As he did with his own son before them, Old Joe pushed Mack Jr., John, and even Erin to learn what hard work meant from an early age. All three grandkids did their time with Old Joe but only John showed interest beyond making pocket money in the summer. John worked every summer, spring break, winter break and any other time he could carve out at the Hound. Old Joe quickly made John his protégé and tried to teach him everything he knew about the business and, more importantly, about people. Old Joe knew people inside and out. He could tell if someone was genuinely bad or just a little misguided. He treated everyone he knew well and was extremely generous to his customers and staff.

Joe had a million sayings, but one of his favorites was not to mistake kindness for weakness. A good boss can be kind, generous, and approachable without being a soft touch. Most of Joe's contemporaries believed you must manage with an iron fist. Keep your staff scared and on their toes. Old Joe knew loyalty and mutual respect went much further than intimidation and threats.

John modeled himself after Old Joe. He saw first hand how his grandfather worked with people. He witnessed Old Joe's staff's unwavering loyalty. He also experienced the dedication Old Joe's customers had in good times and bad. John knew the formula of success and his aim was to follow closely in his grandfather's footsteps. Only John's summer in Ireland the year before he took over the Hound had any other significant influence on his managerial style and overall approach to his life.

After many summers and countless other vacations and school breaks working at the Hound, John had to break the news to his grandfather that he was going away to college. Old Joe was not exactly against college but he also believed if you had a calling and a good opportunity, college might not be necessary for success.

Of course, Mack Sr. was not as open minded on the subject. To him, college was the only option. If you did not go to college, your future would consist of digging ditches or shucking oysters.

John wanted to continue his education and was looking forward to the experience of living on his own away from home. His grades had always been good and his SAT scores gave him a lot of options. He also knew Old Joe was getting older and there was no one lined up as his successor. Joe was mostly counting on John, and John always saw the Flying Hound as his calling.

After considering his college options and choice of majors, John had settled on Cornell, and their extremely prestigious Hospitality Management program. John was tempted to go to the West Coast or maybe Florida, but he knew that Cornell was close enough that he could make it home for the weekends and holidays to help his grandfather at the Hound. After all, it wasn't like Cornell was a second string institution. Surely, Old Joe would understand.

"Joe" John started, always calling his grandfather by his first name. "I am sure by now you know that I want to make the bar business my profession. I think I will have more to offer if I get a proper education in restaurant management."

Old Joe didn't say anything at first. John could tell he was pondering what he was just told. John also knew Old Joe might be concerned about waiting four years for his successor to return. There was also the chance that college would change John and he may decide to go in another direction.

Joe did not take long to respond. "I'll be waiting." Joe said without looking directly at John.

John decided to keep his response just as limited. "I'll be back."

Chapter 5

College did change John. It might be impossible to spend four years studying everything from microeconomics to creative writing and not be changed. John was exposed to many different people from many different backgrounds. Opinions, attitudes, perspectives, biases, prejudices, and points of view ran the gamut. John was intrigued and very engaged. He grew as a person and evolved as an individual. However, John never stopped thinking about the Hound or his old grandfather. He looked forward to coming home on the weekends and for various breaks. After all, Lawrenceville, Pennsylvania was only a couple hours from Cornell so John managed to get home more often that many of his classmates. He always headed straight for the bar even before going home to his parents. Old Joe took comfort in this and began to believe that destiny would keep John on course.

On Friday afternoon in the spring semester of his junior year, John noticed a booth outside of the cafeteria promoting various summer abroad programs. He was intrigued by the idea of spending time studying overseas and thought the summer prior to his senior year was the right time. Many of his friends had already done a semester or summer in England, Italy, France, Australia or some other wonderful place.

John decided, not surprisingly, to do a summer in Ireland. The pretty co-ed in the information booth told him about a program based in Dublin that she heard was "kick-ass." It consisted of three intensive courses, each two-weeks long. John found himself interested. Perhaps it was a combination of her flirty attitude and delivery along with John's affinity for Ireland based on his heritage but, whatever it was, he was sold on the idea. He knew Old Joe would be sorry to not have him for the first six weeks of the summer but he knew this was an opportunity that would not likely present itself again.

Five minutes after talking to Miss "kick-ass," John was in the Semester Abroad office filling in forms and signing up for classes. He considered asking his parent's permission before going through the motions but convinced himself that his parents and, in particular, his father, would only be too delighted to approve this arrangement. He also knew that one of the three classes would appeal to Mack Sr. above all others, the Irish Hospitality Tour, HRM 300. This class would take him all over Ireland on an investigative tour of its hospitality industry. What an awesome experience it would be, he thought.

A week after the spring semester ended, John was getting ready for his trip. He booked his tickets through the Semester Abroad office at the school and was scheduled to leave from Newark on Continental Airlines at 7:48 the next evening. John's mom and dad were peppering him with advice and giving him the names and addresses of distant cousins who he must look up while back in the "old sod."

John's mom cautioned him to "keep your money in your front pockets and only carry as much as you need at one time", Mack Sr. warned him about getting trapped by "street-walkers who might take advantage of a kid who is brand-new". John's mom scoffed at Mack Sr.'s advice reminding him that John was going to Dublin, not military leave in some German backwater.

John had not been overseas before and was only out of the country briefly when he went to Cancun during his sophomore year spring break. Something told him there would be few similarities between Cancun and Dublin. He patiently took in all of his parent's insights and advice but had some trouble focusing. The excitement of the coming experience was a bit overwhelming and all he could think about was getting on the plane and hitting the road.

John had his bags packed, filled with more clothes than he could possibly need for a six week trip thanks in large part to his mom. He kept his tickets and passport in a new travel wallet his mother picked up for him at Brookstone's in the mall. He had his class schedule, the instructions to follow upon his arrival, his student ID and 50 euro his dad gave him to have "a little pocket money when he got there." Everything was set, so he decided to make a quick visit to the Hound.

Chapter 6

Old Joe was behind the bar with Patrick, his lead barman. It was a Sunday night and it was fairly slow. Old Joe perked up when John came in and quickly waved him down to the end of the bar by the service station.

Are you ready for your trip?" Joe started. "Do you need a little cash?" John shook his head. "I'm fine. I am 21 and have hardly been anywhere. I can't wait to get there and experience for myself what I've heard about my whole life." John's enthusiasm was beginning to surge.

"Just remember," Joe cautioned, "those old stories your dad and I filled your head with are just that, stories. Ireland today is not what it was when my dad emigrated here a century ago. Best to go with an open mind. Keep you eyes open and your mouth shut, at least at first."

John nodded and took in the advice. It was not his style to be an ugly American anyway but the point was well taken.

John was about to say his goodbyes and head home to bed when Patrick stopped him. "You can't leave without at least toasting the homeland."

John glanced at Joe who nodded his approval. John was legal to drink but never liked drinking too much in the Hound. He always felt it was more prudent to party somewhere else. Too many things could go wrong when drinking where you work. All that being said, John also knew that when you run a bar, it is bad form and even rude to turn down a drink from a guest. In this case, his barman made it clear he was expected to have one for the road.

Pat put a shot glass on the bar and reached behind him for a bottle of Power's Irish whiskey. Pat was a couple of years older the John and had traveled extensively. He was a perfect lead bartender; he was very responsible, friendly, and full of shit. He could talk with anyone about anything and had enough experience to back it up. He graduated from a state university and hit the road for two years. He even spent six months in Ireland and gave John the names of a few pubs to visit. One of the best things about Pat was his lack of traditional ambition, or, in other words, his happiness did not depend on entering upper management or it's responsibilities. He was happy where he was and did his job well.

The shot burned as it went down. John was mostly a beer guy and really shied away from shots. However, under Pat's scrutiny, there was no escape. The burn turned into a warm glow as it settled in John's gut giving him a comfortable satisfied feeling. Before he could enjoy the buzz for too long, another shot was being poured. This time, it was courtesy of Billy Mullins. Billy had been a regular at the Hound for years and once visited Ireland in the 70's on a bus tour.

"The food sucks so enjoy their whiskey." Bill shouted from across the bar. This shot went down a little easier.

Joe had seen enough and shook John's hand and wished him luck. "Remember to do a little research while you are there. Check out the famous pubs and see what makes them special. Oh, and bring back a fine Irish lassie for yourself." Joe chuckled as he put on his coat and shuffled out the door. Just before he stepped outside onto Frankford Avenue, Lawrenceville's main street, Old Joe called back to John. "Don't forget to come back. I hear Ireland can be enchanting. I can't afford to lose you to the "old sod." Old Joe's voice was light but John sensed he was, at some level, serious and maybe even a little desperate.

John felt the words as much as he heard them and knew what Old Joe really meant. It was as if he wanted to say "don't let me down; you are the future of the Hound."

An hour or so later, things were beginning to get out of hand. A third shot was being hoisted. This time it was Brian Flannigan raising the glass. Brian was a retired New York cop who was also a daily regular at the Hound. He retired to the "country" after forty years in the big city and enjoyed a quieter life out here even if it was not exactly the country.

The shots were now suddenly smooth and going down easy. In the back of his head, John knew this was not going to end well unless he could find an escape. Eventually, John did escape. It was 2 AM and Pat was giving last call. John had six shots in total and was now sitting glossy eyed at the end of the bar. Pat would close up and drop John at home. Even through his clouded mind, John knew tomorrow would be rough.

Chapter 7

One saving grace for John was his flight to Dublin was in the evening. Most flights to Ireland flew overnight leaving you at your destination early the next morning. John was extremely grateful for the opportunity to sleep the prior night's whiskey fest off in the morning and was even more grateful that he should be able to sleep for the six hours across the Atlantic.

"Are you getting up soon dear?" John's mother called from the bottom of the stairs. "Breakfast is on the table and getting cold. We still need to stop by the drug store for your toiletries before going to the airport."

John tried to respond but his brain was not fully functioning just yet. An hour later, his mom was up in his room.

"What is that stink?" she said covering her nose and mouth with her hand with only a slight exaggeration. "What in God's name happened to you?" She opened the blinds letting the sun hit John right between the eyes. It felt like someone was shooting lasers into his head.

"A proper send off I think they called it. My head is splitting." John complained.

"Well, it serves you right." his mom said giving him a small scolding. "Now get up so you can finish packing. We can't be late for an international flight. They want you at the airport at least two hours before the flight. Your dad and I want you there even earlier in case there is a problem." John wondered what kind of problem his parents might be expecting. Maybe his name would pop up on the FBI Watch -List and he would be held for questioning. He smiled in a smart-ass kind of way at the thought. He knew his parents were a little old fashioned and a trip overseas was still a big thing for them. Since he himself had never been overseas, or even on a plane for more than a couple of hours, his parents' concerns were understandable.

After a minute or two of attempting to focus his bleary eyes, John attempted to get to his feet. His mother left him to wallow in his own misery but he knew she would be back soon if she thought he went back into the rack. His first attempt to stand resulted in a spinning head, causing him to quickly sit back down.

"Holy shit. I will never make it. Maybe I can postpone this until tomorrow." he thought to himself. In reality, John knew he had to suck it up and work through the hangover. Even though he was not a huge drinker, he had dealt with severe hangovers before. He was sure he would be fine by the time his plane took off.

It was noon by the time John made it downstairs. A hot shower got him back to feeling somewhat human. Now a cup of coffee and a little bite to eat would set him straight. At least, that's what he hoped.

In the kitchen, Mack Sr. was drinking what was probably his third or fourth cup of the day. One look at his son and he knew the reason for his "lie-in."

"You look like hell. Are you trying to get into drinking shape for the Irish?" John made no attempt to respond. Instead, he poured the coffee and tried not to sweat. His eyes were still a little out of focus so his attempt to read the paper was aborted. He opted for a toasted onion bagel with butter and cream cheese. Surely this would help to cure his ills. Mack Sr. tried again. “Do you have everything? Check to see if you have your passport, wallet, student documents and directions to the school. I don’t want to get to Newark and realize something is missing.” Mack Sr. thought a pragmatic conversation would be more appreciated than any attempt to preach or lecture on the evils of booze. He knew his kids would have to make their own decisions about these things. He also knew there were so many things to worry about these days that at some point you just had to hope for the best.

“I have everything.” John assured his dad and his mom who had now joined them in the kitchen. “My bags are at the bottom of the steps and I have all my documents in my travel wallet. Now I just need a quick trip to the drug store and a final stop at the Hound.”

“Don’t you think you’ve had enough of the Hound for now?” John’s mom protested.

“I just want to say goodbye to Old Joe before I go.”

John and his parents hit the road at 3 PM. Newark was only a two-hour drive so they should be at the airport by 5. This would give John almost three hours until the flight. While John would usually protest the idea of being so early, he was actually looking forward to being alone in the airport where he could relax.

John ran into the Hound to see Joe. His dad came with him while his mother stayed in the car. Miriam liked the bar well enough, but she preferred the country club for her dining and socializing. She was happy enough to wait in the car reading the “Martha Stewart Living” magazine she bought for the ride.

Inside, Joe was sitting at one of the tables talking to Bob Gleason, his account sales manager for Sysco Food Service. Bob’s been in charge of the account at the Hound for years and always enjoyed stopping in to talk to Joe. When he saw John and Mack Sr. heading over he jumped to his feet and stuck his hand out to shake.

"I hear you're off to Ireland today. Try not to drink too much Guinness." he said laughing.

"I think he'll stick to tea for a while after last night's performance." Mack Sr. piped in.

"I heard you were a little tight last night." Old Joe said using one of his old fashioned terms.

"I am fresh as a daisy now. Can we please move on?" John said hoping to move the focus of the conversation off of him.

Pat was just getting in for the evening shift when John and his dad came in. He immediately reached for the Powers with a shit-eating grin on his face.

"Don't you dare!" John said putting his hand up for affect. "I am never drinking whiskey again."

Pat withdrew the offer or threat depending on your perspective. He asked John to bring him back a special bottle of Whiskey, which was not sold in the States, Paddy's. John wrote it down and promised to pick up the bottle but insisted he would not share any with him when he got back.

Old Joe and Bob wished John well. Joe pulled John aside and told him to forget about the Hound and enjoy himself. The bar would be here when he got back. He sounded more confident and less sentimental than last night, which went a long way to alleviating John's lingering sense of guilt.

"For now, just enjoy yourself and stay out of trouble."

They all said their goodbyes and headed out. Joe and Bob returned to their conversation and Pat got busy setting up the bar. John knew the Hound would keep going with or without him, for now anyway.

The drive from Lawrenceville to Newark was surprisingly quiet. John's mom read her magazine while Mack Sr. listened to

ESPN and local news radio. Every now and then, Mack Sr. would respond to a news story or some sports report with a snort or a quiet "Jesus."

John mostly looked out the window and wondered about Ireland. Occasionally, he drifted back to the Hound but mostly he thought of Ireland.

Mack Sr. and Miriam walked their son as far as security. It's been a long time since friends and family could actually escort loved ones to their departure gates and for this, John was secretly happy. He knew he would miss his parents and even though he loved and adored them, he wanted to get the journey started. His mom grabbed his shoulder and turned John towards her.

"Be good, John. Try to make it to mass on Sunday. Don't forget to look up your cousins." she said as tears welled up in her eyes.

Mack Sr. finally broke in. "Give the guy a break, Miriam. Of course he'll be good, after all, he is a Frawley."

Miriam looked at Mack Sr. with a "that's what worries me" look. Mack Sr. just laughed and slapped his son on the back. Mack Sr. was not much of a hugger but John knew this was his father's way to show affection.

"I'll be fine, don't worry. You won't even know I'm gone before you'll be back here to get me in six weeks." John said. Finally, he grabbed his hand luggage and turned to go up the little escalator leading to security and the "C" gates for most of the international gates leaving Newark. From the top of the escalator, John turned and gave a little wave. He could see his mom was now full on crying and thought he even detected a gleam in his old dad's eyes as well.

Chapter 8

John had made it through security without any trouble. His parents had already left since there was not much to do in the Newark airport on the other side of security. They offered to stay a while but needed little persuasion to head home when John told them he'd prefer to wait inside. They were anxious for him to be on time and John was anxious to have some time alone.

As he put his belt, shoes and watch back on following the near strip act now required when going through security, John looked at the flat panel video displays listing hundreds of arrivals and departures. He quickly looked at his tickets for the flight time so he could check the status on the departures board. Flight CO 179 was scheduled to leave Newark at 7:48 PM from gate C 112. John scanned the terminal map and found gate C 112 towards the end of a long concourse. It was now a little past 5 in the afternoon so he had plenty of time. He decided to go directly to the gate first, just to get his bearings and then find somewhere quiet to think.

Gate C 112 was just where the map indicated it would be. A few people who had also arrived early were waiting patiently for their departure. A flight going to Berlin was boarding at C110 adjacent to his gate. On the other side, Gate C109, a Boeing 757 was waiting to load travelers heading to Mexico City. This all felt a little exotic to John who suddenly realized how within reach the world really was. All you had to do was drive to Newark and you could board a plane to just about anywhere.

Now that he was comfortable knowing his gate's location, John headed to one of the many Hudson News outlets to pick up some reading material for the flight. He had a copy of James Patterson's Double Cross that his mother slipped into his bag but wanted some magazines and a newspaper to pass the time. Realizing that his head was still hurting, he wanted something light to read which would hopefully lead to a long nap on the flight over. The USA Today, Rolling Stone and Maxim felt about right for the job.

John was heading back to the gate when he noticed the Garden State Diner. Like most modern airports, Newark had many full service themed restaurants to go along with a wide array of mall-type shops. The Garden State Diner was a full-scale replica of the type of old diners found throughout much of this part of the country. John's hangover subsided enough for raging hunger to present itself. He had not eaten since he got through half of his bagel at noon. A diner looked like a good option to kill off the rest of his hangover.

With his bag from the newsstand and his carry-on luggage in tow, John found a spot at the counter and looked over the menu. Like most diners, the vast assortment of food offered was intimidating and impressive. John calculated the diner had five times the number of menu items available at the Flying Hound. He wondered how they could possibly handle so many items to prep and serve.

"What can I get you to drink?" a pretty Latin looking waitress asked.

John looked up and saw her nametag: Gabriella. John thought quickly and, on impulse, ordered a Miller Lite. He was not intending to drink before the flight but he felt odd ordering a Pepsi from this sexy Gabriella. The beer came and John ordered Buffalo wings and fries. He immediately regretted his entire order considering his lingering hangover and the prospect of a six-hour flight and a stomach full of fried food. But then again, maybe it would help him doze and he could arrive in Dublin a new man.

The beer was cold and went down surprisingly well. The remnants of his hangover were suddenly gone and for the first time since yesterday, John was excited for his trip. He began to think about being abroad for six weeks in a place he had heard about his entire life. He worried about the Hound but he spent even longer periods away when he was in school. He knew nothing big would change while he was away but as he neared graduation, he became more obsessed with the Hound. He knew that soon, he would take over the operation and became more protective of the place as that day neared. He had so many plans, a new menu, a spruced up interior, live music, and maybe even re-opening the guest rooms upstairs which had sat mostly unused since the 1970's.

All of these plans created an excitement in John that overshadowed most other aspects of his life. Even this trip to his ancestral homeland did not give John the same sense of anticipation and exhilaration as running the Hound did.

John got a little lost in the moment. The combination of cold beer, a dissipating hangover and the lovely Gabriella created in John an elevated mood that made time fly a little. Out of habit, John finally checked his watch.

"Shit, 7 o'clock already. They might be boarding." he said half out loud. He summoned pretty Gabriella and asked for his check. "Thanks. Keep the change." he said and quickly headed for the gate.

Much to John's shock and horror, the gate was empty except for one agent at the counter. "Has the plane already boarded?" he asked desperately.

"Which plane?" the agent asked without looking up.

"Dublin." he replied trying to convey his sense of urgency.

"Flight 179 to Dublin had a gate change. That flight is now leaving from gate C 79 on the other concourse. And, yes, they have boarded."

John was panicked. His parents would kill him if he missed a flight he was nearly three hours early for. He began to run scenarios in his head with all of the potential excuses he could come up with. Suddenly, the agent broke his trance.

"You better run, I'll call the gate to tell them you are on your way but they won't hold the door for you for long." John flew into action. He gathered his things and began running to the other concourse. He ran with great effort but he felt his progress was painfully slow. The wings, fries and beer were threatening a revolt. Sweat was pouring down his face. Every geriatric, woman with a stroller and kids, and cell phone talking business guy seemed to go out of their way to block him. It was as if there was an announcement to block John Frawley's progress at all cost. At some point he realized he left his bag from Hudson news but didn't entertain the idea of returning to the diner. Instead, he figured maybe Gabriella would enjoy reading the mags.

He got to C 79 as the agent was shutting the door. Thankfully, the agent spotted John and surmised this was the guy the other agent was calling about.

"You Frawley?" he asked.

"Yes." John replied gasping for air and resisting a growing urge to throw up.

"I need your boarding pass right away." the agent snarled.

Panic again gripped John. For a split second, he thought he left his travel wallet with the magazines in the diner. A quick check of his back pocket and the discovery of the wallet put his fears to rest. John fished out the boarding pass and handed the agent his ticket. The agent scanned the boarding pass and told him to hurry. John got to the jet way and was relieved when he saw the Boeing 757's door was still open.

The flight attendant looked at John's ticket: 38 B. All the way to the back she instructed. John was a novice at air travel. He did not ask about emergency exit rows or bulkhead seats. He did not try to check in online 24 hours ahead to find the best seat. These tricks of seasoned travelers were all but unknown to John. As he made his way back to near the end of the plane and settled into his middle seat in between a woman carrying a baby and an older Irish man, he could not help to wonder how he got stuck with such a shitty seat. His new travel companions gave John a quick scan as he was sweating profusely and breathing heavy. The lady with the baby gave him a "how in the hell did I get stuck next to you?" look even though she was probably expecting it to be directed at her initially. The old man kept his nose in his New York Times. John was just happy to be on the plane and even more happy that he didn't hurl in the jet way.

John relaxed and settled in as the plane climbed to its cruising altitude. The 757 was new and had all of the newest equipment including video screens playing movies and sitcoms. The head flight attendant came on the speaker to inform the coach passengers that they would be through the cabin with a drink and dinner service soon. She also reminded them that cocktails cost money and they should stay out of the first class toilets.

The flight passed without incident. The baby fell asleep soon after takeoff, and it didn't take long for the woman to follow. The older Irish man next to him said very little and once he finished his paper, mostly just looked at the back of the seat in front of him. This was all fine with John who enjoyed the silence and the time to think.

As always, his thoughts returned to the bar. He considered all of the changes he wanted to make but wanted to be careful not to ruin a good thing. If it ain't broke…. was all he could think sometimes.

Soon enough, John was asleep. He managed to sleep through the movie, The Vacation, and even the dinner service. When he did wake, he was stunned to see the start of the sunrise. It felt like late evening but here was the sun starting to show itself. The flight attendant was back on the public address system announcing the service of breakfast and the passing out of immigration cards.

Chapter 9

As the plane descended, John looked intently out the window. The lady with the baby blocked most of the view but John could see green fields and country roads. He thought that things looked very rural for being this close to Dublin but he figured it was the same way in many parts of the States. After passing through lower level clouds, John saw the plane was back out over water. He surmised it was the Irish Sea since they had already passed the Atlantic. A minute or so later, the plane made a hard right turn as it returned toward land. Within minutes, the plane landed in Dublin.

John officially arrived in Dublin at 6:35 AM. He was a little groggy and stiff but was energized by the sight of Ireland from his limited view from the plane. He waited a long time to exit because he was so far back in the plane. The wait was excruciating but he figured it would mean less time waiting for his bags.

Dublin airport was busy. It was Monday morning and business people clogged the coffee bars and duty free stalls. John passed along a glass hallway that separated new arrivals that had not cleared immigration and customs from those who were leaving or flying domestically. The line at passport control was long, but by the time John got to the front, the Irish passport agent waved him to his booth. John slid his passport and immigration card towards the clerk who asked in a rough Dublin accent what the nature of his visit was.

John replied he was studying at the American Institute in Dublin.

"How long you here fir?" came the next question but the combination of the thick accent and strange structure of the question confused John.

"What? I am sorry, what was the question?"

"How long you here fir? When d'ya leave back for the States?" the agent repeated.

"Six weeks." John stammered. The agent stamped his passport with unnecessary force and mumbled something about the schools in the States. John ignored the comment but couldn't help to wonder about the "friendly Irish" after his first impression in Dublin.

He got his bags and headed through customs and into the arrivals hall of Dublin's airport. Just behind the security rope, a tall man with a sport coat, tie and sweater was holding a sign: American Institute Students. John waved and the driver waved back.

"You here for the American Institute program abroad?" the guy with the sign asked.

"Yes, I'm John Frawley."

"Lovely, let me help you with your bags." replied the man whose name he would later learn was Dermot, the college's official greeter, driver, handyman, soccer coach and all around representative on student matters.

They walked across the street to the parking garage. Dermot was driving the school's minibus with the school's crest blazoned across the doors. Dermot opened the "boot" and helped John put his bags in the tiny minivan. John then headed for the right side of the van and pulled open the door. Confused, he stepped back and looked at Dermot.

"You driving?" Dermot said grinning like an idiot. Clearly, Dermot relishes this moment when "yanks" first arrive and always go to the wrong side of the car. John knew Ireland drove on the right side but instinct and habit are hard to break.

They left Dublin airport and headed into the city via the M1. For most of the ride, John flinched at the approaching cars because he had the feeling they were on the wrong side of the road. Fortunately for John, traffic came to a near standstill as Dublin commuters clogged the roads. Dermot cursed saying he was hoping to get in before the heavy traffic. These days, rush hour starts before 7 AM and goes until after 9 AM. If you are unfortunate enough to be on any of the roads going into Dublin between these times, you are likely to be sitting in traffic.

Once they got closer to the city, Dermot used his local knowledge of Dublin streets and took several shortcuts. Old Georgian squares with wonderful townhouses passed by John's gaze. The bustle of the city was now in full swing. John took it all in while Dermot gave an impromptu history lesson about the places they were passing. He also told John about places to shop, drink, send a letter, and most other topics that would normally be covered during a formal orientation. As they crossed the River Liffy, Dermot pointed up river toward Temple Bar.

"I'm sure you'll find Temple Bar soon enough but it's just up the way a bit. Be certain though, to stay on this side of the river until you get to know the city better. The North side is grand but some spots are a little dodgy."

John was surprised to hear anyplace in Ireland was dodgy but Dermot sounded serious in his advice.

Dermot drove up Westland Road away from the Liffey. Eventually, they came to the corner of Merrion Square, the location of The American Institute. Dermot pointed out the main administration buildings including 1 Merrion Square, which was the boyhood home of Oscar Wilde. They did not stop, however.

"We'll head straight for the residence hall so you can get settled and maybe have a rest before orientation."

John couldn't fathom taking a rest. Several people told him back home to try to sleep for a few hours when he arrived to ward off jet lag, but he was way too excited to think of following this advice.

Dermot pulled into an alley behind Merrion Way off of the square. A remote control opened an electric gate that led to a parking area behind the residence. The residence itself was a collection of inter-connected Georgian houses that were converted into a youth hostel. The college acquired the buildings just before Dublin real estate became insanely expensive. The hostel was easily converted into a dormitory and living space for students.

The residence was buzzing. It was 8:30 in the morning and students of all nationalities were making their way out of the building. John was immediately nervous that he was late for something.

"Dermot, am I supposed to be somewhere now?"

"Not at all." Dermot assured him. "There are several different programs on in the college in the summer. Most of these students are English language students. They are on an intensive English program. There is also a hospitality management certificate program on that caters to the Chinese market. Summer abroad students began arriving yesterday and today. Your orientation will be this afternoon. For now, let's get you your room so you can relax a while."

John already could see Dublin and maybe all of Ireland was not the same place his ancestors spoke of. Dublin was a modern international community that felt more like New York than Gloccamora.

Dermot helped John again with his gear. His room was on the third floor overlooking Merrion Road. The room was simple with two twin beds on opposite sides of the room. A washbasin and dresser rounded out the furnishings giving the room a feel of a seminary more than a dorm.

"Right." Dermot pronounced. "This is it then. Toilets and showers are at the end of the hall and the dining room is in the basement. You can still get a cooked breakfast if you're hungry. Lunch won't be on until noon. If you want to have a stroll around, stay close and don't get lost. Last year we lost a student for two days before she turned up in the Conrad. At least she got lost in posh surroundings."

John thanked Dermot and shook his hand.

"All the best," Dermot said as he left "back to the airport."

John shut his door and opened the window to the street. Dublin traffic was loud but not as loud as most cities in the US. He figured there just was not as much honking. He unpacked his bags and began to feel a burning in his eyes. He decided to lie on the bed for a minute to take it all in. Within minutes John was in a deep sleep. His booze laden sleep the night before combined with a restless doze on the plane gave way to a real slumber. He would sleep for four hours only to be woken by a light but persistent knocking at his door.

Chapter 10

"John. Are you all right there?" a soft voice began to penetrate John's subconscious. "May I come in John?"

The door opened slightly and the request was repeated.

"Can I come in please?"

Now John heard the words and was able to process the question. He popped up in the bed and looked around. He was in a deep sleep and woke very disorientated. He looked for clues and saw his luggage piled in the corner. A quick flashback played in his head to Dermot and his arrival at Dublin airport.

"Yea, Come in." was all he could muster.

A figure appeared in the doorway that got John's attention. Suddenly he was aware of his wild nap head hair and generally scruffy appearance. This realization is generally made when you're facing a beautiful woman for the first time and are literally caught with your pants down. "Oh. Sorry. Just give me a second." the door closed a little giving John the chance to pull on his clothes and find a baseball hat to cover his head.

"Come in. Sorry, I'm a little out of it." John apologized.

"No worries. I'm sure you are knackered from the trip." The voice was distinctly American but her words and speaking cadence was Irish.

"I'm Katy Welsh, the semester abroad student coordinator. I will be giving the orientation just after lunch at 2 o'clock in the student lounge. You need to try to be there or you'll miss out on important information."

Katy was young, maybe a couple of years older than John but with the presence of a much older person. She had auburn hair that fell below her shoulders and wore a white sweater with a brown pencil skirt. The sweater and skirt highlighted a near perfect body only to be outdone by her perfect face. Katy was a natural beauty and now had John's full and undivided attention.

"Of course I'll be there. Do I need to bring anything?"

"Just your good self." Katy replied with a stunning little smile. "Come down for lunch when you are ready. We'll meet across the hall from the dining room in the student lounge." She closed the door behind her.

John was intrigued. None of the administrators at Cornell looked like Katy Welsh.

Chapter 11

Katy Welsh came to Ireland to do her graduate work at Maynooth College, just outside of Dublin. She was raised in Columbus, Ohio and lived a typical upper-middle class life. Her parents brought her to Ireland a couple times as a child to visit family. Katy always loved Ireland and decided a two-year stint in graduate school would be perfect following her graduation from Dartmouth. She was a serious student who wanted to become a professor. She studied liberal arts with a specialization in early American literature. Her plan was to get her M.A. from Maynooth and try to get an instructor's position in a small liberal arts college in the States. She preferred New England to the mid-west but was realistic to know that any higher education job in the arts would be a blessing.

Two years at Maynooth proved not to be enough of Ireland for Katy. As graduation loomed, she began to look for ways to extend her stay. Dublin had become her home and she felt more comfortable here than anywhere back home. Liam, who she'd been seeing for most of her first two years in Dublin, was also motivation to stay longer. Liam would never consider moving to "the cultural wasteland" he considered the USA to be. He was a graduate assistant at Trinity College in the English department. He was, in his own mind, the next W.B. Yeats, even though he had yet to publish anything.

Liam was a product of Ireland's recent success and his snobbish behavior came with that territory. The Irish had long been Europe's poor and downtrodden. With the Celtic Tiger and Ireland's appeal in popular culture, Irish citizens now had a swagger and even arrogance. This is not to say everyone in Ireland took on this persona, but it was common in Ireland's more esteemed universities.

Katy had a friend who taught sociology for the American Institute. He told her the college was looking for a new student activities director after the last one went back to the States homesick after six months. It was not teaching literature, but it was a job in a college. It would keep her in Dublin for a while longer despite the objections of her parents.

Katy met with the Dean of Administration, Mary O'Neil. Mary was a South Dublin snob who may have been referred to by many Irish as a West-Brit. She recognized the college's commitment to American principals and educational styles but secretly thought of them as second rate compared to Ireland.

Mary met Katy over tea and cookies in her office. Katy was not nervous or intimidated having dealt a fair amount with the Irish elite in the past. Mary was professional in the interview and outwardly friendly, but had no real intention to hire Katy. She felt she had enough Americans to deal with already and wanted to fill the position with a capable Irish person. The interview ended with a promise to be in touch. As Mary walked Katy to the door, the president's office door had swung open. The president's assistant came rushing out followed by the school's American president, Dr. Timothy Adams.

"Good afternoon Dr. Adams." Mary said stiffly.

"Good day, Mary. Who do we have here?"

"Oh, this is Katy Welsh; she was in to apply for the student activities job." Dr. Adams shook Katy's hand.

"It's a pleasure to meet you Dr. Adams. I have heard many good things." Katy gushed.

Dr. Adams smiled broadly. Katy's unmistakable American accent was just what he wanted to hear. Unlike Mary, Dr. Adams wanted as many Americans on staff as possible.

"Come into my office for a moment if you can." President Adams said.

"Dr. Adams, you have an appointment with the Hungarian ambassador in five minutes." His assistant objected.

"Just for a minute." Dr. Adams insisted.

As promised, they emerged five minutes later. Katy was all smiles and Dr. Adams seemed equally pleased.

"Say hello to our new student activities director." Dr. Adams announced to everyone in the hall.

Mary smiled but did not appreciate being stepped over. Dr. Adams assistant mumbled "congratulations" and hurried the president towards the door. Katy thanked him and promised to do a good job. Dr. Adams waved and was suddenly out the door. Katy turned to Mary sensing her displeasure and offered no explanation.

All she could come up with was "Sorry."

Even though the job was not on the faculty, Katy took her role very seriously. She was well liked by the staff and faculty and even Mary came to appreciate her professionalism. She put together parties, outings, tours, orientations, housing, and a wide range of other endeavors. Because the college was small, she was expected to do more than the title might suggest. She even found herself in charge of classroom assignments and course schedules. Katy was happy to be able to stay in Dublin and actually enjoyed her job. She convinced herself and her parents that it was a good résumé builder.

Chapter 12

John had showered and changed his clothes before lunch and, more importantly, the orientation. He wanted to improve upon his first impression with Katy and took extra time to pick out an appropriate outfit. He denied to himself that Katy had caught his attention. He was in Ireland to study and learn to appreciate Ireland's culture. He was there to absorb his heritage and experience the wonders of the "old sod". Unfortunately, all he could think of at this point was Katy's ample breasts and that wonderful little smile.

After a quick sandwich, John found the student lounge where the meeting was to take place. He was a little early and the room had a mix of students from different programs in the college. Several Chinese students were watching reruns of Father Ted, an Irish sitcom, laughing hysterically at everything Dougal had to say. A couple of Irish guys were playing cards while a blond haired blue eyed California type girl read on the couch. John sat at the other end of the couch and waved but got no response. The beach blond gave him a quick look but quickly turned her attention back to her book. John could see she was reading a tour guide for

Dublin and wondered if she was in his group. If all of the women he would encounter looked like this girl and Katy, he thought he would enjoy the trip even more than he hoped.

Katy walked in. John immediately confirmed in his own mind that he had been right about her stunning good looks. In a way, he was hoping jet lag skewed his perception. He did not want a girlfriend or even someone to lust over. He wanted a true Irish experience without personal complications. He resolved to stay focused and remember he was here for the good of the Flying Hound.

"If you are not part of the summer abroad orientation, please move to the dining room or somewhere else for the next half hour." Katy announced to the group. A collective sigh was audible prompting Katy to apologize. She hated moving the students out of "their" lounge but knew there was no other place to hold the 27 students registered for the summer.

Slowly, the lounge emptied. Everyone was gone except John and Miss California. Katy called upstairs to find out where the rest of the group was.

"Dermot? Where are the rest of the Americans?"

"Most are in Murphy's next door and a couple are still in bed."

Katy rolled her eyes "For fuck sake." she said half under her breath. "Could you please go collect the group at the pub and I'll get the others out of bed."

At first, John was startled by Katy's use of the f-word. He would find out, however, that in Ireland, fuck might be the most common word you could hear. He could not recall anyone of authority use such strong language back in Cornell. Katy quickly headed for the door. As she walked out, she looked over to John and the California girl and said, "Stay put, I'll be right back."

Suddenly, it was just John and blonde.

"I take it you're American." John asked in an attempt to break the awkward silence.

"I'm from LA." she replied as if LA was its own country. John was pleased he guessed her home state but decided against further attempts to communicate.

Slowly, the other Americans arrived. Most of those in the pub had arrived the day before and were reasonably acclimated to the time change. They stopped in for a pint at the pub next to the residence hall taking advantage of the lack of drinking age. John was one of the older students and had already lost the novelty of being able to drink out in the open. The others that were roused out of bed arrived on a later flight than John and had not had the benefit of a long nap. John scanned the group wondering who he might become friends with. Collectively, he did not think any of them stood out.

The group settled in. John estimated about a fifty-fifty split of girls to guys. Most did not appear to know each other but some seemed to have become friendly.

Katy called the meeting to order and laid out the points to be covered. She discussed the fact that we were guests in this country and were expected to act accordingly. She noted that laws, rights, and the legal process were all different in Ireland and they should all be careful to stay out of trouble. She went on to discuss the currency, Euros, the two big papers, "The Times" and "The Independent", near by shopping (Spar and Centra) and a litany of other helpful tips. She put up a big map of the city and highlighted points of interest as well as areas to stay away from. John was still amazed Dublin had crime. His impression came from his older relatives, who remembered an Ireland united against one enemy, England. In reality, he figured, with prosperity came all of the vices.

Katy spent the better part of an hour outlining everything a young American first-timer might need to know to get by in Dublin. She reviewed the rules of the college as well as class schedules and planned activities. At the end, she took a few questions and wrapped things up.

"Remember, classes start tomorrow. Don't go out on the piss all night. Professors here take attendance seriously. Classes are on an intensive two-week format so missing one day is the equivalent of missing a week."

She knew most would ignore this warning and would be out on the town tonight. Hell, she would be out tonight herself.

Chapter 13

It was now 4:00 in the afternoon. John felt good and decided to give himself a tour of the city. He had the latest edition of Fodor's Guide to Ireland and outlined a list of places he wanted to visit in Dublin. It was getting late so he decided to pick off some of the closer sights first. This time of the year, it was light out until after 10 PM so he decided to walk up to Grafton Street, Dublin's premiere pedestrian shopping street, and tour Stephen's Green.

He walked out of the residence hall and onto Merrion Row. He was surprised by the sunshine, expecting Ireland to be chronically damp and rainy. As he headed up Merrion Row towards Merrion Square, he studied the faces of the people whom he passed. Certainly, Ireland and Dublin in particular had become more diverse over the past decade. However, John was still struck by the overwhelming majority of white faces. Growing up in the northeastern part of the US, John was used to seeing many races and colors, particularly in a big city. While Dublin had some cultural diversity, it was still far behind most of its European contemporaries.

Merrion Square looked like a well preserved Georgian square steeped in history, albeit English history. In the center of the square was a beautiful park once reserved for the exclusive use of Merrion Square residents. Now, since it's a beautiful sunny afternoon, the park is filled with young couples openly displaying the affection for one another, old people reading books or newspapers, and young professionals having a smoke break from one of the many converted houses on the square that have become offices. John took it all in. He was amazed at how clean and crisp everything looked. His preconceived image of Dublin aside from the rain was a drab, dull place shrouded in mist. Here, however, Dublin was bright, sunny and full of color.

John cut through the park making his way past the Merrion Hotel, one of Dublin's finest, and took a left onto Baggot Street by mistake heading away from Stephen's Green. As he realized his error, he stopped and turned around. A woman wrapped in what looked like blankets and scarves appeared in front of John sitting against a building. She was holding a baby who looked to be no more than a year old. The woman looked too old to be the baby's mother but it was hard to tell. John was a little startled by the sight but realized when she held out her little paper coffee cup that she was begging for money. John had read a little bit about the "travelers" and other folks that solicit hand outs on the streets of cities and towns alike. This, however, did not prepare him for the reality of being faced with mother and child on a posh street in Dublin.

John hurried by not making eye contact. He was a little ashamed of himself but was not sure what to do. He had no change and wasn't sure if he should giver her money even if he had it. Despite the sun and the beauty of the park and Georgian Dublin, this encounter brought John back to reality. Dublin, and Ireland in general was not Disneyland.

Once he got his bearings again, John found himself in front of one of Dublin's oldest and best-preserved Victorian pubs, Doheny and Nesbitt, one of barman Pat's highly recommended spots. After a very brief consideration of his options, John decided the best choice was to begin his pub research and put off his cultural tour until he had more time. He reasoned with himself that part of the reason he was even in Ireland was to learn why pubs are part of Ireland's heritage. He also wanted to see how he could bring back and apply this information to the Flying Hound. This is what John told himself but in reality, it was late in the afternoon on what had been a busy day and he was ready for a drink.

John pulled open the heavy wooden front door of the pub. His eyes needed a minute to adjust to the dim light of the pub after being in the bright sunshine. Immediately, John noticed a very familiar smell. This 150-year-old establishment smelled a lot like the 100 year old Flying Hound. Over a century of smoke, spilt beer, and human occupation had given the Hound and this pub a similar bouquet. The smell however, was where the similarities ended. Just inside the pub, along the front window was a little room with a door and a hatch to the bar. Two small tables with little backless stools furnished the little room known in Ireland as a snug. The bar ran the length of the front room but was partitioned in several places separating two or three bar stools per section. At the end of the bar was another little snug. There was a rail for drinks along the other side of the pub but no stools. The bar itself was dark polished wood well worn with time. The back bar was ornate with glass mirrors and display shelves for the bottles. The walls were rough plaster with a yellowish sheen that was a remnant of pre-smoking ban days. There were no televisions or music playing. In fact, there was no attempt at adding atmosphere at all, but Doheny and Nesbit did not need any added atmosphere. The place itself oozed all of the character needed.

The pub was fairly empty. One old man with a newspaper, "The Evening Herald", was sitting in the far snug. Two men in business suits sat at the bar discussing something to do with local politics. The lone barman was stocking bottled beer in the refrigerator behind the bar.

"So much for warm beer." John thought to himself. Another fallacy. John took a seat at the bar next to one of the partitions. The barman noticed John and stood up from the refrigerator.

"Are you alright there?"

John was confused by the question. "Yea, this seat is fine. Do you want me to move somewhere else?" John asked trying to accommodate.

The barman laughed realizing his Irish way of asking John if he wanted a drink often confused the "yanks."

"Can I get you a drink?" the barman asked and smiled at John as a way of being hospitable.

"Oh, yea, I'll try a Guinness. Thanks."

"Pint of Guinness." the barman said taking a tulip shaped pint glass from the stack of glasses under the taps. He placed the glass at an angle under the tap head and "pulled" the stout into the glass. When the pint was a little over half full the bartender stopped and set the glass down. The old man with the newspaper called for a Shandy, and John watched the bartender pour half a glass of beer and top it off with lemonade. John was confused again. Back home, it would be rude to stop making a drink for a customer to make a drink for someone else. He figured it must have something to do with being foreign. Maybe the Irish took care of their own first. He decided to let it go and not make a scene.

A few minutes passed and the barman came back to the Guinness. This time he filled the pint placing the glass flat on its bottom under the tap. He put it down in front of John on a beer mat or coaster.

"Now," the bartender announced as he put the glass down. "$4.50 please."

John took out his travel wallet and handed the bartender a $20. He put John's change on the bar in front of him. John, following bar protocol from home, grabbed the .50 and said; "Here ya go," reaching out to the bartender. The man behind the bar looked at John making him feel a little uneasy. Maybe it was not enough.

The bartender smiled, "Look mate, bartenders in Ireland are professionals and don't take tips. Save it for the next round." John was a little embarrassed and decided his best option was to observe the behavior of the locals and try to learn how things were done before making any assumptions.

The two businessmen called for another round "two more pints please" they said not specifying the brand. The barman began the same ritual as with John's Guinness. This time, no one interrupted him but he still stopped pouring about half way through the pint. After a minute or so, he came back and finished the job. The barman was not slighting John; this he realized was just the way to pull a proper pint of Guinness. He wondered if his regulars at the Hound would get it.

After two more pints, John decided he had better move on. It was now a little after 5 and too early to get loaded. He wanted to ask the barman about the pouring of Guinness and a few other things that struck him as strange as he sat there. After all, he was intimidated and a little embarrassed. He ran a busy bar and he served Guinness. So, he decided that his technique of learning by observing was a better option.

John wandered the streets for a couple of hours just enjoying the new scene. At one point, he realized he was hungry but was not clued in enough yet to know where to eat. There were plenty of options on and around Grafton Street but the decision was daunting. He eventually did what a lot of Americans do when they first get to a foreign city; he played it safe and went to McDonald's.

Chapter 14

The next morning John was up very early. Jet lag forced him to bed by 9:30 so, by 6 a.m. he was wide-awake. The bed opposite of his was still unoccupied. He was told after he applied that everyone would be assigned a roommate. Maybe his was just late and would arrive today.

He dressed and went to the dining hall for breakfast. The woman at the counter asked if he wanted a "full cooked breakfast" John hesitated but thought he'd give it a try, he wasn't sure what other options there were anyway.

He found a table near the back of the room. Only two other students were in for the early breakfast, and they seemed to be eating cold cereal and juice.

"I guess there were other options after all." he thought to himself.

The woman from the counter brought over a tray with his breakfast. Placing the plate down in front of him she asked,

"Tea or coffee?"

John, a little mesmerized by the giant breakfast in front of him blurted out "coffee please."

He stared down at two fried eggs, four breakfast sausages, two other sausage patties (which he later learned were called black and white pudding), two rashers, and a half broiled tomato. He was overwhelmed.

"Now" the counter woman announced setting down his coffee and beginning to leave. She turned back and pointed to a table against the wall. "Juice, milk, brown bread and toast are over there. Help yourself and enjoy your breaky."

John was just about done with his monster meal when another American that he remembered seeing yesterday came into the room. He was average size and about John's age. He wore jeans, a plain t-shirt and a Red Sox hat. His name was Tony Keller from North Adams, Massachusetts.

"Mind if I join you?".

"Not at all." John replied moving his chair over a little. "I'm John Frawley." he reached out to shake hands with Tony.

"Hey, I'm Tony Keller. You here for the summer program?"

"Yep. Just got in yesterday." John said.

"I've been here two days already. I can't eat another of those fuckin' breakfasts. I don't know how they do it. After last night, I'm sticking to toast." Tony moaned.

John remembered him coming in with the other pub revelers for the orientation. He figured he liked to party and judging from the look of him, he had been partying for a few days now.

"Classes start today, right?" Tony asked.

John was amazed, Tony had been here for two days, gone to the orientation, received all of the information in the application, and still was not sure if classes started.

"It all starts today." John replied. "Are you taking Irish Lit or International Relations?" "

I think Irish Lit. I can't really remember." Tony looked dazed.

John was amused and amazed.

"I am really just here for the cocktails and the babes. There is some real talent around here. My goal is to sample as much of it as I can get away with. In six weeks, I'll never see any of them again."

John just smiled and figured no reply was the safest way to proceed.

John got his books together and mentally prepared himself for two weeks of intensive Irish Lit. For the middle two weeks, John had signed up for a study tour around Ireland, followed by two weeks studying Principles of International Business. He was ready to get started but wished he had more time to acclimate to Dublin before getting right into his studies. Unfortunately, that wasn't in the plans.

Chapter 15

The first week of class flew by. Class started at 9 AM sharp and Dr. Sally was not the type to be lax on promptness or attendance. He taught this section to the semester abroad students each term and felt it his duty to get them "up to standard" quickly. Dr. Sally felt the US educational system coddled students too much and he was here to get them on track. His Oxford educated mind gave him an air of intellectualism that made up for the fact that he was not yet thirty. He quickly earned the respect of the students based on his knowledge of the subject and his strict classroom management. Teaching Yeats, Joyce, Wilde, Behan, and Swift to a bunch of red-eyed hung over and still jet-lagged yanks required a good system. Dr. Sally had perfected his system over the years and managed to get the most from his tired subjects.

John really enjoyed the class. He found the teaching style in Ireland less participatory than in the States, but he appreciated the traditional approach and style of Professor Sally. He wasn't sure his classmates were as enthusiastic; given that they regularly bitched about his strictness and the amount of work he piled on.

Out of all of the Americans studying abroad that summer, John gravitated to only three. Even at Cornell, John had a few close friends and had never in his life been a part of a big crowd. In Dublin, John's buds were Tony, whom he had breakfast with at the start of the term; Mike Mullen, from the University of Vermont, and his roommate at UVM, Jeff McInnis. All three shared some traits with John but were also quite unique in their own right. Tony led the party. He had tremendous energy and could get by on only a couple of hours of sleep. Any night the group promised to stay in for a "health night," Tony found a way to convince them a pint or two couldn't hurt. Mike was quieter than the rest. He liked to party but was less likely to lead the charge. He had a serious girlfriend back in Burlington so he was not as interested in chasing girls as the rest. Jeff was a serious athlete. He was on the hockey team at UVM and had a bit of the jock mentality, especially when it came to girls. He would talk to and hit on any girl anytime. For John and Mike, this worked out well since neither of them was too aggressive when trying to meet the ladies.

John and his group also spent time with another subset of Americans comprised of three of the girls. The two groups did not spend all of their time together but more often than not ended up doing shots together in one of their favorite pubs. Nancy Conty, the California girl from orientation, was their ringleader. She was from LA but no one could figure out where she went to school. She often ducked the question saying she was enrolled in the Open University of life. Like her male counterparts, she loved to party. Her surfer girl California looks appealed to the Irish lads who were not used to seeing tall blonds with a dark tan dressed in pink and wearing flip flops while drinking the boys under the table. They were more used to seeing dark haired pale Dublin girls dressed mostly in black. She knew how to use her looks, and while she never seemed to go home with any guy, she rarely paid for her own drinks.

The second week of class was coming to an end, and John's roommate never materialized. Something about a last minute change of plans. John didn't mind, though, since now he had a room all to himself.

Exams were coming up in a couple of days and most of the Americans were hunkering down to study. John was on his way to the library when he bumped into Mike coming out of the residence. Mike had just got back from a jog and was heading in to shower.

"Are you ready for the exam?" John asked as Mike caught his breath.

"Yea, I guess so. I'll be happy to get this over with. The next class should be a blast." Mike said referring to the study tour all four of them had signed up for. "I am really looking forward to seeing more of Ireland. Dublin's great but after a while, its just another city."

Rachel, one of the other girls in the group, appeared at the door of the residence. "Heading to the pub?" she asked with a sly smile in her cute southern draw.

"Fuck no; I'm trying not to puke as it is. Last night almost killed me and anyway, I've got to study a little." Mike protested still gasping after his run.

"Maybe later," John replied "I was mostly in control last night so I could handle one or two later."

Rachel said she'd call with "the plan" as they referred to their drinking arrangements. John headed off to the library while Mike and Rachel went inside the residence. It was early afternoon and a light rain was falling. John was dreading the idea of studying and decided to put it off for a little while so he at one of Dublin's newest institutions, the coffee bar.

As he waited for his latte to cool down a little, John wondered how things were going at the Flying Hound. The weekends were usually slower during the summer since most people headed down to the Jersey shore. The staff would also be trying to fit in their summer vacations. He thought about his days in Dublin so far. He thought of his new friends and how it felt like they had known each other for so much longer. He thought of the pubs and the new rituals like drinking in rounds. He thought of how pubs here rarely have televisions or background music. The "craic" as the Irish refer to a good time, comes from the people and their interactions. Distractions and outside stimuli are unnecessary provided the pub pulls a good Guinness and you are with your friends. He considered how many times he left a great old pub after a "session" and could not explain why he had such a good time. There was no band, no game on the TV, no karaoke, no booming dance music; hell the lights weren't even dimmed, but still, an awesome night. John thought of how this could be used in the Hound once he took over. He thought of his customers back home and whether they could enjoy just enjoy being together shooting the shit.

His thoughts were suddenly interrupted.

"Shouldn't you be studying?" a voice pierced his trance.

Katy Welsh stood above him smiling and waiting for him to say something. As he snapped out of it, he caught himself staring at her breasts pushing through a tight white buttoned down shirt.

"I'm on my way to the library" he stammered. "I just needed some caffeine" he offered trying hard to keep his eyes on her face.

Katy chuckled a little knowing she caught him and enjoying the fact that she did. She ordered an espresso.

"Join me if you'd like." John said but instantly regretted the offer as maybe being too forward. Even though she was only a little older, she was a member of the college staff.

"I'd love to. Thanks." she said sitting across from him.

"How do you like Dublin so far?" she asked.

John thought the question was interesting as it pertained to Dublin and not the college.

"I love it. What's not to like? The people are friendly, even to yanks, the Guinness is addicting and I've made some new friends. It also doesn't rain as much as I expected." John stopped himself realizing he was stringing pointless small talk together. He decided to switch tactics. "How do you like living here? I mean, isn't it tough being a foreigner all the time?"
John asked with genuine interest.

"I don't mind. Dublin is so mixed now that running into an American or any foreigner for that matter is no big deal. I really enjoy Dublin and can't really imagine moving back."

John listened but couldn't help being distracted by Katy's beauty.

"Anyway, my boyfriend would never leave. I can hardly get him to even leave the city." The mention of her boyfriend broke the spell a bit. John thought, however, that he picked up a slight tone of dissatisfaction in her voice when she mentioned him.

"Sounds like a bit of a drag." John said suddenly, wishing he hadn't said anything negative about her man.

"Yea, I know" Katy started but was cut off.

"Hey dude, let's get lit." Tony said coming through the coffee bar's door. He didn't see the person John was with until he got to the table. "Oh shit, I mean, fuck, I'm so sorry." Tony fumbled and started to laugh.

Katy smiled but used the interruption to break off the conversation. She didn't want to get too friendly with a student, or confess too much about her personal life.

"I better get going." she said pushing her chair back.

"No, no, I am going." Tony said but it was too late.

John could not help but feel a little miffed at Tony for breaking up the mood.

"I've got to get back, or Mary will give out to me for being gone too long." Katy said as she waved goodbye to both of them.

Tony turned to John, "Fuck man, how did you get her to talk to you. She likes to keep her distance."

"I don't know, I just invited her." John said, acting as cool as possible.

"Maybe I could invite her to suck my dick." Tony said but didn't continue, as John clearly wasn't interested in his remarks about Katy. They both left heading to the library. John was determined to study at least a little before temptation took over.

Chapter 16

The "plan" came together as usual. Nancy, who by now had established herself as the leader of the female contingent, left a note on John's door that was short and to the point; The Long Hall, 9PM. It was just after 7PM when John got back from the library. Tony had left an hour or so earlier saying he was going to get something to eat. John knew he would stop at McDonalds or Burger King, something he had not done since his first night in town. Tony, however, liked his comfort zone and was not as interested in experiencing real Ireland.

John had found several places he liked to eat, none of them on a typical tourist's itinerary. For lunch, he frequented "Take Five" on Lincoln Place. It was similar to an American diner and had great burgers. He also liked the "Apollo" up on Camden Street because of their famous mixed grills. Most days, though, John stopped in one of the many newsagents that had small deli counters in the back. His new favorite treat was tuna with sweet corn and butter on white bread. Not a typical concoction you would find back home but not nearly as foreign as black pudding.

For dinner, Dublin had a fantastic range of options. There were very trendy places like “Balzac” or “Shanahans” around Stephen’s Green. Either of these places could easily be in New York City. There were also Irish bistros like “Dobbin’s” where many scenes from Educating Rita were filmed, and “Roly’s” in ultra posh Ballsbridge. Of course, there were many local chippers where a student on a budget is more likely to be found than in any of the high-end options available throughout the city. Chippers were a Godsend before and after the pubs offering everything from batter-burgers to fried chicken to curry fries.

Tonight, John decided to skip dinner and hit the chipper on his way home. He went to his room and took a power nap before going out. He set his clock for 8:30 and drifted off to sleep. He kept thinking how easy it was to settle into Dublin life and it felt like he had been there far longer than his two weeks. With four more weeks to go, John began to regret not being able to stay longer. He was even beginning to regret signing up for the study tour. He was really starting to embrace Dublin and was enjoying the experience. A part of him even considered the fact that he might miss Katy. He made an effort to run into her whenever possible and their rapport was getting stronger. He knew nothing could come of his crush but he was exhilarated by the thought of her.

Chapter 17

John jumped to his feet when the buzzer on his clock went off. It took him a second to get his bearings.

"What time is it? Where the hell am I? What day is it?" all of these questions went through his head as he looked around his room for a clue. Nancy's note brought him back to reality. He recognized it on his nightstand and remembered "the plan."

John showered and changed. His clothing choices had evolved since he first arrived. John would now wear jeans and a t-shirt with a sweater most of the times he went out. He stopped wearing his baseball hats and sneakers when he learned they were associated with Yanks. John had no interest in passing himself off as Irish but did not want to stick out either. He realized that the Irish in Ireland did not consider Americans with Irish backgrounds Irish at all. Americans were "Yanks" and it didn't matter much what your last name was or when your grandfather left Ireland. It also didn't matter if you were from New Hampshire, Nevada, or Mississippi; all Americans were "Yanks."

John knocked on Jeff and Mike's door.

"If you're going, let's go!" he knew no further explanation was necessary, as everyone in their little group knew the "plan."

John could hear the two of them scrambling around getting their things together. Mike opened the door but said nothing to John. John could see they were hurrying to get ready but Jeff was still in a towel and Mike was brushing his teeth.

"Have you guys seen Tony?" John asked.

Mike spit out his toothpaste. "He already left. He said he wanted to get a head start."

"Great, he'll be an obnoxious pain in the ass." John said.

Jeff nodded but said nothing. They all knew what Tony was like. He was a great guy but he was not going to change or try to fit in. You could be sure Tony would be waiting for them in the pub wearing his Red Sox hat and Converse All Stars drinking a Jack Daniels and Coke.

They left the residence refreshed, showered, and ready to go. They passed Trinity College on their way to Grafton Street, which was still packed with shoppers and people on their way home from work. John was amazed at how busy the city was on virtually every night of the week. In the summer, tourists swelled the city population to an extreme. Every store, pub, restaurant, and street seamed to be constantly packed.

Up Grafton Street, the troop cut down a side street past the Royal College of Surgeons and on to George's Street. A couple of blocks up George's Street and finally, they arrived at the Long Hall. This was one of John's favorite pubs despite its distance from the college. Certainly, the three of them passed many great pubs along the way, but this place was always worth the extra effort. The "plan" could have been to meet at any number of places the friends enjoyed. Most of the time, they gravitated towards old established Victorian or Edwardian pubs with their well-worn beauty. Places like Kehoe's, Doheny and Nesbitts, Toners, The Flowing Tide, McDaid's, and the Stag's Head to name a few.

Occasionally, they would go to one of the newer lounges or even a nightclub, but more often than not, they settled on the quieter and more social atmosphere of a pub. Somehow, the seven new friends were as comfortable together as people who grew up together. Perhaps that is why they tended towards the established well-worn atmosphere of Dublin pubs as opposed to their fellow students who were found more often in trendy nightclubs.

The three guys arrived expecting the girls and Tony to already be there. The pub was busy with business types, still working on their after work pints, and some students from Trinity debating which American president was worse, Nixon, Reagan, or W. John and company looked around but did not see the rest of the crew. John spotted a table at the back of the long narrow bar with a few open stools and one older man finishing a pint. In the States, this table would be deemed occupied, but as John and his friends learned, here in Ireland, a space to put down your pint was communal.

They made their way to the back of the Long Hall. John caught his reflection in the massive antique mirror and ran his hands through his hair. Even though none of the guys were actually dating or even hooking up with the girls, he still wanted to look good for them. Jeff got to the table first and asked the man if the stools were taken. The old man who appeared to have had a few, mumbled something and gestured for the guys to take a seat. Mike and Jeff pulled a couple of the stools together and watched in amazement as the old fella tipped his pint back and swallowed the last two-thirds of the pint in one gulp.

This talent came from drinking many pints, as many as 30 in a sitting, almost every night of the week. Serious pint drinkers knew how to open their throats and just let it flow back. The guys, having seen this a few times by now, were nonetheless still impressed.

The old man was getting up to go by the time John arrived with the drinks. John had a pint of Guinness while Jeff ordered a pint of Smithwick's, a brown Irish ale, and Mike, the consummate athlete, settled for a Coor's Light. John put the round on the table as the old man finally vacated. He said something to the guys as he left but none of them could understand him. Even though the majority of the Irish speak English as their primary language, it can be very challenging for Americans to understand what they are saying. Most Irish who are used to dealing with Yanks will attempt to talk slower but two Irish people speaking to each other, or after they've had a good few pints, they may as well be speaking French as far as an American's ability to understand them goes.

"I wonder where the girls and Tony are?" John asked. "They must have stopped some where on the way or they'd be here by now."

" Knowing Tony, he has the girls doing body shots at some club." Jeff added.

"Too early, even for Tony. Maybe they stopped to eat. They did have to walk right past Burger King you know." Mike said with a little chuckle.

The three guys sipped their beers. Without Tony and the girls, the table was quiet. Jeff and Mike were good guys but much like John, they were not apt to carry on detailed conversations. None of them were bumps on a log but they definitely needed the others to spark the conversations.

Just as they were finishing their first round, John spotted Nancy coming through the front door. As if on cue, most of the heads in the bar turned and stared at the tall blond smiling as if she was walking down the catwalk of the Miss America contest. Nancy knew most of the bar was watching her, but you'd never be able to tell by her expression. She was confident and a little stuck up. These traits didn't make her obnoxious at all, but did create an aloofness that made people keep their distance. John got a taste of that the day he arrived during orientation when she gave him a funny dismissive look as they sat together on the couch. By now, John knew that that was just her defense mechanism to keep guys from constantly trying to chat her up. Once she trusted you, though, Nancy was as sweet as could be.

Emily, the other member of the girl's half of the little group, followed close behind with less of a grand entrance.

Being a New Yorker, Emily had a certain urban chic look about her. In fact, more than any of the others, she looked like a Dublin local. She tended to dress in black and could easily be confused with a posh Dublin girl from Foxrock or some other fancy neighborhood on the Southside of the city. Emily was also a strong and confident person but more understated than Nancy. She was petite and pretty, but without the stunning good looks of Nancy.

The girls saw John wave and made their way to their friends with most of the patron's eyes still glued to them.

"Where are Tony and Rachel?" Jeff asked.

Nancy rolled her eyes and Emily sighed and shook her head.

"You don't want to know." Nancy said waving her hand as if to say 'no more questions please.'

The boys looked at each other but none bothered pressing the subject. With Tony involved, anything could happen.

John got the girls their drinks, Bulmer's ciders as usual. The stares subsided but every punter headed for the toilets took an extra look. It's not as if Ireland doesn't have its share of beautiful women but the chic Emily and the blond bombshell Nancy were pretty exotic in these parts.

The pub had now shifted gears. Most of the business types and early crowd had given way to a younger group made up mostly of student types. Dublin is a young city as far as its population goes, and students or young professionals dominate most of the more popular city pubs by 10PM. The feeling of the pub almost becomes that of a bohemian coffee house but with Guinness being consumed in place of coffee. Most of the conversation was general covering politics, business or the arts. Of course, gossip is also a key component to many of the conversations. Most of the crowd is organized into groups of three to six people sitting on small stools crammed around small tables. The bar itself is full but with mostly single drinkers. People wanting to socialize with other people dominate Irish pubs. Anyone on their own is waiting for someone or trying to engage someone in conversation. Perhaps it is the "gift of the gab" but it sure is more interesting and rewarding than playing a trivia game anonymously on a television screen with hundreds of other anonymous people.

Back home, none of their new friends would likely be sitting around a crowded bar with no music or television to entertain them. However, after only a couple weeks in Dublin, they quickly adopted this behavior. They talked about everything one could imagine. In many ways, this type of personal interaction brought them much closer as friends than would normally occur back home. John particularly enjoyed this aspect of pub life and often thought about how it would play in the Hound.

What if he got rid of the televisions, stereo, live bands and other distractions and forced people to sit on small stools around cramped little tables and talk to each other? He tried to envision some of his regulars being asked to sit together and just talk.

The scenario always went something like this:

"Hey John, can you turn the lights down a bit, it's like a classroom in here?" regular number 1 says.

"Yea, and how 'bout some music for Christ sake. And turn the Eagles game on it started a half hour ago." chimes in regular number 2.

"What's with the fuckin' little stools, I feel like I am back in school. For God's sake John, you're killing my back." regular number three adds.

Eventually the bitch session in John's minds eye escalated to an all out barroom brawl. At that point, the fantasy ends and John accepts that a few Americans sitting in a 200 year old pub in Dublin can carry on like their Irish counterparts but a wholesale importing of this element of the culture would simply not work.

"What's up John? You spaced out." Emily asked giving John a poke with her index finger.

"Oh, nothing. I am just trying to imagine how this scene might translate back home." John replied.

"I'll tell you, it might have been the way back in our grandparent's day but today, a bar needs pool tables, darts, video games and a dance floor just to compete. Americans want television so they don't have to talk much with the guy next to him. Today, it's about personal space and boundaries." Mike stated.

"I'm not sure that's always the case." Nancy protested. "My friends like to hang out on the beach and talk. We don't need all of the bells and whistles."

"That's because you're high most of the time." Mike said.

"Not most of the time. I'm just saying, California's not like the East Coast. We're not as uptight." Nancy said.

"New York has a bad rap but believe it or not, we are not so uptight either. I mean, if the Yankees are playing, it better be on the TV in the bar but we know how to relax and talk too." Emily offered.

"I don't know, we're so worried about being p.c. that we avoid real topics like politics and religion and have to stick to sports or trivial stuff just to keep from getting into a fight. Here, at least, they can agree to disagree." John said.

"Yea, that's true. It's not like religion or politics have led to a thousand years of war and strife here." Jeff said sarcastically.

"I know but it's different somehow." John said.

The conversation was cut short when Tony announced himself at the front of the bar.

"I'm here, assholes!" he yelled.

Again, most heads turned but were not as impressed with this entrance. Tony made his way to the table ignoring the shaking heads.

"It's your round dumb ass." Mike said. "Where have you been anyway?"

"My ass my round, I just got here." Tony protested.

"Well, you need a drink and we're about done with the round so it looks like your timing is perfect. Anyway, we didn't mention where you snuck off to so you best shut it and belly up to the bar." Emily said.

"Whatever. You don't know dick." Tony replied. "Anyway, I guess I'll buy. Let me guess, orange whip, orange whip, orange whip…three orange whips." Tony quoted John Candy.

"Two Bulmer's, pint of Guinness, pint of Smithwick's, a Coor's Light and Roy Roger for you numb nuts." Emily ordered.

"Whatever." Tony replied and ordered the drinks.

John considered the way they all spoke to each other. The abuse, insults and general slagging was amazing for people who have known each other for so little time. He enjoyed the closeness. Even after three years of college, he didn't have this many people he could be this comfortable with. It was strange but in a way John recognized this was a special time and a special place. He knew he was changing, just like many people said he would when he went abroad. He did know, too, that the change was not intellectual or about maturity, he was growing as a person and as a soul.

The night was going well. Round after round kept coming and they were all getting well lubed. Finally, Emily suggested they call it a night. They still had exams the next day and she wanted to check on Rachel. Tony assured her Rachel was feeling "no pain" which again piqued the interest of the other guys.

"You didn't stuff her in a bag and throw her in the Liffey I hope." Mike said.

"No, I left her in my closet." Tony laughed.

It was now clear that Rachel did meet up with Tony earlier, which, in some way, eliminated her from joining the party.

" I am sure she is still passed out in front of the TV." Nancy assured everyone but they decided to call it a night just the same.

John breathed in the cool wet, fresh air out on the street. After several hours in the crowded pub, the fresh air perked the whole group up a bit. As per their usual ritual, they decided to hit the Abra Kebabra on the way home. It was funny that they all knew they would regret this choice in the morning but like zombies drawn to the living, they went as if they had no choice.

Chapter 18

Curry fries, gyros, bun burgers, and fried fish were consumed with glee. The choice of food was the perfect antidote for pint after pint of stout and cider. They ate as they walked back to the residence. John enjoyed watching legions of other college-aged people walking the streets home or to the late bars. Many of them were also carrying little brown bags from the chipper or fast food joints. John felt a sense of being one with all of these people sharing a common experience. The feeling gave John a wonderful sense of belonging. He thought how strange it was that he was so at home and happy so far away from home, his real friends, and his family.

As they got close to the residence, a familiar figure was approaching the group from the other direction.

"Way to rally bitch." Nancy called. "Thought we'd seen the last of you for the night."

"You wish." Rachel replied. "I just needed my beauty rest, y'all. Where's the party?"

"The party is over." Jeff said.

"A bunch of wusses. You didn't even get me some fries." Rachel said.

Tony held out his bag of curry fries offering Rachel some.

"Stop whining. I'll go to Scuffy's with you for a drink if you really want to go." Tony said.

"I think I am ready for one or two." Rachel accepted.

Jeff looked at his watch. "Shit man, it's already midnight. I got to get some sleep or I'm going to fuck this exam up royally."

"They don't flunk the Americans. Don't you know we keep this place running? They charge us like five times what they charge full time students." Emily said.

"Just the same, I'm calling it. Later." Jeff said as he climbed the step to the residence. Despite her interpretation of the college's finances, Emily called it a night, as did Nancy who almost said nothing since downing her gyro. John was on the fence, however.

"Scruffy Murphy's, huh?' He asked. "I guess it is the closest place. Maybe I'll join you for a night cap." John said looking for a clue in Tony or Rachel's response.

He was getting some kind of vibe from the two of them but he was not sure what it was. Even though he was fairly drunk, he still perceived that the two might be starting to hook up.

"Don't be a *fage* like the rest of them, have one drink. Your only here once." Tony said giving John just enough motivation to convince himself it would be ok and he really would stay for just one.

Chapter 19

Scruffy's was just a block away. John wouldn't consider it one of his favorites but the friends often ended up there because it was close to the residence. None of them spoke much during the short walk but John could sense the two of them were starting something. He would try to pry a little when they got to the pub.

The pub was still very crowded. The three of them found a spot at the end of the bar with two bar stools.

"I'll stand." John offered. "I need to stay vertical for a while.

They ordered drinks and settled in. Surprisingly, none of the other Americans were there. Usually there are at least a few. John suddenly got a pang of guilt.

"What if everyone but us is studying?" he thought. "I am really going to stay for just one." he told Tony and Rachel. "I can't afford to fuck up my first class."

Neither Tony nor Rachel replied. They seemed busy looking at each other and giggling.

"OK, what did happen to you two earlier?" John asked.

"Tony got me so high I had to lay down. The next thing I know, these guys are gone and I have a post-it stuck to my forehead telling me to meet at the Long Hall. I was walking there when I ran into you guys coming home."

"It's a good thing you didn't make it all the way there and we had already left." John said.

"It would have been good exercise for her." Tony joked.

"Hey!" Rachel shoved Tony Elaine Bennis style almost knocking him off his stool.

The playfulness and timid flirting was getting to John. His concerns about feeling like a third wheel were starting to be confirmed. He lifted his pint and was about to try the open throat technique he witnessed by the pint-man earlier when he spotted Katy and some guy huddled around a small table in the back. He hadn't seen her earlier because of the crowd, but as Scuffy's began to empty, she was there as plain as day.

"Isn't that Katy Welsh?" John asked fully aware that it was.

"Fuck man, here's your chance. Go buy her a drink or something." Tony said.

"Are you still high? She's clearly with her boyfriend who, by the way, does not look overly friendly." John said.

"Go kick his ass, she'll be impressed. She'll probably want to do you on the spot." Tony laughed and Rachel shook her head.

"Do you like that teacher?" Rachel asked.

"She's not a teacher first off, and no, I don't even know her." John said.

"It sure looked like you two were chummy in the coffee joint. Didn't you have your hand on her leg when I caught you there?" Tony teased.

Rachel's mouth was wide open in surprise mode.

"You dog. Doin' the teacher." Rachel piled on.

Finally John gave up trying to defend himself. As the Irish say, he was getting slagged and he knew it. The only defense was to go with it.

"She's coming over, stud." Tony said.

"Fuck off." John said.

"I am not kidding. Her goofy ass boyfriend is reading the paper and ignoring her. She's coming our way."

Suddenly John was nervous and even began to feel beads of sweat on his forehead. He thought, "Great, I stink like curry, I'm clearly shit canned, and now I am sweating. She'll be so impressed." John caught himself in mid-panic. "She's here with her boyfriend, she's older, she's an employee of the college, and she's way out of my league. What am I worried about?" he thought to himself.

"Hey guys, how's it going?" Katy said smiling like a den mother checking on her cub scouts.

"John's much better now that you're here." Tony said trying not to laugh.

John kicked Tony hard under the bar.

"Dude, why you kicking me under the bar?".

John felt like killing him but was also amused by Tony's balls.

"Can I get you a drink?" John asked hoping to change the direction of the conversation.

"Thanks." Katy accepted. I'll have a hot whiskey. I've become addicted to them since I moved here

"What about your boyfriend?" John asked motioning to the figure at the table with the newspaper in his face.

"He'll have a mineral water. He doesn't drink. I make him come to the pub once in a while just to get out." Katy said looking a bit pathetic.

John ordered the drinks and again looked over to Katy's boyfriend. He didn't look up from the paper. Katy had been gone long enough where most boyfriends would have looked. He didn't seem to care at all, and Katy didn't seem to be in a hurry to get back either.

"Never trust a fucker that doesn't drink." Tony said half into his pint.

Again, John gave him a kick.

"I'm just saying, unless you've got a problem or something, why not have a beer if you're in a bar?"

Katy appeared not to be paying attention to Tony's opinion. Instead, she smiled and looked at the bartender making her drink. John thought it was a little curious that she didn't try to defend her boyfriend. Why not tell Tony he's a health nut or running a marathon or something. At least tell him to fuck off. The lack of defense was a bit telling, he thought, maybe hoping that was the case.

"Shouldn't you guys be studying?" Katy asked sounding as if it were her duty more than out of real concern.

"We're ready." John assured her. He was doing his best not to slur, spit, and drool or even breathe on her. He was pretty sure that he was doing all of the above, however. He glanced back to the table with the boyfriend still sitting there, seemingly unaware of Katy's absence.

"Don't worry about him. As long as he's got something to read, he'll be fine." Katy said.

John didn't mean to keep looking but he couldn't help but feel a little self-conscious. Tony and Rachel were in their own world leaving him to engage Katy alone.

"So, I'm looking forward to the study tour; it should be a lot of fun. I'm ready to see more of Ireland."

In truth, John was only partially truthful. He was having a blast in Dublin and part of him wished he were staying. Even though all of the new friends were going on the trip with him, he still was not as enthusiastic as he was when he first signed up.

"The trip will be awesome. You are staying in some great places and should really enjoy the countryside." Katy said.

She was closer to John now almost pressing up against him. He had calmed down thanks to Katy's easy manner but the fact that she was so close and the boyfriend was so near still made him uneasy.

"Another whiskey?"

. "One more and them I'm done." Katy replied.

"I think I'll try one myself." John said.

Chapter 20

The whiskey was warm and sweet. It didn't resemble the shots of Powers that Pat had poured for him back at the Hound at all. This whiskey soothed him and didn't make him feel like his gut was on fire.

"This stuff is not bad." He said.

"It's a cure-all. If your sick, hot whiskey, if you're hung, hot whiskey, if you're cold, hot whiskey, and so on." Katy said.

She was exciting, John thought. He was also starting to believe she was flirting a little. He refused to confirm this thought, though, thinking it would be conceited but he did get some kind of vibe just as he had earlier with Tony and Rachel.

"We're outta here." Tony announced and stood up.

John was a little startled as Tony never was the one to suggest ending the party. Perhaps Rachel's hand on his leg prompted him to move their party behind closed doors.

John glanced at his whiskey and then at Katy.

"You can go if you want. I should get back to Liam anyway." Katy said.

"I'm going to finish my whiskey first." John said. "But you can go back if you need to."

This feeling out did not go unnoticed by Tony

"If you get her good and liquored up, maybe she can get you a good grade on tomorrow's final."

Katy smiled but didn't laugh.

Rachel said goodnight and then they were alone.

They finished their whiskies and ordered two more. Katy was starting to feel the effects of the booze and was now sitting on the stool vacated by Tony. His knees kept coming in contact with his legs. John was enjoying this but still kept his suspicions in check. Finally, a voice from behind him broke the spell.

"We should go. It's late."

"Liam, this is John. He is one of the Americans studying here this summer." Katy said.

John stood and turned. Liam was much taller than he expected. He was thin but not at all scrawny.

"How's it going?" Liam said extending his hand. His accent was definitely D4, very posh. He looked at John but didn't seem too interested.

"I'll be done in a sec." Katy said pointing to her drink.

"I'll be outside for a smoke. Good to meet you." Liam said and walked to the door.

Katy rolled her eyes a little indicating that she had to go but did not really want to.

"Guess you'd better go."

"Yep." Katy replied throwing back the rest of her drink. She put down the glass and stood up. She stumbled a little feeling a little light headed. She swayed towards John who caught her before she fell. Her entire upper body pressed against him, which he enjoyed thoroughly. However, the thought of Liam charging back in the pub motivated him to get her upright and steady.

"Woops" Katy said giggling from the buzz.

"Easy does it." John said still holding her by the shoulders.

"I'm fine, I'm fine. Just drank that last bit too fast. Thanks for catching me." Katy said.

"No trouble. Anytime. Have a good night." John said.

Suddenly, Katy stepped forward and kissed him on the lips. The kiss lasted only a second but far too long for just a friendly peck good night. Her lips were soft and smooth. He wanted to grab hold of her and press her against him but managed to control himself. Katy backed away and smiled without any shame.

"Don't stay too long. Remember, exams." Katy said and started towards the door.

John was gob smacked, as the Irish say. He was certain that Katy was flirting and would have been up for more if Liam were not just outside the front door of Scruffy's. He sat on the bar stool and tried to settle himself. He ran through the details of what just happened trying to make sense of it all. Maybe she was just the friendly, flirty type. Maybe it was the booze but still? He picked up his whiskey and finished it off just like Katy had done a moment earlier. He sat a while replaying the events over in his head. After a while, he realized he was alone in the pub. It was nearly 1:00 am and he outlasted all of his friends in spite of the fact that he was only going for a pint or two. He stood up and started home to the residence. Again the cool misty air refreshed him as he walked and thought. Katy was now firmly on his mind.

Chapter 21

The next morning, exam day, John was grateful to have a room to himself. He needed a little time to think on his own to try to get last night's events straight in his slightly aching head. Somehow, he felt guilty. He wasn't sure if it was because of Katy or because he let himself be corrupted by his friends and hadn't studied one bit. Whatever it was, he wanted to and needed to think. Unfortunately, his window of opportunity was about to close. Staring at the ceiling, John was trying to decide if his head and stomach would tolerate an attempt to sit upright. He hadn't felt this bad since the morning he left for Ireland. That was also the last time he vowed never to go drinking again. John had been in a bar and around alcohol all of his life. He certainly was no teetotaler but he had a healthy respect for the booze. An uncle once told him never to drink so much that one day he'd have to stop. John listened to that advice and generally lived by it. However, from the time his trip to Ireland began, the drink had become a more prominent part of his life. The hangover had also gained in frequency.

"Johnny boy, you up?" A voice from the hall called.

John recognized Tony's voice but was surprised to hear him up so early. Usually, Tony rolled out of bed at the last possible second but here he was, an hour before Sally's exam, knocking at the door and sounding frighteningly chipper.

John opened the door.

"What the hell are you up so early for?" John asked.

Tony took an exaggerated look into the room pretending to be cautious as not to walk in on anybody.

"Oh, get the fuck in, no one's here."

"Just trying to be sensitive, you know, respectful of our elders, teachers, etc."

"She's not a teacher and she's only four years older, anyway, what difference does it make, nothing happened and nothing will. Have you forgotten newspaper boy?" John said.

"Yeah, what's with that? She seems too clued in to be hooked up with some pseudo intellectual snob." Tony said.

"I don't know and I don't even know if he's a stiff, but I do know I would not let a hot piece of ass like Katy talk to a bunch of drunks at some bar while I did the crossword." John said as he pulled on his jeans. "Let's get some coffee. Is anyone else ready yet?"

"They're all downstairs. Jeff already left for the classroom building. He is very nervous for some reason. Mike's a little freaked out because if he fucks up, it could affect his scholarship"

Nancy, Emily and Rachel were sitting on the residence steps smoking Silk Cut cigarettes. Mike was on his cell phone talking to his parents. John overheard him telling his mother that "he loved her too" and thought it was nice. His parents were not overly affectionate and he didn't remember telling either of them that he loved them since he was a little kid. In a way, John envied Mike and that closeness.

"Ready girls?" Tony asked as they put their smokes out on the sidewalk and walked up Merrion Road towards the college.

To people passing them going the other way, they must have looked like prisoners being marched to the gallows. They were all a bit haggard and tired looking. Nancy was basically in her pajamas while Emily was still wearing what she had on the night before. Only Rachel was put together reasonably well. Something about her southern upbringing did not allow for ever leaving the house without proper attire, full makeup, and the right accessories. She might have been as tired as the others but you would never know it by looking at her.

Chapter 22

The exam was not as bad as John had expected. Perhaps they did dumb things down for the yanks or maybe John absorbed more than he thought. In any event, he had completed his exam in under the two-hour limit. He thanked Dr. Sally and genuinely meant it. John had not taken many arts courses since his freshman year at Cornell and was enjoying the break from business and hospitality classes. His first two weeks in Dublin actually did expand his cultural base and he was glad for it.

John walked down the steps of the academic building. As he turned at the landing, he was still thinking about the night before as he literally ran into Katy.

"Whoa, big guy" she said smiling. No trace of guilt or embarrassment on her face.

Was he imagining their little moment last night? Did she remember? Did it mean anything? John thought of these things all at the same time rendering his ability to speak useless.

"Hey, sorry, the test…" John stuttered and stopped.

"Oh, relax! I know exams are stressful and after last night, I am sure you're in bits."

John was confused. Was she acknowledging last night's kiss?

"Oh, about that." John started trying to collect his thoughts.

"I mean, out on the piss with the lads and a couple of whiskey night caps could not have been good for the old head this morning." Katy said using little Irish terms that John just loved. She had a grin on her face that told John she was letting him off the hook but she seemed to be holding back.

"How did you do anyways?" she asked.

"Good, fine I think."

"Grand. You'll enjoy your study tour more than being in a class. Plus, you get me for part of the trip. The regular professor has to leave part way through so they asked me to finish the tour."

John just about had a nervous break down. Katy would be on the tour, sleeping in the same hotels, riding on the same bus, drinking in the same pubs. His excitement had to be transparent.

"Liam's thinking about coming along too. He knows a lot of history and stuff and will add a lot to the tour." she added taking the wind right out of John's sails.

John went from the top of the mountain to six feet under in seconds. Feckin' Liam was coming. Excitement turned to acute disappointment, which was also likely to be transparent.

"Aren't you happy I'm coming?" Katy asked with a hint of desperation in her voice.

"Yea sounds good. Liam will be great." John replied sounding unconvinced and disappointed.

"He'll be fine, don't worry." she was acting like John's girlfriend all of a sudden. John heard it in her voice but thought it would be best to ignore it. Instead, he played it cool.

"It'll be good to have someone who really knows the lay of the land with us. I am looking forward to his input." John said.

Katy looked at him with a strange combination of relief and disappointment. She stepped back a little and smiled.

"I'll see you on the second Monday of the trip, John. If I read the itinerary right, I will be meeting up with the group in Clare." Katy said.

John thought it was interesting the Katy said she would meet the group and not "we will meet the group." Maybe he was grasping at straws but he found the phrase curious and hopeful.

Chapter 23

John walked back to the residence. He had finished the exam first and was not expecting to see any of the others for a while. However, when he was about half way home, he heard an American accent calling after him.

"John, wait up!" it was Nancy walking quickly behind him "How did you do?"

. "OK, I guess. Thankfully, I recovered surprisingly fast from last night's session." John answered.

"I heard things were getting chummy with you and Miss Katy late in the night but I'm sure it was just a rumor." Nancy said with a big grin.

"Nothing to report." John cut her off. "Just an arbitrary thing. I'm not in the market and even if I was, her lame-assed boyfriend was there."

"You've already figured out the boyfriend. How interesting." Nancy said egging him on, or as the Irish say, taking the piss.

John had an odd feeling Nancy was more than just playing with him. In a way, she was acting a little jealous. He was trying hard not to let his ego go off unchecked but there was something flirty in the way she grilled him with questions about Katy. John blew the idea off but he still felt Nancy and he had come a long way from the orientation on the first day.

They walked back together to the residence. Nancy kept smiling at John and even gave him a little punch on the shoulder as if to say "way to go." John did not feel Nancy's enthusiasm for the "affair." he wanted to kill Tony for even saying anything. Katy was definitely beautiful, but she was taken and he was trying to keep his trip in focus. He didn't want a girlfriend and Katy wasn't the type to have a casual fling. She certainly would not be a fuck-buddy. He decided to try to make a statement to Nancy who would certainly inform the rest of the group about the situation.

"I have a serious girlfriend back home. In fact, we are engaged to be married right after graduation. She has my promise ring." John regretted this rouse as soon as it came out.

"A promise ring? What are you, fourteen?" Nancy replied "Fuck off, I'm not buying it." she said deflating John even more.

Unfortunately, he was now committed, at least to the lie.

"No, really, we got pre-engaged last Christmas over break." he explained. The look on Nancy's face made John regret this line of bullshit even more.

"Pre-engaged? Promise ring? What's next, a pledge pin?" she pressed with amusement.

"Look, Nancy, give me a break, I want to keep everything here simple. I don't want a romance or a scandal. Katy and I have done nothing and I want to keep it that way. Being with her, if it were even possible, would be a nightmare. Tony and Rachel didn't see shit because there wasn't anything to see, so cut me some slack."

. Nancy saw he was desperate, so she agreed to let him off the hook but she could not help but recognize that someone so anxious to bury something might just be trying to hide something too. She would let it go, but would not forget what she felt.

Chapter 24

The weekend after the exam went by quickly. By Friday, the gang wanted to celebrate, but all they could manage was a few jars at Scruffy's before fatigue set in. Tony and Rachel appeared to be becoming more of an established couple tempering Tony's desire to stay out all night. Jeff and Mike needed a break and only stayed out for a little while. Nancy and Emily were subdued enough and went to bed by 11. The week leading up to the final saw so much action that the weekend following it was anticlimactic.

On Saturday, John was up and out of bed early. Since the evening before was as close to a health night as he'd had since arriving, he felt good Saturday morning and decided to make the most of it. He even considered cutting out the booze for the rest of his time in Ireland, which, of course, he didn't consider too seriously.

John showered and got dressed. It was only 9 in the morning, which meant none of his friends, with the exception of Jeff, would be up for hours. He did not exactly have a plan but since he felt well rested and full of energy he went downstairs and headed out the front doors. As he stepped into the morning sunlight, he took a deep breath of clean air. Little traffic on Saturday morning meant fresher air. John even thought it had a certain country quality to it. In any event, John stood there for a moment trying to decide what to do. After a few minutes, he set off towards the city center. Two blocks from the residence, he saw a familiar figure jogging towards him.

"You're up early." John said as Jeff came into earshot.

"I like to run in the morning before I get too distracted. Since we all behaved ourselves last night, I figured I'd take advantage of the opportunity."

"Yea, I'm kinda doing the same thing but actually exercising is just too ambitious. I was thinking more of a coffee and the paper or something." John said.

"I'll meet you. Just let me run back to the dorm and get changed." Jeff said.

John was happy for the company. They agreed to meet in a half hour at Bewley's up on Grafton Street.

John took his time walking towards Grafton Street. He decided to cut through the back gate at Trinity College. He walked past the science buildings and out along the sport's fields. A few students were jogging around the track while others played Frisbee. John was amazed how such a park-like setting was right there in the middle of the city. He thought of Cornell and his time there. Inevitably, his thoughts turned to his family and, for the first time since arriving, he felt a little homesick. There was something about the peaceful setting and the students enjoying a Saturday on campus that made him miss home. It was a little strange but the feeling persisted until he exited Trinity through the front gate and came out onto busy Westmorland Road. Once back in the city vibe, John's thought of home escaped him as he headed towards Grafton Street.

As John approached from the bottom of Grafton Street, he marveled at the exterior beauty of the ornately decorated building, no wonder Bewley's, aka Bewley's Oriental Café, had been a landmark on Grafton Street since 1927. The front doors were constantly opening and closing with customers from all walks of life stopping in for coffee, tea, or their breakfast. Starbucks was not yet a fixture in Ireland and John wondered how they would be able to compete with such a coffee palace.

Inside, John found a table for two and ordered a pot of coffee. He was not too sure if Jeff drank coffee but figured he could polish off most of it himself. He unfolded the "Irish Independent" that he picked up in the newsagent just across the street from Bewley's and settled in to wait for Jeff. The news had a more international angle than the US papers typically had, and for a while, John had trouble following the reports. He decided to focus his attention on the "Living" section of the paper and read about the fighting Gallagher brothers from the ridiculously popular band, Oasis. He drank the strong hot coffee while he read and blended into the ebb and flow of the café. John realized, at one point that he almost felt like a local, or at least, a regular. There was no self-consciousness or concern that people were looking at him as a stranger like he had felt almost continuously for the first couple of weeks whenever he was in public. John relaxed and enjoyed the feeling while he waited.

A full half hour had passed with no sign of Jeff.

For a while, John enjoyed the tranquil time alone but now, the coffee was cold and he worked his way through all of the paper that he could follow. Just as he was folding up "The Independent", he spotted Jeff rushing through the front door of the café. John waved to get his attention. Jeff saw him and rolled his eyes as if to say "what a nightmare getting here was."

Jeff came over and sat down.

"I had just about given up on you."

"Sorry, man. There was no hot water for a shower for some reason and then I got stopped by Nancy coming out of the residence. I was shocked she was even awake but she would not let me go." Jeff said breathing a little heavy still.

"What the hell did she want this early? Surely she didn't have a plan put together for tonight already." John said.

"No, nothing like that. She was giving me the third degree about you. Or, you and Katy Welsh to be exact."

"What the fuck?" John said a little exasperated.

"I know! Dude, she wanted to know your every move. I mean, where you were, who you were with, was Katy there, and on and on. Finally I told her I wasn't your frickin' mom and I didn't keep tabs on who you are fucking."

"I'm not fucking or doing anything else with Katy Welsh for God's sake but why does she care?" John's voice was growing higher by the minute.

"She's snooping around for some reason. Who knows." Jeff said.

"I guess she just wants ammo to give me shit with." John said and then decided it was best to just let it go.

Chapter 25

"The coffee's cold." John said trying to change topics.

"I'm just going to get some orange juice. For now." Jeff answered and called the waiter over. John ordered more coffee but wasn't sure he could stomach much more. He was hot after the conversation about Nancy and hot coffee did not seem to be the best choice of beverage but it was too early for a beer.

The two friends sat for a while making small talk. Eventually, the subject of friends and family back home came up. John realized he knew very little about Jeff and, for that matter, all of his new friends.

He learned Jeff and Mike were friends since grade school and played junior hockey together. Jeff said Mike was the best hockey player around, even better than him but a knee injury in high school ended his aspirations to play in college and maybe even the pros. Instead, Mike became content as a fan and now is the sports information director for UVM's college paper, "The Vermont Cynic". After high school, the two decided to go to college together and have been roommates all three years that they have been at UVM. Neither knew what they wanted to do when they graduated but both thought they would stay in Vermont. Mike considered journalism or coaching hockey while Jeff was holding out some hope to further his hockey career in one of the professional leagues.

"I know I wouldn't make it for long but I want to try at least for a while." He said looking down at his shoes.

John sensed Jeff was a little embarrassed by this admission.

To Jeff, saying he wanted to be a pro hockey player sounded a little like a little kid saying he wanted to be an astronaut when he grows up, but it was how he felt.

John and Jeff spent the better part of the morning getting to know each other. John brought Jeff up to speed about his own background and history. John was happy to know a bit more about Jeff and Mike. It was another level to connect on and he began to feel he might stay friends, real friends, with some of his Dublin buddies.

By the time John and Jeff made it back to the residence, everyone was up and around. Emily and Rachel were on the steps having their morning smoke. Mike was coming across the street from a newsagent with a copy of "USA Today" folded under his arm.

"When did they start carrying the "USA Today"?" Jeff asked Mike as he came into earshot.

"I guess today. I heard you can find it around town once in a while but that newsstand never had it before." Mike unfolded the paper and handed the front section to Jeff.

"What about the sports section?" Jeff asked. "Yea right. You can have it when I get out of the crapper." Mike said.

"Nice." Rachel chimed in.

"Pig." Emily added with a sneer.

"Where's Tony?' John asked to everyone present.

"He's still getting dressed. Sometimes, I think he's worse than a woman." Rachel said rolling her eyes.

"I'm sure he wants to look his best for you." Mike joked. By now, everyone accepted that Tony and Rachel had become a couple.

The doors to the residence swung open. Nancy, in her customary pajamas sauntered out.

"Where have you been?" she asked John with a mischievous little smile.

"Having coffee with Jeff." John said dryly back to Nancy.

"Just you two? How gay."

"That's right Nancy, we've gone queer. Something about being around bitches like you." Jeff said.

Nancy flipped Jeff the bird and faked a laugh. "Just because you can't get any, don't get pissy with me." Nancy said putting an end to that conversation.

"Anyway, the plan for tonight…" Nancy started but was immediately interrupted.

"The plan for tonight is we take another health night." Mike said. "I am not going on a two week tour with a massive hangover. I vote we go to the movies or something and take it easy again."

John found himself agreeing with Mike. He felt good for the first time in days, or even weeks, and the feeling appealed to him.

"I'm up for a movie. It might be lame but I don't want to feel like shit on the road. I'm sure we'll be drinking like fish for the trip anyway." John said. Emily and Rachel shrugged in a gesture signifying they didn't care.

Nancy said she was rested enough and wanted to go to some club on Leeson Street.

Jeff said nothing mostly because he was paying attention to the newspaper Mike had given to him earlier.

"What's up?" Tony asked walking from the residence front door.

"Ah, the beauty queen has arrived." Nancy said.

"You should take notes." Tony said back.

"These losers want to go to the movies and lay low tonight so they can be fresh for the trip. I want to go out. We can rest again tomorrow before the tour starts anyway." Nancy pleaded her case.

While the guys were tempted, ultimately they decided to opt for a second health night. Mike was the one who persuaded Jeff and John but Tony remained uncommitted. He seemed to be hedging based on what Rachel decided to do. Emily already signed on with Nancy who was busy chiding the guys.

"You're all so lame. You can rest and worry about your health when you're old fucks. Let's live it up while we can." Emily said. "I'm in."

Tony said nothing but looked at Rachel. Finally, she said she was up for going out prompting Tony to say he would keep his options open until later.

After a brief discussion, John, Jeff, and Mike agreed on X-Men: 3, which was playing at the Ormand Cinemas in Stillorgan at 7:45. By 6:30 they had not heard from Tony and assumed he was going to the club with the girls. None of the guys were surprised. The chance to party and hook up with Rachel was just too much for Tony to pass up.

The movie was packed. John was happy they decided to reserve seats in advance, something unheard of back in the States. When the movie ended, they caught the bus back to Merrion Square. Once they got off the bus, it was just after 10:00 pm. The temptation to go out for a pint or maybe even catch up with Tony and the girls was strong.

"So, what are we going to do?" John said coaxing out the discussion.

"I'm still going to take it easy." Mike said sticking to his guns.

"Yea, it's late enough to chill. If we go out now, tomorrow will suck." Jeff agreed.

"Fine." John said with mild disappointment. He knew it was best to stay in but he was getting restless.

Back at the residence, Jeff said he was turning in. Mike said he was going to the computer lab to check his e-mail. John said he was just going to hang out and see what happened. They all went their separate ways.

John hung out in the residence lobby for a few minutes mentally going over his options. He could go to bed but he didn't think he could actually sleep. He could find Tony and company but he only knew they were planning to hit some club on Leeson Street. There were dozens of clubs on Leeson Street and he did not exactly feel like turning his night into a quest. Most of those clubs charged a cover anyway so he decided to keep his money in his pocket for better things.

Eventually, John found himself walking towards Srcuffy's. He didn't exactly know what his motivation was but could not think of anything better to do. Maybe on some level he hoped he'd run into Katy again but knew that even if she was there, Liam would likely be with her.

Chapter 26

Scruffy's was very busy. It was, after all, Saturday night. John pushed through the crowd looking for an opening at the bar. To his surprise, a bar stool opened just as he made it through the crowd. He grabbed it before the people around him even realized the spot had opened. He pulled the stool under him and settled in.

John ordered a Guinness and had a quick look around. He didn't recognize anyone and immediately regretted going out. He decided to just stay for one and call it a night. Half way through his pint, he noticed a couple back in a dark corner of the lounge section of the bar. The woman's back was to John blocking the face of the guy she was sitting next to. John could tell they were having some sort of animated discussion. He tried to look away and focus on something else but he kept returning his attention to that dark corner. The female looked a little familiar. She had long dark hair that was tossing back and forth as she appeared to emphasize some point in their discussion. Suddenly, she reached down under the table to fish something out of her bag. As she did this, John saw the face of her male counterpart and instantly recognized him. It was Liam. He looked a bit bewildered and drawn but it was him. The woman, whom John now knew was Katy, shot back upright and wiped her eyes with a tissue that she just pulled from her purse. They were fighting and it was nasty, John thought.

"Another pint?" a voice cut through John's attention.

"What? Ah, yea, why not?" John replied to the barman, now too riveted to leave. He watched knowing they could not see him. He felt a little strange like he was seeing something he was not supposed to. The scene, however, was just too compelling.

For the next half hour or so, John watched. No one came into the bar that John knew so, except for ordering two more pints, John's voyeuristic entertainment went on uninterrupted. He was ashamed of himself not just for watching, but also for rooting for Katy and for the argument in general. He didn't fully understand why these two fighting in a prolonged battle was so appealing to him. On some level, he had to know that he had a little crush on Katy and, based on that realization made Liam his foe. But, for whatever reason, John just sat back and smiled as the war waged.

Without a hint of notice, Katy was suddenly up off her stool and grabbing for her purse. Liam shot up and tried to grab her by the arm. She pulled away from him and for the first time, John could make out what she actually said.

"Fuck off. Leave me the fuck alone." she hissed in a muted but highly agitated tone. Liam recoiled and sat down. Katy turned and was heading for the door. She was about ten feet from John when she turned and looked his way. Tears streamed down her face, which had taken on a reddish hue. John was not sure if it was anger or sadness or both but the color in her cheeks made her look somehow even more beautiful.

Katy looked right at John as she passed him. To John, though, she was looking right through him. He looked at her and made a little gesture indicating concern but she made no reaction. Maybe she was too angry or upset to acknowledge him or maybe she hadn't seen him. John could not imagine she didn't see him or recognize him. Now she was out the door and into the cool Dublin air. He wanted to chase after her but knew this was not his place. He sat tight for the moment and returned his attention to Liam. He sat looking down and into space. He made no attempt to follow Katy. His inaction brought only one word to John's head. "Putz."

John finished his pint and headed out. Once outside, he scanned the immediate surroundings to see if maybe Katy was still around. He was disappointed that she wasn't and decided not to linger. Liam would be coming out soon and he had no interest in running into him.

John cut down the back alley towards the residence. He was thinking about the night and thought how the X-Men: 3 movie seemed like weeks ago. He found himself smiling again at the thought of the fight and again felt a little ashamed.

John turned the corner in the alley to cut through a little alley that lead back to Merrion Way. As he turned the corner, he felt someone put their hands on his shoulders from behind. Before he could process what was happening, he was forcibly turned around and thrown up against the brick archway of the Via. His very first thought was that it was Liam who must have seen him watching them and was coming to kick his ass. This theory, though, was quickly dispelled when his attacker pressed against him and started kissing him hard on the mouth. Now John really hoped it wasn't Liam. He tried to push back but the attacker held tight. John recognized he was being kissed and manhandled by a woman. He relaxed enough to see long silky hair. He felt soft hot cheeks pressed against his. He succumbed and let himself enjoy the moment even though he wasn't too sure who had him in her grip.

Voices from Merrion Way could be heard coming close to the alley. All of a sudden, John recognized one of the voices.

"I can't believe you bitches dragged me to a male strip club. I need a hot shower after that shit."

Just as John was processing the voice, his attacker pulled away while simultaneously turning John away from her. She pushed off without revealing her face and hurried up the alley and out of sight. John's head was literally spinning. The pints, the attack, the dark alley and Tony's protesting voice made him dizzy and a little disoriented. He tried to focus on the retreating figure that was now just a shadow in the alley. Then, he heard his friends again.

"Hey, shit for brains, are you lost?" Tony asked laughing.

"What the hell are you doing?" Rachel chimed in as the three of them stared at him stumbling around in the alley.

"Oh, hey" was all John mustered up.

"Are you loaded?" Rachel asked.

"What? No, no. I'm just going home. I went to Scruffy's and…" he trailed off without knowing how to finish.

"Maybe you should come with us." Emily said sensing John was not quite right.

"Yea, ok." John said as the four of them started back again.

After a block or so, John's head had cleared. "Where's Nancy?" he asked.

"She ditched us about an hour ago. She said she had enough and decided to go to Scruffy's. Didn't you see her there?" Tony asked.

"No. I didn't see anyone, really." John said.

"That's weird." Emily said. "Maybe she just went home.

"Maybe." was all John could say as he walked the rest of the way in contemplative silence.

The next morning, everyone was up early. There was not much partying so they were all well rested and looking forward to their trip the next day. John, Jeff and Emily were in the dining hall first. Tony and Rachel then walked in together followed by Mike a few minutes later. Finally, Nancy sauntered in still in her customary pajamas.

"Look what the cat dragged in." Jeff said.

"What the hell happened to you last night?" Tony asked. "I mean, first you drag me to some gay bar then you take off. What the f?"

"It wasn't a gay bar. It's a new club and it was lady's night. They do male dancers on Saturdays to get the girls all worked up for the late night action. I didn't need the dancers to get worked up so I took off. No biggy." Nancy said dismissively.

"Well, where did you go?" Emily asked. "I thought you went to Scruffy's?"

"I was around, don't you worry." Nancy said smiling. "I was under cover." Nancy said and then looked directly at John.

John felt like his blood had turned into ice water. Did she see him at Scruffy's? Maybe she saw him in the alley. Maybe… John's thoughts were interrupted by Tony.

"Under cover. Under who's cover is more like it." Tony said drawing laughs from the guys. Nancy said nothing more and let her comment just sit there for John to ponder.

John regained some of his enthusiasm for the trip even though he had a nervous feeling in his gut every time he thought of Katy joining the crew. These concerns become more amplified after last night's surreal encounter even though he could not say for sure if it was Katy in the alley. Regardless of who accosted him in the alley, John simply felt a change of scenery would not be a bad thing.

Chapter 27

Monday morning came fast and furious. At 7 am, the residence hall manager woke the twelve people who had signed up for the study tour. The plan was to have an early breakfast, a brief orientation with the professor in charge, and then head off. Three of the ten, none of which were John's friends, made it to breakfast and the residence hall manger had to make another round of knocking on doors to get the other 9 in the student lounge for the orientation by 8:00 am.

John made it to the lounge first. The professor, Dr. Jim Carney, was there, setting up some handouts to be distributed if the rest of the group ever materialized.

"Good morning." John opened.

"Top of the mornin' to ya." the professor answered with a terrible faux Irish accent. Dr. Carney, from upstate New York was a Yank with just enough Irish background and heritage to make him embarrassing. He had conducted this tour several times but he never engaged with the real Irish to know that his warped idea of what Ireland was really about was way off. He enjoyed the cartoonish stereotypes of the Irish that were so pervasive in the

U.S. a generation or so earlier. Drinkers, fighters, talkers and schemers would be the way Dr. Carney would likely describe the Irish. He was not exactly an ugly American; he didn't mean any harm at all, he was simply ignorant, and seemed to enjoy being so.

John sat in the back of the lounge. Tony and Rachel came in next followed by several of the other Americans. Finally, Nancy, Jeff, Emily and Mike joined them. Dr. Carney welcomed them all and proceeded to hand out his syllabi and itinerary.

"Top of the mornin' to ya." he tried again. "Ya look like you could use a bit o' the hair o' the dog this fine mornin'." The fake accent was excruciating.

Most of the students tried to laugh a little but John just squirmed in his chair. Carney did not notice or even seem to really care that his act was bombing. Eventually, he went into "professor" mode and started going over the syllabus and some of the ground rules for the trip. Most of these were straightforward "you are representatives of the USA and the college" kind of stuff. He didn't attempt to be too heavy handed though, acknowledging that they were adults and he couldn't stop them from having a "wee jar" now and then. He only asked that they show up when and where they were supposed to and that they treat the properties and the people they visit with respect.

"I have taken hundreds of students through Ireland over the years and have not had a major incident. However, I do reserve the right to send anyone who is disruptive or who causes embarrassment to the school back to Dublin."

John laughed to himself wondering if the good doctor would follow his own rules of behavior. One use of his fake accent or hackneyed quips would be embarrassing enough to merit a bus ride back to Dublin.

The meeting was over in about an hour. Dr. Carney asked the group to bring their bags, limit of one per person, to the back parking area of the residence. Dermot would meet them there to help pack the bus and get everyone on board. The goal was to be on the road by 10 AM. They had a fairly long first leg and he did not want to be late to their first stop. Like a parent, he asked everyone to use the toilet before they left to avoid unnecessary stops. Even though Dr. Carney was a little goofy, he had been doing this for a few years now and knew how to organize and operate a tour.

Chapter 28

John was in his room getting a few last minute items together. As he closed his bag, someone knocked on his door. "I'll be right down." he hollered assuming it was Dermot hurrying them along.

"Sorry, I didn't mean to interrupt." Katy said as she opened the door. John looked at her with his mouth open trying to formulate a sentence. "I guess you're ready to head off then." she said.

"Yea, just a few last things." John said. He immediately started to sweat and stammer a little. "What are you doing here?"

"I need to make sure you all get out alright and I want to talk to Dr. Carney about some details for when I take over the trip."

The thought of her on the trip again excited and terrified John. Another knock at his partially opened door startled him back to the moment.

"Let's hit it, sport." Nancy said. She spotted Katy and broke into a broad "I gotcha" smile. "Oops, sorry, I didn't mean to interrupt." she said as she backed out the door looking at John with delight.

"We're just talking, Nancy. I'll be right down." John called after her. "Shit." he said half to himself.

"What's the problem?" Katy asked.

"No problem, my friends are just jackasses."

"Well of course we were just talking, what else would we be doing?"

John suddenly felt worried he had said the wrong thing. He was not trying to imply something else might be going on. In any event, he thought he better let it go. He also felt that Katy might be trying to put out a little signal. Even though there was no discussion about the first night he saw her at Scruffy's or about whatever went on in the alley, she could not deny something indeed happened. This may or may not have been have been her way of saying that nothing more would be happening.

Dermot hauled the girl's bags on to the bus. "Jeezas, what is in these bags, bricks?' He asked.

"Mostly shoes." Emily chimed in.

"Well, I hope you have more than shoes."

Emily was joking but Carney was clueless. She laughed and quickly retreated to the back of the bus. After the last of the bags were loaded, Dermot slammed the rear hatch giving Dr. Carney the thumbs up.

"All aboard, we have a schedule to keep." Carney announced. The remaining students began to fill the bus. John and Tony took up the backbench. Jeff and Mike sat a couple of rows in front of them. The girls were camped three across in the middle. The other three, two girls and one guy were spread out in the front. Finally, Dr. Carney sat behind the driver. He had an oversized brief case that he kept next to him with all of the confirmations, room assignments, and other related details for the trip.

Just before they pulled out, Nancy pointed out the window towards Katy who had joined Dermot at the back of the residence.

"There's your girlfriend." she said chiding John with a smartass smile. "Maybe she forgot to kiss you goodbye."

The three girls chuckled and acted as if this topic had been well covered. One of the other girls, Becky Hamilton from Bennington College in Vermont looked at John with genuine surprise as if to say, "Are you really screwing one of the staff?"

John shot Nancy a look.

"Sorry," she said. "sensitive, are we?"

"I have nothing to be sensitive about but these people don't know you're just full of shit." John said motioning towards the other students.

"They'll know soon enough." Tony joined in.

"Let's just have a good trip and forget all of this…" John started but was interrupted by the Professor.

"Remember what we talked about in the orientation. No smoking or drinking on the bus. Sleep if you want to but you'll miss some beautiful countryside. We'll have a pre-arrival meeting when we are about fifteen minutes from our destination. This drive should take around three and a half hours. We will be making one stop in a couple of hours. Does anyone have any questions?" everyone looked around but no one had a question. "Good." Carney sat down and started discussing something with the driver. They were nodding in agreement.

Dermot, who was now the official college's bus driver, cranked the door closed and put the bus into gear. The bus lurched forward throwing everyone forward and then back in their seats.

"Hold on." Dermot said. "Turbulence ahead."

John considered this comment and could not help but wonder if it was a premonition or prediction.

Chapter 29

The bus and its occupants did not get very far. Their vehicle was too big to navigate the alleys and small side streets many locals use to avoid the main arteries while massive Dublin traffic chokes most of the main entrances and exits of the city. They had to be content with crawling along the Liffey, past the different quays towards the new M50 motorway. John watched as throngs of people poured over the Ha'Penny Bridge and through the archway leading to Temple Bar. How many nights had his little band of drinkers gone through that arch for a night out at one of the numerous rowdy bars and clubs in that famous part of town? He reminisced about all of the good times he'd had so far on this adventure and was even now starting to look forward to this tour of the country. He was not sure if his newfound enthusiasm for the trip was because of, or in spite of Katy Welsh.

The traffic got a bit lighter after they passed Heuston Station. Dr. Carney pointed to the entrance of the Phoenix Park and asked if any of the group had visited here. All but one of other girls, Carol Vogel, were embarrassed to admit that they had not ventured that far from the city center. Carol's parents had brought her to the park when they visited earlier in the term. They were invited to meet the US ambassador for some kind of political reception. The ambassador's residence is in the park just across from the Irish President's residence. Carol's mother worked for the US State Department but Carol wouldn't say or didn't know in what capacity. In any event, she had been to the park but hardly as an adventurous student. Like her classmates, Carol found her comfort zone in Dublin and didn't stray too far from that place.

Once the little group reached the outer environs of Dublin, they all began to drift into their own little worlds. Most of the group fell asleep blocking out the noise with their Discmans. John and Tony talked a while but Tony eventually moved up to sit with Rachel. John watched as towns like Lucan and Leixlip, which now looked like Dublin suburbs, passed by the bus's window. A sign for Maynooth made John's stomach twinge with nervousness. Next came Enfield and then Kinnegad and John began to notice that all hints of Dublin had faded. No more double decker city busses were to be seen. Traffic was now considerably sparser. Fields with sheep and cattle now became the norm. John enjoyed the change of scenery. Heading "into the west" was a ritual for many Dubliners, a kind of physical and emotional escape from the city. John was beginning to recognize why. He felt more at ease, more at peace. He enjoyed the change of scenery and let his thoughts return home for the first time in a couple of weeks. Of course he spoke to his parents and made a couple of calls to Old Joe in the Hound, but he had not really thought of home much. He reminded himself that part of his reason for being in Ireland was to study the pubs and their culture, but he mostly did this out of duty or obligation. He was experiencing Ireland and this obsessed him at the most fundamental levels. The Flying Hound would certainly benefit from this experience, as would John himself. However, these benefits would not result from a clinical study or research project but rather from simply immersing oneself in the experience.

Chapter 30

The bus traveled west on the N6. Dermot told Dr. Carney that they were coming up on the town of Kilbeggan, the first scheduled stop on the tour, and home of Locke's Distillery, which dates to 1757. Although they no longer produce Irish whiskey here, the distillery has survived as a museum, which has helped Kilbeggan draw tourists to this otherwise unremarkable town in the Midlands.

"Everyone up and alert please. Take off your radios and give me your attention." Dr. Carney ordered. "We are scheduled to have our first tour of the trip. We will be touring an old Irish whiskey distillery with a tasting at the end. After, we will have lunch in the café. Everyone is to be on their best behavior. Also, please limit your drinking to the official tasting as well. We still have a ways to go after this stop."

The students began to wake up and focus a little.

"Where the hell are we?" Nancy asked.

"Oh, this looks like fun." Emily added looking out at the small industrial town.

"Hey, there's free whiskey, how bad could it be?" Tony chimed in.

Dermot pulled the bus into a dusty lot across from Locke's. "Right you be." he said opening the bus door.

The group filed out of the bus yawning and stretching. Dr. Carney led them across the busy road to the entrance of the museum.

"Remember, best behavior. Also, please try to formulate reasonable questions at the end of the tour. Try to act like college students." he said. Becky made a face at Dr. Carney's comment. Of course she would act like a college student. She, after all, went to a "real" college with real intellectuals.

As Carney checked in at the group sales desk, the students wandered around the reception area and the gift shop. John was looking at the vast array of Irish whiskies on display.

"Man, I've been in the bar business for a while but I had no idea there were so many brands and varieties of Irish whiskey. Back at the Hound, it's usually just Jameson or Bushmills. I never knew of these others." he said looking at the bottles of Tullamore Dew, Red Breast, Paddy's, Powers, Jameson 10 and 12 year old, Bushmill 16, Midleton, Knoppogue, and Locke's own brand.

"I wonder if they all taste the same?" Jeff asked.

"Not likely." answered Charley Robertson, the other "new" guy on the trip. "They're probably as different as Beam and Jack." he said referring to two great American bourbons from rival states.

Charley hailed from Kentucky and likely preferred Jim Beam or Makers Mark to Jack Daniels. He spoke with a pronounced drawl that was distinctly southern but not exactly like Rachel's softer accent. His family was in the horse breeding business and had sold some horses in Ireland. He had been to Ireland a few times before but spent most of his time in or around Kildare, racehorse country. He hadn't said much prior to this observation, which caught John a little off guard. John wondered how he knew so little about this guy. He then realized that Charley only joined the program for this course. He had only just arrived in Dublin the day before the trip.

"Everyone, please take a ticket and wait by the sign marked 'Group Assembly'." Dr. Carney instructed.

The group gathered together and was met by a young portly woman dressed in a green and brown uniform that made her look a little like a flight attendant.

"Good morning. You are all very welcome to Locke's." she said with a strong midland accent. He name tag read "Orlagh." she seemed to be genuinely friendly and excited about whiskey.

John noticed during his time in Ireland how fiercely proud the Irish were about all things Irish whether it was writers, actors, musicians, history, education or, in this case, whiskey.

The tour was about an hour long. Some of the students were interested and attentive. Others were just going through the motions. John was very tuned into what Orlagh was saying despite the fact that he lost about half of what she said to her accent. At the end of the tour, Orlagh asked if there were any questions.

"When do we get our sample?" Tony asked. Dr. Carney shot him a look but Tony either didn't see him or just chose to ignore him.

Orlagh smiled although it was not the first time she had been asked this question. "If you would like to come to the tasting room, I will give you each a voucher for either a whiskey or an orange juice if it's too early for some of you."

They all happily took their vouchers and went into the tasting room. This looked like a new addition to the ancient distillery building. Tables were arranged in long rows along a long and narrow space. Old photos and posters hung on the wall depicting scenes from the distillery's prime sometime around the turn of the 20th century. A cafeteria-style line along the back wall dispensed mineral water, orange soda, and finally, Irish whiskey.

Chapter 31

All but two of the group went for the whiskey. Carol gave her voucher to Tony who gladly helped himself to two whiskies. Becky decided on a mineral water saying she only drank after five in the afternoon. John wondered if she drank at all.

After the whiskey, the group went into the little café next to the distillery and gift shop and had a light lunch. Several students bought bottles of various whiskies. Dr Carney reminded them that the bottles were to stay sealed until after the trip. John picked up an expensive bottle of Midleton Whiskey for Old Joe. He knew if anyone would appreciate something as fine as this rare whiskey, it would be his grandfather.

"A gift for your pre-fiancé?" Nancy said as John paid for the whiskey.

"Yea. She's a real drinker." John shot back.

For a minute he forgot the little lie he told Nancy earlier but it was clear she didn't believe him anyway.

The journey continued west through the Midlands, past Athlone towards County Galway. The terrain got rougher as they made it into the West with rocky walls replacing hedges and fences. John could see why the British were more prominent in the eastern part of Ireland and why the west remained wild for so long. While the West was beautiful and rugged, the land for farming was generally poor. Still, John really felt like he was now entering the Ireland he'd expected when he left the USA.

As the bus approached Galway city, urban sprawl again appeared. Galway, a large town a generation ago, had grown into a significant city. On the outskirts, new shopping centers and modern houses dominate the landscape. Some of the students started to come to life at the sign of the city buzz. However, before they came to the city proper, Dermot left the N6 at the roundabout just past Oranmore and got onto the significantly smaller N84. Just as quick as the city life had appeared, it had now retreated and the group was suddenly back in the country.

"Galway looked like it would be fun." Mike said as he watched it fade in the back window of the bus.

"Tell him to turn around." Nancy added.

"I'm looking forward to a little country experience." John said. "We've been in a city for over two weeks now and I need a break."

"I'm a city girl." Emily said. "Give me the clubs, shopping, restaurants and keep Green Acres to yourself."

John wondered why some of them signed up for the trip. Most of them slept through the countryside even while Dermot pointed out interesting sights as they traveled. Sometimes he was really only talking to Dr. Carney and him. Why come all the way across the Atlantic to sleep or wish you were back home?

Dr. Carney turned and asked for everyone's attention. "We are about fifteen minutes from our next stop. As you have seen in the syllabus, our first night is in a farmhouse B&B. Ireland is famous for its B&B's and the one we have picked is an excellent example of a farmhouse operation. Remember, this is a working farm so stay out of the way of the family running the place. You will have time to relax before dinner so take a walk and enjoy the fresh air."

The bus struggled with the steep and winding roads. A small sign planted in a sheep's pasture pointed to a very small dirt road leading to Casey's Farmhouse B&B. Dermot pulled the bus onto the road creating a minor dust explosion. The students looked at each other with a mix of dread and anticipation.

"What does 'en suite' mean?" Emily asked to anyone listening.

"It means this is a nudist B&B and all chicks have to arrive topless. You'd better start stripping." Tony said.

Jeff and Mike laughed causing Becky to shoot them one of her now famous looks.

"It means there are bathrooms in every room." Carol said. "In the old days, most B&B's had shared toilets. Now, many have upgraded to appeal more to Americans."

The bus continued to spread a dust storm as it made its way to the paved drive leading to the farmhouse. A middle-aged woman with short red hair and wearing a flowered apron was waiting at the sliding glass door entrance into the house's windbreak. She was smiling as the bus approached. John felt it was strange pulling up to some stranger's house to spend the night. The woman's smile, though, was welcoming and gave the impression that they were expected.

Dr. Carney got off the bus first and greeted the women warmly.

"Good afternoon Mrs. Casey. It is so good to see you again." he said as he shook her hand.

"You are very welcome back, professor. You are all very welcome indeed." she said welcoming the group as they got off the bus. "Please come into the parlor and we'll get you sorted."

The parlor looked as if it might have been the same for a hundred years. Large, flower print sofas faced towards a picture window looking out into a wooded area. An ancient looking TV sat against the wall with paintings of country scenes hanging on the wall. All of the lights were off except for a small naked bulb that hung over the little reception desk. The desk had brochures offering gillies for trout or salmon fishing, a homemade craft shop located in Cong, a nearby village, and horseback riding options.

Dr. Carney conferred with Mrs. Casey about the rooming lists.

"Right then, professor, I will leave the details to you." she said and handed Dr. Carney a handful of keys. She turned to the group sitting quietly in her parlor. "Breakfast is at half 7 tomorrow. If you are not coming, please let your professor know. Feel free to walk the grounds and relax. There is tea in your rooms. Have fun." she said and went into the room behind reception.

"I have assigned you rooms randomly." Dr. Carney started. "If you want to change, it is up to you. It is now 4 PM. Dinner is at 7:00 pm and we will need to leave around 6:30 to get there. Dress casual." he started to call out names according to room assignments. John was assigned a room with Charley. He hadn't had a roommate so far and was hoping he'd be with someone he knew. Tony and Jeff were assigned together leaving Mike a room to himself. Eventually, after everyone got a roommate, they went to the bus to get their gear. Dermot had already unloaded the bags and lined them up neatly on the tarmac driveway.

The rooms were small but neat and definitely "en suite." The bathroom was a tiny closet that made it physically possible to shower and take a leak at the same time. Charley was unpacking and not saying much. John decided to take a walk around to stretch his legs. "You feel like checking the farm out?" he asked Charley.

"Man, I was born and raised on a farm. I've seen enough, thanks. Besides, I have to write some postcards home or my ma will kill me."

John thought there was something old-fashioned about Charley. He figured it was his country demeanor but could not exactly pinpoint it. The strange thing was, he might be country and born and raised on a farm, but he wore expensive designer clothes and carried Tumi luggage. He might be country, but it looked like he was rich-country.

John went downstairs to the parlor. Becky was on the couch reading a travel guide. None of the others had come down yet. He went outside into the fresh air. It was technically summer but the air was cool and misty. John enjoyed the freshness of it as he set off for his walk. He found a path down into the woods. The big oak trees were covered in neon green moss at their bases. The light was partially blocked by the tree's giant canopies giving a kind of enchanted feel to the place. John half expected a leprechaun to jump out from behind an oak guarding his pot o' gold.
The trees thinned out as he came to the edge of a large lake. John could see small fishing boats, fishing skiffs, trolling for salmon. Beyond the lake, jagged mountains rose framing the spot in a beautiful, peaceful, and mythical setting. John imagined it was scenes like these that made immigrants to the US pine for their homeland. He could not imagine how bad things must have been a century or so ago that would drive people from this place.

"Going for a dip?" Jeff's voice broke the silence.

"No." John answered. "Just admiring the view. Could you imagine this back home? The place would be full of high-rise condos, speed boats, jet skis and tiki bars."

"Yea, probably." Jeff replied now taking in the sweeping landscape.

"Where are the troops?" John asked.

"Mike went for a run. The girls are camped out in their rooms for the most part. That Carol girl is on the phone with her mother I think. I saw Charley go into the barn with some farmer looking dude."

John thought it was weird that Charley now seemed interested in the farm despite his earlier protests.

"Do you think Charley is odd?" John asked. "I don't mean in a bad way but I don't get the whole country thing and"

"His Gucci shoes." Jeff finished John's thought.

"Yea, what's with that? I mean, whatever, but it seems strange."

Jeff and John walked along the lake for a while. They came to another path that looked like it went back towards the farm. As they headed up the path, they noticed a couple embracing in what looked like from a distance, a romantic embrace. As they got a little closer, they could make out Tony and Rachel's features. The new couple was kissing and holding each other close. There was no denying it; Tony and Rachel were more than casual hook ups. John thought they made a strange couple but who could say why certain people end up together. Jeff appeared to agree with John as he shook his head a little and turned to head back towards the lake.

By the time they got back, Nancy and Emily were sitting on a stonewall overlooking a small pasture with new lambs grazing below. Becky was now reading outside a little further down the wall.

"Where'd you guys go?" Emily asked.

"Out looking for wild life." John said.

"Yes, and we sure found some." Jeff added.

What are you up to?" John asked.

"The farmer lady said we could feed the lambs. She went to get the bottles." Nancy said.

Almost on queue, Mrs. Casey came from one of the small outbuildings carrying three large glass bottles with rubber nipples. She handed one to each of the girls and went into the pasture to corral the lambs. She gave each of them a lamb and showed them what to do with the bottles. Even though these girls were young adults who smoked, drank, experimented a little with weed, and were not exactly virginal, they did look like little kids in a petting zoo. All three had expressions on their face that made them look like little girls playing with dolls. For that moment, the clubs and pubs of Dublin gave way to a much simpler pleasure. Feeding the baby animals in this bucolic setting was a natural high for all of them and would prove to be a life long memory for all of them.

By 6 o'clock, most of the group had gathered in Mrs. Casey's parlor. John was talking with Mike when Tony came down the stairs.

"What's up?" He asked.

"You tell me." John responded.

Tony scanned the group. "Have you guys seen Rachel?" he asked.

"She's not down yet." Mike replied.

John smiled a little finding Tony's clear infatuation amusing.

"What's so fuckin' funny?" Tony asked.

"Nothing." John said. "I just think your little crush on the southern belle is amusing."

"Kiss my ass. This little situation is strictly for convenience. Don't go getting me married off."

John was not buying Tony's line of bullshit. He may not be an expert on such matters, but he was certain that Tony really liked Rachel. As far as he could tell, and for reasons he could not explain, Rachel seemed to feel the same way.

Chapter 32

Dr. Carney gathered the last of the group in the parlor. “Listen up for a second. We will be heading into a little village just up the road for a pub style dinner. You can dress casually but please, no baseball caps. I need everyone on the bus in five minutes.”

Dermot had already fired up the bus by the time the group made their way outside.

“A pub style dinner? What do you think that is going to be like, Guinness and brown bread?” Jeff asked.

“Hopefully, it will be filling. I am starving.” Mike added.

“I wouldn’t mind just staying home be to be honest.” Emily said. “I’m coming down with something.”

“Stay away from me.” Tony said. “I don’t need to get sick.”

“God forbid, you might spread it around.” Rachel said as she smiled at Tony and pinched his ass.

The bus pulled onto the dirt road and rumbled up to the main road. Dermot pulled the bus up onto the street and headed for the very small village known as “The Neale.” The pub there, Hayden’s, was well known locally for their outstanding pub grub. Most traditional pubs in Ireland served little or no food but

Hayden's, a little country pub in the wilds of Mayo, was drawing tourist from Galway and even away from the nearby Ashford Castle.

John could not wait. He wanted to experience the full range of Irish hospitality and this would be a great start. As the bus arrived, he noted that The Neale was comprised of a few bungalows and cottages, a gas station with a small market attached, and Hayden's pub. This place would hardly be called a village back home. It was more like a crossroads. However, in Ireland, a gas station and a pub often make a village.

Dr. Carney gave them the now usual warning about good behavior and escorted the crew into the pub. It was just past six when they entered. The pub itself was not at all like the older pubs in Dublin. Hayden's did not have ornate Victorian features. It was not full of young professionals and hip college types. Hayden's was comprised of a single front rectangular room with the bar dominating one end and booths and tables the other. It was dark and a little drab but clean. There were a handful of locals scattered around who all turned to have a look at the Yanks and kept looking for a long time. John could not get over the fact that they really seemed interested in the group. Even though this part of Ireland gets its fair share of tourist, Hayden's doesn't often cater to busloads of them.

A relatively young curly haired man came from behind the bar.

"Professor Carney," he said. "welcome back. I see you've a fresh group of students with you. It's great to have you back."

The man and Carney shook hands and exchanged pleasantries. He had been bringing students to Hayden's for a number of years now, which the owners appreciated.

"Please say hello to Mr. Morrissey everyone."

"Roger, please. Mr. Morrissey is my da'."

The group went around and introduced themselves. Roger Morrissey was a charming man who had a playful sense of humor. He flirted with the girls who did not seem to mind at all and told off color jokes to the guys. Everyone settled in and Roger returned to the bar to get everyone their drinks. Most of the group ordered Guinness or Harp. John asked for a Paddy's Whiskey, which prompted a "Good man yourself" from Roger. Tony asked for a white Russian that prompted a blank stare from Roger. Dublin may have been up to speed with the rebirth of the cocktail but it had not yet caught on in Mayo.

"Well," Roger said, trying to be accommodating "you tell me what's in it, and I'll make it."

Tony realized that a white Russian may not be a good idea after all and asked Roger for something that would "wake him up."

"I've just the thing for ya." Roger disappeared into the back room.

John looked at Tony "You're in for it now. A White Russian? Are you fucking kidding?" "I don't know? I can't drink beer; it will put me to sleep." Tony said.

Roger came out of the back room carrying a short glass with a grayish liquid filling half of it.

"Now, here's just the thing to get you going." Roger handed Tony the glass, as Tony looked at it nervously.

"It looks like dish water." he said worrying that it might be a practical joke.

One of the locals sitting at the end of the bar smiled and raised his glass of beer, "good luck and God speed."

"Now, drink it straight down and you'll never be better." Roger instructed.

Tony, aware that most of the bar was now watching him raised the glass and shot its contents in one gulp.

"Ahhh. Good stuff." Tony said. "Not too strong though."

"Just wait lad." Roger said and went back to his orders.

Emily was slouched at a table near the bar. Her head was down but she was not asleep.

"Love, are you alright there?" Roger called over to her. "Too much fun last night?"

Emily raised her head with her eyes watery and squinting. "Just a little under the weather."

"How 'bout a hot whiskey or hot port? That'll fix you." Roger offered.

"Maybe just some tea." she replied.

With a quick nod, Roger began to put together a pot of tea. He came around from the bar putting a little pot of water next to a teacup and strainer. He put loose tea in the pot.

"Let that brew good and strong." he said.

"Do you have any honey? My throat is killing me."

John was watching this scene play out. He watched Roger go out of his way for the sick student and, without hesitation, told Emily that he had honey even though he suspected he didn't. John watched Roger walk into the kitchen behind the bar. Instead of getting the honey from a pantry or storage area, Roger put on his jacket and hat and walked out the back door. He was quiet and no one else saw him go. John watched as he went across the street to the gas station, walk into the little market, and emerged a few minutes later with a little brown bag. He hustled back across the street and into the back door. He took off his coat, his hat and put down the package. He proceeded to take out a small service plate, put a lacy doily on it, take the jar of newly acquired honey out of the bag, unscrew the top and place the jar on the plate. He put a teaspoon on the plate next to the jar and came out to the front bar.

"Now, your honey love."

John was amazed. It took only minutes from the time she asked for the honey until it was produced on a service plate with a doily and spoon. The tea was just finished brewing and no one except John noticed the effort Roger went to in order to comply with the simple request. Emily barely managed a “thanks a lot.” As Roger went back behind the bar, he saw John watching this transpire. He winked and cocked his head as if to say, “all in a day’s work.” All John could think was how that scene would likely never happen in the States. What would likely happen, even in the Flying Hound, would be to simply say there was no honey. It would not even occur to a good server or bartender to take on the problem and handle it. Just a simple “no” would be the answer. Here, hospitality rose to the level or really looking after someone. Back home, it’s more of a chore than a pleasure.

Chapter 33

After a couple of pre-dinner rounds, Dr. Carney ushered them into a back dining room. Tony, now feeling a little bleary from the potchin, stumbled a little as he got up from his stool. John noticed but decided to keep it to himself.

The room itself was brighter than the bar and had a newer feel. A long table was prepared for the group, which took up about half of the room. The table setting was simple enough but had a certain country elegance. Roger was standing at the head of the table while two women servers stood by with pitchers of water. Dr. Carney took the spot at the head of the table and asked everyone to be seated. Once the group settled in, Roger passed out menus and announced a few specials.

"Tonight, we have some lovely Turbot just in from Cliften on the coast, we also have local lamb, and finally, homemade shepherd's pie. The soup is cream of veg. Would anyone like to see the wine list?"

John was surprised at the sophistication of the menu. Ireland had only recently joined other European countries as a culinary hot spot but he had assumed this would be limited to the cities and main tourist spots.

The students were hungry. It had been a long time since lunch at Locke's and the drinks at the bar brought out their appetites. Dr. Carney ordered a bottle of red and a bottle of white for the table. Roger proceeded to take the orders of the ladies first and then the guys. John looked over the menu finding it hard to decide. He wanted to try new things and really experience rural cooking. Finally, he settled on a half dozen of local Galway oysters and the lamb special.

"Poor little lamb." Nancy said overhearing his order. The thought of the girls bottle-feeding the new lambs earlier today was a bit unsettling but John stuck to his guns.

Roger continued around the table until everyone had ordered. Tony caused the only hiccup when he asked Roger if there was any pasta. Roger looked at him straight-faced and said he'd check with the chef.

The food was truly exceptional. John could not believe the quality and simple elegance of the meal. His oysters were fresh out of the Atlantic, their briny tang and plump texture was a treat. The lamb, a four-chop rack, was a perfect medium rare with an herb coating that locked in the flavor. Mashed potato with turnips added to the local flavor. John finished his meal with a cheese plate made up entirely of cheeses produced within fifty miles of the pub chased with a Hennessey Cognac.

John was in heaven. He had not eaten so well since he arrived in Ireland. His curry fries and tuna fish with sweet corn sandwiches could not compare to this feast. He wondered if it could be topped in the ten nights left. If this was pub-grub, what would the gourmet meals be like?

He was intrigued by the fact that Roger came around during the meals to ask if anyone needed more of anything. What would happen in the States if the waiter asked if you wanted more steak, or fish. Places would be overrun. Here, though, it was simple hospitality.

“Man, I am stuffed.” Tony said rubbing his gut. “I can’t believe the chef pulled together a lasagna for me. It’s not like Mom’s, but damn it was tasty.”

The rest of the table looked well satiated. Dr. Carney looked like he was ready for bed.

Roger made one last appeal, “Will you join us in the bar for a wee night cap? It’s on the house.” Half of the table groaned a little but most were delighted at the thought of free drinks. Even Dr. Carney suddenly looked refreshed.

Chapter 34

There were no late night antics at Casey's that evening. The day of travel combined with a big country meal made everyone's decision to turn in easier. John spotted Tony kissing Rachel goodnight and he could not help but think they looked more serious than just traveling buddies.

He went into his room and found Charley already under the covers, reading a book called McCarthy's Bar.

"What's that about?"

"It's about an English guy who comes to Ireland to visit all of the pubs named McCarthy's. Its actually real funny but it makes fun of Americans a little."

John suddenly wished he had a book to read. He had not anticipated any reading time on the trip so he left his books back in Dublin. He decided to just call it a night and fell asleep before Charley even turned off his light.

"Everyone up and At'em." A voice called down the long hallway. "Breakfast is served."

John now recognized Dr. Carney's voice. He was so sound asleep; he was disorientated and needed a minute to figure out where he was. He had not slept so soundly in a long time. Carney's voice, the farm sounds and smells, and the sight of Charles struggling to get his bearings brought John back to reality.

"Man, I slept." John said as he stretched and yawned.

"I usually get up by 6 in the morning, but I am struggling today." Charley said.

They got up, showered and dressed in time to meet Mrs. Casey's breakfast time of seven thirty. Seven of the ten students were in the little breakfast room off of the parlor but three had yet to surface. Tony and Rachel were up early and had gone for a walk. Emily was still in bed nursing her flu. The tea and several hot whiskies got her through the night but this morning, she could not answer the early bell.

Mrs. Casey whizzed around the room delivering various breakfast items to the table and taking orders. John had stayed at a couple of B&B's back home where breakfast usually constituted coffee, tea, and some pastry. Here, breakfast was elevated to another level. In front of each place setting, a bowl of cold cereal, mandarin orange sliced and fresh strawberries and cream were set. Coffee and tea were set with brown and white sugar, milk and heavy cream. Next, porridge was brought out and served with raisins and dark brown sugar. Finally, a full Irish cooked breakfast complete with warm toast and extra rich butter arrived. Everything was so fresh that John and his travel companions had trouble pacing themselves.

When it was over, Dr. Carney sat smiling at the head of the table. "That was a no-lunch special." he said as he got up to settle the final bill.

Dermot had pulled the bus up to the front entrance. Dr. Carney gave them their marching orders right after breakfast. They would leave by 10 AM for their short trip into Cong, County Mayo. He asked that they dress neatly as their hotel, Ashford Castle, was substantially more formal than the B&B. They would be on the road for only a few minutes but they had a full day planned.

Emily finally resurfaced, just as Tony and Rachel walked in from the woods hand in hand. They coaxed some toast and coffee from Mrs. Casey and went upstairs to get their things together.

"Ah, romance." John said.

"I can't believe those two are a couple. They are as different as chalk and cheese, as the Irish say." Nancy said as she watched them go up the stairs. "I would have put Emily with him before Rachel."

"Screw you." Emily said from the couch, sitting with her head in her hands.

"I'm just saying. You're both city people, city folk and all." Nancy said.

"Just because we're both from the city does not mean I would ever have anything to do with him romantically. I'm from Manhattan, he's from Boston for Christ sake. Talk about chalk and cheese." Emily said as she ran out of energy and stretched out on the couch.

"Let's roll." Dr. Carney said as he put the credit card receipt in his big folder in the file marked 'Casey's.' "We have our first meeting at 11:30 this morning." A collective groan went out. The trip was designed to be educational. Dr. Carney believed in the experiential aspects of the tour but tried to anchor the learning elements with lectures and demonstrations. Of course, students always liked the experiential element of the tour over the old-fashioned lectures.

Chapter 35

The group assembled with their bags next to the bus. Dermot began loading up the gear and the students piled in.

"Do you know where we're going next?" Tony asked John.

"Ashford Castle, it's just a few miles down the road." John answered. "It's supposed to be awesome."

"Why didn't we stay there the first night if we were so close?" Tony asked.

"Probably because Carney didn't want to set the bar too high." Rachel chimed in.

"You're probably right. Anyway, I can't wait to see it. I am glad it's close so we don't waste the whole day driving." John said.

The bus pulled out of the drive. Mrs. Casey waved goodbye much the same way she waved hello, smiling with a cheerful look. Dr. Carney asked for everyone's attention as they pulled on to the main road. "We will be at Ashford in a few minutes. This property is one of two castle hotels we will visit. We have arranged a meeting this morning with the hotel's managing director, Martin Dunn. Mr. Dunn will give you an overview of the property, its facilities and amenities. He will then take us on a property tour followed by lunch. After lunch, we will meet with Seamus Lydon, the food and beverage director, and Fiona Chandler, the director of sales. We should be through by 3 PM with the official itinerary, which gives you the afternoon to yourselves. We will also tour the wine cellar with a tasting just before dinner. Men, jackets and ties please. Women, dress appropriately."

"A jacket and tie?" moaned Charley. "I hate getting dressed up."

"What do you mean? You have all of those fancy clothes." Nancy said.

"They're just play clothes my mother buys me. I make my livin' with my back; I don't need a jacket and tie where I come from."

Nancy shook her head and let it drop. The rest of the group just looked out the window as the bus passed some of the wildest, most rugged and beautiful scenes in the West of Ireland.

The bus slowed as it came along a tall curtain wall that looked like something from a King Arthur's fairytale. A thin red and white striped pole manned by a young man wearing a peaked military type of hat secured the massive entrance gate. Dermot opened his window.

"Checking in."

"The name of the group please?" The guard asked.

"Carney, or the American Institute, maybe?" Dermot said.

The guard looked at his clipboard paging through his list of expected guests. "Right, here we are." The guard said as he mechanically opened the poll barricade.

Dermot waved as they passed through. The bus started down the very narrow drive going through a heavily wooded area that eventually opened onto the hotel's golf course. As the bus negotiated the driveway and came around a bend, the group had their first 'holy shit!' moment. The castle sat a few hundred yards down the sloping, winding drive. Everyone was awed by its massive structure. The castle itself faced Lough Corrib, a substantial fresh water lake that dominates the area. Apron walls with watchtowers and turrets surround the back of the castle with a drawbridge over a swift moving river at its front. The lawns spread out as far as one could see. The entire setting was enchanting. The students kept looking at each other mouthing "oh my God" and "holy shit."

John turned to Tony, "this is a long way from the farm."

"You said it. The B&B was fine but this is off the charts."

The bus meandered down the hill passing the staff quarters and stopped just short of the drawbridge. Dermot lined the bus up to navigate the narrow bridge. Lake cruise boats and small fishing skiffs lined one side of the bridge where the river opened up to the lake. An open green field with a helicopter pad flanked the other side. The students were mesmerized.

"This is like a fairy tail." Becky said.

"It reminds me of castles in England and Wales." Carol added.

A horse and trap waited on the other side of the bridge. Several guests milled around the front of the hotel taking pictures and taking in the scene. A Japanese bride was posing with her new husband who was dressed in a formal Scottish kilt.

Two doormen and a porter awaited the group's arrival.

Dermot pulled up to the main entrance. A wooden sign announced that the castle was reserved "For Residence Only" written in old English script.

"Shit, people actually live here?" Jeff asked.

"I think the sign means registered guests." John offered.

Dr. Carney was up to give his two-minute speech "Remember, best behavior. Stick to the schedule and don't be late, and please, try to come up with an intelligent question or two."

They got off the bus. The porter, a short stocky man whose age was hard to determine, welcomed the group and offered to help with the bags.

"Tips are up to you." Dr. Carney announced reminding the group that gratuities were not included in their fees.

The doormen also welcomed the group and showed them into the reception area. A suit of armor guarded the entrance into the hotel. John wondered about the historical accuracy of the prop and decided it was likely done for effect. The hotel itself dated to the mid nineteenth century and was largely built as a hunting lodge for the Guinness family. It was true that the oldest part of the castle dated to the twelfth or thirteenth century but most of the place came to be long after the last crusade.

The reception area and main hall were elegant. The wood paneling, leather, tapestries, and old oil paintings mixed with the aromatic scent of burning peat gave the place a very old world atmosphere. It was easy to imagine this place with kings and queens from the middle ages. Of course, that imagery was hard to reconcile with the Japanese wedding party that crashed through the main entrance following their photo shoot. The Japanese men were dressed in formal Scottish Kilts while the women wore fashionable cocktail dresses. John found it hard to rectify the image of the wedding party and the atmosphere of the castle.

The front desk manager welcomed Dr. Carney back and turned to welcome the rest of the group. "

They sure do like to welcome you a lot." Charley said. "Why do they all say welcome home?"

John didn't reply but thought it was a way to endear Irish-Americans. Back home, the Irish-Americans romanticize about the "homeland" and the Irish in Ireland probably figured out a way to capitalize on this nostalgia.

After the rooms were sorted out, Dr. Carney said the group had about a half and hour to settle in.

"Bring your things to your rooms and have a quick look around if you like." he said.

This time, John and Tony were assigned a room together.

"I'm carrying my own stuff to the room." Tony said and John agreed.

Unlike a modern hotel tower, Ashford was an irregular sprawling property. Guest rooms were scattered throughout the structure and no two rooms were alike. Tony and John's room, 214, was a very large room with two queen beds and a Murphy bed built into the wall. The room overlooked the pristine lake and the mouth of the river. The space was recently redecorated but still felt like you were staying in a museum.

"Can we drink this?" Tony asked pointing to a crystal decanter filled with some type of chestnut brown liquid.

"I don't know, I saw the same set up down in reception. It might be sherry."

Tony pulled the stopper from the crystal and took a deep sniff. "Whoa. Smells potent. I'd better test it out."

"Don't get shit-canned before the meetings." John suggested.

"No, just something to take the edge off. I got to keep myself together for Rach anyway."

"What's with you two anyway? It looks like things may be getting a bit more serious that just someone to fool around with on the trip."

"Yea, maybe, I don't know. It started off casual enough but she's pretty cool. We'll see. I think she has a boyfriend back home anyway." Tony said looking out the window.

John thought this was the right time to drop his line of questioning. "Hey, we better get back down stairs before Carney sends out the guards." John said. "I hope you have thought up a good question."

"Oh, I did." Tony responded. "When does the bar open?" They laughed and headed back downstairs.

The group had reassembled in the reception area. Some came from their rooms while others returned from outside where they had a quick look around.

"They have horse back riding, fishing, jogging trails, and a spa!" Nancy yelled walking in from the main door. "This joint rocks!"

"I need to sit in a steam to kick this feckin' cold." Emily whined.

"Maybe a few more hot whiskies are in order?' Tony said as the group assembled.

"Is everyone here?" Dr. Carney asked. "Who's missing?"

"That Carol chick is off on her cell again." Jeff said. "I saw her outside a few minutes ago."

"Please go get her; I don't want to keep Mr. Dunn waiting."

Jeff ran outside but Carol was nowhere in sight. He took a quick walk to the end of the building towards the formal gardens but she was not there either. He ran back to the entrance and just before he came back in, he spotted a figure sitting across the bridge down by the boats. The person was slumped over with her face in her hands. Jeff knew it was Carol but he couldn't quite figure out what she was doing.

"Carol, is that you?" he called over the bridge. The roar of the river kept Carol from hearing Jeff. He jogged across the bridge and walked straight up to her. "Yo, Carney is waiting on you." Carol did not move. She sat still until Jeff thought he noticed her heave a little. "Hey, you ok or what?" he asked coming closer.

"Just go away. Tell Carney you couldn't find me."

Jeff could tell from her quivering voice that she was upset and crying. He didn't really know Carol and only had spoken to her a little but he couldn't help but be concerned.

"Hey, what's the matter?" he asked sitting down beside her, their feet dangling towards the river.

Carol still didn't say anything.

"Look, I'll sit with you but you need to tell me what's up." Jeff said.

Carol stayed quiet for a few more minutes. Finally, she looked over at him and smiled. Jeff was taken aback.

"Are you fuckin' with me or what?" he asked.

She kept smiling but Jeff could see she had been crying and was upset.

"Sometimes I laugh or smile at inappropriate times. I can't go to funerals because I tend to laugh. I dunno, its some kind of nervous response." Carol explained.

"God, that sucks." Jeff said. "Do you want to try to go back in?"

Carol rubbed her eyes.

Jeff suddenly realized how pretty she was. She was always a little conservative and even business like in her manner but now, sitting on the ancient wall in front of this romantic place, Jeff could see her plainly.

"What are you looking at? Do I have something hanging out of my nose?" she asked, smiling again.

"No, no, sorry. You just looked so bummed. Can I get you something?"

"I'm fine. Just stupid family crap. My mom just informed me that we are moving to South Africa or some shit. This will be my fourth country in ten years. We lived in the Sates for the past three years and I was starting to feel settled. I even managed to make a few friends."

"What is it that your family does anyway?" Jeff asked genuinely interested.

"It's a little involved but my Mother works with foreign governments to promote US policy abroad. She has been assigned to Washington since we moved back from Panama and I thought we would be there for good. I mean, I don't have to go with them if I don't want to. I am in college and could just be on my own but I've never been away from them before and to have them so far away…" her voice trailed off and her eyes again filled to the brim.

"Boy, that's tough. My parents moved from Hartford to Boston when I was in the seventh grade and I thought that was a pain, but your situation sucks."

"It's been great, don't get me wrong. I've lived in some wonderful places and met fascinating people. I even know several languages, but being a foreigner all of the time is tiring and I just want to just stay put."

"Well, if we stay put much longer, Carney's going to shit a brick." Jeff said motioning towards the hotel.

"You go, I'll be along soon. I just need to get myself together."

"I'll just tell him you are on your way." Jeff said as he got to his feet and brushed the gravel from the back of his pants.

Carol smiled up at him, which confused Jeff because he was not sure if this was her sad reaction or if she was cheering up. "Thanks" she said and gave him a little wave.

Chapter 36

Mr. Dunn stood in front of the assembled students and began his opening remarks. John thought he looked young to be in a senior position at such a prestigious property. In a way, John was envious. He desperately wanted to run the Hound, but was he aiming high enough? After all, here was Martin Dunn who could not be more the five or six years older than him.

John thought of his Father pushing him towards the corporate world and then thought of Old Joe who was counting on him to carry on the family legacy. John was conflicted and worried for the first time since he arrived in Ireland. How could the simple sight of a young executive cloud his plans for his future?

Suddenly, the group was on the move. John snapped out of his trance realizing he heard none of the opening remarks.

"Where are we going?" he asked Tony.

"What the fuck? Are you drunk?" Tony laughed.

"No, I just spaced out."

"We are doing the property tour. The manager dude said we would start outside and work our way in."

They filed out the front door and reassembled across the parking lot next to the helicopter pad. Carol quickly and quietly rejoined the group without drawing anyone's attention. Jeff, however, watched her and was amazed at how collected she looked. He nodded at her but held back the urge to wink fearing she might think it would be weird.

"Now." Martin Dunn started. "Please do not hesitate to stop me with any questions. I have done this tour once or twice so I tend to rush things."

With that the group embarked on a whirlwind tour of the magnificent place. They walked up a long lane to the riding center passing rows of ancient oak trees on their way. They visited the Falconry and the formal gardens. They walked to the lake and climbed a twelfth century crescent shaped battlement that is believed to be the oldest structure on the grounds. They learned of the castle's history including visits from famous people like Ronald Reagan and Pierce Brosnan.

Dunn, a talented guide and historian, kept the students interested throughout the hour-long walk. No one complained or asked for a break while a few even managed competent sounding questions. Dunn finally returned the group to a private room off of the main dining room.

"I am going to leave you in the good hands of Fiona Chandler, our director of marketing and sales. She will be with you in a moment. I have arranged coffee while you wait. Thank you for your attention. It has been a pleasure to show you around our little place." Mr. Dunn concluded as he left the group to sit and relax before their next tour.

"This place is awesome." Nancy said. I can't wait to hit the spa."

"I can't wait to hit the bar." Tony said in reply. "All of this walkin' around has given me a terrible thirst."

John nodded in agreement but was still looking forward to the next tour. Martin Dunn had energized him and although meeting him fogged his notion of his future, he was learning and experiencing new and wonderful things. Things he hoped to bring to his professional life at some point.

The door to the little breakout room swung open. A middle-aged woman wearing a fashionable business suit walked in and started talking to Dr. Carney. The two were nodding and smiling at each other exchanging pleasantries. John noticed the two didn't seem to know each other that well but Carney was still giving her his best bullshit.

After a few minutes of this, the good professor asked for everyone's attention, "Everyone! Please quiet down and say hello to Ms. Chandler. Please give her your full attention."

Fiona Chandler welcomed the students and thanked Dr. Carney for bringing another group of "future hospitality professionals."

John smiled a little at this comment noting to himself that he was the only one in the group that was actually studying hospitality. The others took the class as a free elective because the only other option offered during this session was Quantitative Business Analysis.

Ms. Chandler gave a brief overview of the hotel's operations, facilities and history. She discussed the role of marketing, who their target clients were, and how the hotel competes with other exclusive luxury properties. John was interested and tuned into what she was saying. Most of the rest of the group was thinking about the spa, the bar, or some other pursuit that so far, they'd only heard about.

Ms. Chandler took the group on a tour of the hotel itself. They visited several types of rooms and discussed rack rates for each. They saw the main suites including the Ronald Reagan suite that was built for the former President when he visited in the eighties. They toured the public rooms, the two restaurants, the Prince of Wales Cocktail Bar, named after a visit by the prince in 1890, the library, tearooms, spa, and famous Dungeon Bar. The students were chomping at the bit to experience all of these wonderful things and were having trouble focusing on the academic nature of the tour.

"When will this end?" Tony moaned. "I need to meet the prince in his bar for a private discussion."

"We still have the chef to deal with." Mike added. "He is going to do some presentation or something.

"Ohhh, for God's sake let it end." Tony droned.

Ms. Chandler concluded the tour at just past two in the afternoon. The group was played out and when it came time for questions, only John had the interest and energy to participate.

"How do you attract guests to the hotel in the off season, the winter for instance?" he asked as his classmates sneered a little.

"Aha! Good question." Ms. Chandler started. "In the old days, the hotel closed in the late fall and did not reopen until spring. Once the owners decided to go year-round, we were asked to create a strategy to fill the rooms. Mostly, we do special packages and events to bring people in the winter."

John sat paying close attention to the answer.

Ms. Chandler described packages and getaways, wine programs and gourmet classes. Her answer went far beyond the interest of the others. Soon, Dr. Carney was forced to refocus everyone.

"Guys, we're not going anywhere until the session is over so pay attention." he snapped. John managed two more questions before he felt the silent pressure from the group to wrap it up.

Ms. Chandler thanked everyone and wished them well in their "hospitality" careers. She announced that the chef, locally born Seamus Lydon, would be with them shortly.

Chapter 37

Dr. Carney told the group to take five minutes for a break. Everyone scattered heading for the bathrooms or outside for a smoke. Carol and Jeff stayed behind.

"How's it goin'?" Jeff asked Carol who smiled at him.

"Oh shit, you're not going to cry again?"

"No, this time it's a real smile. Thanks for sitting with me, it really helped."

"No trouble. Maybe we can get a drink after this if you want?" he asked.

"Sounds good. I think we'll need one after this is all done."

John walked outside to get some fresh air.

"Here comes mister inquisitive." Nancy teased. "Any more questions ace?"

"Sorry if I'm here for more than the sightseeing." he said as he glanced over to the drawbridge. He saw Tony and Rachel leaning against each other against the stone wall.

"Love is in the air." Emily said.

"Who'd a thunk it?" Mike replied. "I thought that would be over soon after the night they hooked up in Dublin." he noted.

"I think they're getting a little serious." John said recalling his conversation with Tony back in their room. Suddenly, Tony noticed them all looking at them. He returned the stares with a double middle finger salute. Rachel laughed and pulled his hands down. They tickled each other and laughed as they embraced.

"I'm gonna be sick." Nancy said. "How does he find a cute girl who is not a moron to like him?" She asked.

"Boston charm?" John replied cynically.

Emily shot him a look. "No charm in that boy at all and no such thing as charm coming from Boston."

Dr. Carney was rounding everyone up. "Let's get going. The chef is waiting."

The group reconvened in the main dining room. The space was huge. Wood paneled walls graced with crystal sconces gave the space the elegance of a country manor. John could not imagine serving so many people at once and was looking forward to the chef's presentation.

A man in his early forties dressed in white kitchen pants and a starched white chef's jacket stood just outside the kitchen entrance. He was holding a high chef's hat and wore white clogs on his feet. He had a ruddy complexion similar to many people from this part of the world. He smiled patiently as the group came back together. Dr. Carney called everyone to attention and then introduced Chef Lydon. The Chef thanked Carney and welcomed the group.

"Anyone considering a career in catering or cooking?" he asked to start things off. No one raised his or her hands. "Good, finally a sane group." he joked and waved the group into the kitchen.

Chef Seamus Lydon hailed from Castlebar; a larger village located about thirty miles north of Ashford Castle. He went to a local culinary school after secondary school at the urging of his mother. He showed talent from the start of his training prompting the school's director to recommend a stint in Germany to further his training. After a four-year tour of continental Europe with cooking stints in Austria, France and Italy, Chef Lydon was ready to come home. He worked in Dublin for a few years earning a name for himself as well as a reputation for his temper and sometimes-outlandish behavior. One story had him physically throwing out an Irish Times food editor from his restaurant for panning one of his dishes. Chef Lydon was Ireland's own Marco White or Gordon Ramsey. His distant relationship to John Lydon aka Johnny Rotten added to his legend.

However, after being the bad boy of fine dining in the Dublin scene, he was looking forward to a quieter gig where he could go back to the cooking he grew up on. When the Ashford job came up, he jumped at it. This was his own back yard where he had even done a six-month internship as a student. It took a little convincing for the owners to take a chance on a maverick like Lydon but ultimately, they couldn't pass up a person of his celebrity.

The group entered the kitchen. John noted the sterile nature of the place. White tiled walls went from floor to ceiling. All of the stainless equipment was spotless. There were aromas of all kinds wafting in the air as perfectly dressed cooks scurried around preparing for the evening's meal.

"Get me my drink, Tommy." Chef Lydon said to a young cook wearing a stripped blue and white apron over his kitchen whites as he passed.

Without looking, Tommy responded in a well-rehearsed reply, "Yes chef."

Chef Lydon smiled out of the corner of his mouth as if he told an inside joke. He had the group's attention. John knew the feeling of commanded respect that comes off certain chefs or managers who, without saying or doing much, can hold your attention. To John, it was not intimidation but simply an air one gets after reaching the pinnacle of their career. Chef Lydon had done it all and had the Michelin stars and Egon Ronay awards to prove it. Even Tony was riveted when the Chef spoke.

"Being a chef will ruin your life." he started shocking his audience a bit. "You'll work your arse off seven days a week in some God-awful conditions. It might take you years to get a position like mine and you're not likely to have the talent to go this far. But, if you love it, I suppose it's worth it."

Tommy arrived back carrying a brandy snifter full to the brim. Chef Lydon took the glass from Tommy's tray.

"Good man." Chef Lydon said without looking at Tommy.

"Yes chef!" he replied and hurried on his way.

The Chef showed the group around the kitchen, the pastry station, the storage areas and the wine cellar. A tall blond haired man was in the wine cellar when the group arrived. He was wearing a tuxedo shirt with an unclipped bow tie hanging loosely around his neck. He wore black tux pants with polished black shoes. A red captain's jacked hung on the back of a chair indicating the man's position as the sommelier.

"Good morning chef, you're up early." Hugh said.

"Feck off Hugh, I've been up since twelve. I was late getting your mother home last night…"

"Me ma? You had her out again? Can I call you da' yet?" Hugh responded without breaking a smile.

The slagging went on for a bit and John had trouble just trying to understand what the two were saying. Most of the time, it sounded like they were speaking a different language altogether.

Finally, the chef nodded to Hugh and introduced him to the group. "This is our main wine man, our sommelier. He's from just up the road but spent years in France chasing French girls. Now he's here getting Yanks to buy overpriced wine."

"Thanks for that fine introduction. Now go have another drink or sign some autographs or something and let those of us that work for a living have at it."

Chef Lydon smiled at the good-natured ribbing. Hugh invited the group to follow him into a little vaulted room that was lined with bins of wine with different labels identifying the year and type of wine.

"This is where we keep the good stuff. Fine vintages, rare wines of all types. This is also where the chef likes to sleep off his daily hangover."

"With your mother." Chef quickly added.

"Right, dear old ma." Hugh said keeping the joke going.

John was a little surprised at the meanness of the exchanges. It was all in fun but it was still harsh and a little scary. John recognized that these exchanges took place between seasoned professionals who had been together for long enough to have mutual respect for each other. This was the second time John felt a tinge of envy as he watched and listened to these two take the piss out of each other. How great it must be to be at ease and have fun while running one of the most prestigious resorts in the world. Once again, John saw himself in the Hound and tried to imagine what his life would be like if he followed that destiny.

Chapter 38

The tour ended in the Prince of Wales Cocktail Bar. Chef Lydon invited the group to have one on the house provided Dr. Carney had no objection.

"I guess we've worked hard enough today." he said as he bellied up to the bar.

Everyone ordered a drink. Even Emily felt good enough to abandon her hot whiskey for a glass of wine.

Hugh joined the little party as they all toasted each other.

John took the opportunity to personally introduce himself to Chef Lydon. "Thanks for the tour, it was fantastic." John said trying not to sound like he was kissing ass. "I have your last cook book at home. I've even managed to successfully follow a few of your recipes." he said noticing that Tony was listening in.

"You wrote a book?" Tony butted in.

"It does seem hard to believe he was capable." Hugh joked.

The Chef seemed oblivious to all of this. He turned to John and thanked him for buying the book. "I need the cash." he said. He then turned to Tony. "Are you Spanish?" he asked. "You look Spanish."

"Fuck no." Tony replied. "I'm as Italian as it gets. Except for my Dad who's half Italian and half German."

"What part of Italy did you come from?" Chef Lydon bated.

"My grandfather was from Sicily I think." Tony said.

"So you're American. I can't figure out why Yanks don't just say they're Americans. They are Irish, Italian, Polish or whatever but never just American." Chef Lydon said.

"No, where I come from, I am Italian-American. We say we are Italian."

Hugh stepped in. "If you're born somewhere, that's what you are. I was born in Ireland so I am Irish. Chef Lydon was born on Mars, so he's a Mar…"

"Do fuck off wino." The chef interrupted.

They all laughed. John thought this was like the pub conversations back in Dublin. He was enjoying the banter and it took his mind off the Hound and his pending future.

Chapter 39

The party went on until four o'clock when the chef and sommelier decided they had to get back to work.

"Join us for an after dinner drink in the Dungeon if you like." The chef said as he left the group. "I'll see you in the dining room anyway." He waved and headed back to the kitchen.

"That was awesome." John said to Tony.

"I am Italian. I don't care what they say." Tony replied.

"Who cares? We were just drinking with one of the top chef's in the world. I thought he'd be a pompous prick but he was a blast." John gushed.

"Let's see how the food is before we say anything else." Tony said with a shrug.

The party lingered for a while. Eventually, most of the group went their own way. Mike, as always, was going for a run and then to the gym. Jeff and Carol went outside to check out the riding center. Emily and Nancy went to the spa. Becky went back to the library to read and fill out postcards. Tony, Rachel and John stayed in the bar and ordered one more drink.

"What do you think of the trip so far?" John asked.

"It's pretty cool. I hope the nightclub is good."

"What nightclub?" Tony asked looking at her like she was crazy.

"That place downstairs, the Dungeon or whatever..." she said.

"That's just a bar where the old fucks do a sing song after dinner. There's no nightclub. Where in the frickin' sticks here." Tony said.

"We'll see." Rachel said defiantly as she punched Tony in the arm.

"I think this is great, a blast. I hope it's all this good." John said as he went to his room to relax and have a hot shower before dinner. He turned on the television, which was tuned to an in-house station that continuously played the John Wayne and Katherine O'Hara classic, "The Quiet Man". The movie was made in Cong and on the grounds of the castle back in the 1950's but still had a huge following particularly with Americans. John started getting sucked into the movie when Tony and Rachel came into the room.

"Man, your room is bigger than ours." Rachel said looking around and marveling at the spacious room.

"What are you guys up to?" John asked.

"Chillin', getting ready for pre-dinner cocktails in a little while." Tony answered. The new couple sat on the large sofa across from John.

"What's on?' Rachel asked.

"Some old John Wayne movie that was filmed here."

"Why would they make a western in Ireland?" Rachel asked.

John laughed while Tony looked at her with a fake shocked look on his face.

"He did more than westerns." John said. "This is a love story."

Tony reached over and playfully bonked Rachel on the forehead. “Duh.”

“How am I supposed to know? He’s like a hundred.”

“He’s like dead.” Tony said while the two began wrestling around giggling and screeching.

“I’m hitting the shower; you guys are just too cute for me to take.” John said as he got up and went into the huge bathroom. He could hear the two of them outside the bathroom door playing grab ass and for the third time today, he felt another tinge of envy. John had not been serious with a girl in a long time. Most of his college experiences lasted a couple of weeks at the most. This trip had given John a few instances to recognize things he was missing in his life and it had only been two days.

John showered in the massive shower stall and toweled off with the hotel’s oversized bath towels. He listened to hear if the lovebirds were still at it. No sounds came from the bedroom making him a little nervous.

“Anyone out there? I’m coming out.” John grabbed the terrycloth robe hanging on the back of the door and slowly opened the door. “Ready or not.” He certainly did not want to catch them in a compromising position. Tony most definitely would be the type of guy to try to get a quickie in while John was in the shower. However, when he peeked out, he saw no one. The happy couple took off leaving John to dress in peace.

It was 5:30 in the afternoon when John made his way down the steps towards the bar. He saw Becky still sitting in the library reading what looked like an old textbook.

“Hey!” he called. “Do you know when we are supposed to meet?”

“Dr. Carney said 6:30 in the front lounge.” she answered without looking up.

“Thanks.” John said sensing their conversation was now over.

John passed the main dining room, which was a flurry of activity. Waiters and busboys whipped around setting up stations and polishing silverware and stemware. The Maître D' was scanning a massive reservations book at an ornate wooded podium just inside the door. Hugh, the sommelier was busy with a cordials cart setting up port and sherry glasses. John loved the buzz of the place. The staff moved in a kind of synchronized dance with everyone playing a role and carrying out a task without speaking or looking at what the others were doing. This was a professional outfit; John thought to himself and dreamt of conducting his own staff to perform at this level. In a way, it was daunting but it also energized John and made him look forward to the future.

When John finally pulled himself away from the dining room dance, he saw a figure sitting at the bar with his back to the entrance. The figure, that John had not yet recognized, looked uncomfortable and ill at ease. When he got close enough, he saw it was Charley, slightly hunched over his Jim Beam on ice with his arms folded across his chest. Charley actually looked to be in distress when John pulled out the bar stool next to him and sat down.

"What's with you?"

"Oh man, I'm just so embarrassed." Charley said without changing his expression.

John saw Charley was dressed in a new looking blue blazer with a white collared shirt and medium grey slacks. He wore his black Gucci's with navy blue socks showing at his pant cuffs.

"What're you embarrassed about?" John pressed.

Charley unfolded his arms, opening them as he sat up straight. "I can't believe I have to dress like this. Man, where I am from, no one dresses like this. I make my livin' with my back." he said blushing.

John was taken aback. Charley was wealthy and seemingly educated. He wore a Rolex watch and Gucci shoes. He carried expensive Tumi luggage but was embarrassed to the point of pain by putting on a jacket and tie.

"Charley, look around for fuck sake. Everyone in the bar has a coat and tie on. It's a hotel rule."

Charley took a quick look around taking stock of the other guests drinking in the Prince of Wales Cocktail Bar. He looked back at his whiskey and took a big drink. He loosened up a little but was still awkward and uncomfortable. John figured he'd be fine after a few more slugs of his hometown spirit.

"What can I get you, sir?" the barman asked putting a cocktail mat in front of John.

John looked at Charley's whiskey and decided it looked good. "Can I get a Black Bush with a little ice please?"

"You fancy the whiskey from the North of Ireland?" the barman asked with a slight hint of disapproval.

"So far, I've liked it all." John said a little unsure of himself. "Isn't it all Irish whiskey?"

"'Tis, I recon, but, for my money, it can't touch Jameson." he said as he walked over with the Black Bush and ice.

"I'll do a comparison. The next whiskey for me will be a Jameson." John said trying to be diplomatic. He could tell there was a little resentment about the North. He didn't push the subject though, deciding it was a little out of his league to discuss Irish politics.

By 6:00, John and Charley were into their third whiskey. Charley stuck with Beam but John, under the guise of research as well as diplomacy was now drinking Tullamore Dew. His palate was not sophisticated enough to notice a huge difference between Black Bush, Jameson or Tullamore Dew, but he made it clear to the barman that he felt the whiskies from Midleton, County Cork were superior to anything from County Antrim.

Charley was looking less embarrassed and had mellowed enough to have cordial conversation with John. Charley told him that his family made a lot of money in cattle but he still considered himself a hands-on worker. He felt a man's worth was measured in his labor. He had nice things, even drove a Mercedes back home but he did not like "to put on airs" by wearing jackets and ties. John found this all interesting and fun to listen to. Charley seemed like a good guy and John was warming up to him despite the fact that he was new to the group and only with them through the end of the tour.

Becky was the next to arrive. John was surprised to see her in a fashionable skirt and silk blouse. She wore heels and carried a classic Chanel handbag.

"Wow, you clean up nice." Charley said with a casualness that made the comment sound harmless and inoffensive.

"Gee, thanks, you two don't look so bad yourselves."

The comment, however, made Charley wince as he folded his arms back together and slumped forward in an attempt to hide.

"What's with you?" she asked looking at John but talking to Charley.

"He thinks he is overdressed." John answered for him.

Becky looked around and shrugged. "Well, get over it, Chuck." she said as she motioned for the barman. "I'll have a gin and tonic, make it Bombay Sapphire please." she ordered with a sophistication that took John by surprise.

"I wouldn't have taken you for a gin kind of girl." John said.

"What did you think I drank, white Russians?" they laughed at Tony's expense. John was impressed with her sense of humor. He didn't think she was even paying attention.

The three of them talked and joked. John felt strangely comfortable with Becky and Charley given that they didn't even know each other a couple of days ago. By 6:30, however, the rest of the gang had infiltrated the cozy little trio.

Mike and Tony arrived together with Carol and Jeff close behind.

"What's going on there do you think?" Becky asked John quietly before the three split up. John shrugged but agreed the two of them looked chummy.

"Our tour bus is quickly turning into the Love Boat." John sighed.

Next, Dr. Carney walked in talking and laughing with Nancy and Emily making him look like their father or favorite uncle.

John sat back and enjoyed the group dynamic. He was amazed at how this group, many of them virtual strangers, were gelling and becoming fast friends. Hell, some even looked to be more than friends. He considered how this might all play out over the next ten days or so. He hoped the group wouldn't splinter. He thought it would be nice if they could all just enjoy this experience and each other, but only time would tell.

Chapter 40

Dinner was truly a magnificent affair, the likes of which most of the group had never experienced before. The Maître D', Terry Hogan, who worked in the hotel for more than twenty years, had hosted many of Dr. Carney's groups and knew the best location and configuration to accommodate them. He set up a large round table in the corner of the dining room set into one of the gabled windows. The view looking over the river was fantastic. The group was also slightly isolated from the rest of the dining room allowing for lively interaction that would not infringe on the other guests. John picked all of this up. He saw the strategy as soon as they were seated and appreciated how their group's needs were so well anticipated.

The food, wine, service, and atmosphere were exquisite. Each course was a well- orchestrated movement that left each member of the table feeling like the guest of honor. The feast was comprised of exotic starters like Poached Terrine of Duck Foie Gras and Gateaux of Crabmeat and Cream Cheese. Entrees were equally fantastic and featured such selections as Medallion of Irish Beef Filet, Filet of Cod, and Grilled Organic Salmon.

At first, the group was intimidated by such offerings but with the help and gentle prodding of Mr. Hogan, everyone was more than satisfied. Hugh O'Brien brought bottle after bottle of fine clarets, white Burgundies, and big Cabernets. Even Chef Lydon, looking as if he had not had a drink all day, popped out of the kitchen just before desert to ensure everyone had enough to eat. It was magic and everyone knew it. Whatever the expectation was when the tour started, the students now knew this would be an adventure to remember.

After dessert, the group was invited by Martin Dunn to have a nightcap in the front lounge. Everyone was full but not overly so as is often the case after a big meal in the States. The meal was abundant but not over the top. John enjoyed the satiated feeling without being uncomfortably stuffed.

John and Tony sat on one of the couches along the big window overlooking the courtyard and fountain with Lough Corrib glistening in the background. The rest of the group filtered in around them as Martin Dunn and Dr. Carney joined them.

"Well, I hope you all enjoyed your dinner." Mr. Dunn said.

A universal "yes" was the general reply except for Tony who said something like "hell yea!"

Mr. Martin looked pleased and began talking with Dr. Carney about the rest of the group's itinerary. A waiter soon arrived and took the group's drink order. When he returned, Mr. Dunn proposed a toast to the students and Dr. Carney and wished them all well in their hospitality careers. John again smiled at the comment. Clearly, the Irish were not familiar with the concept of a free elective.

Just before Mr. Martin wished them a good evening, he suggested the group join the other hotel guests in the Dungeon Bar for a "sing-song." The students, while getting tired showed that youthful resolve that allows them to push on if there was a slight chance of a good time.

"Let's go. I need a little action." Nancy said. That rallying call was all that was needed to motivate everyone to move the party downstairs to the Dungeon.

John looked at his watch. It was just after 11:00 and he was starting to feel fatigued. The gang was having fun singing along to old pub songs and drinking copious amounts of liquor. Chef Lydon and Hugh O'Brien popped in and did shots of Grand Marnier with everyone taking the party to the next level.

Carol and Jeff were looking increasingly friendly and John even sensed something brewing between Charley and Becky. Tony and Rachel had already disappeared. Nancy and Emily were on stage singing Patsy Cline's 'Crazy' with a couple of young Australian guys that were on vacation with their families. John seized the opportunity to disappear himself and quietly made his exit.

It wasn't that he was not having a good time, in truth, John was having the time of his life. He just had so much swimming in his head that he wanted some time to reflect and sort things out before becoming either too drunk or too tired. He thought he would take a walk in the cool night air and just think. He also wanted to give Tony and Rachel some time alone if they snuck off to his room.

John came up from the Dungeon and stopped in the Prince of Wales Cocktail Bar to buy a Cuban cigar to enjoy as he walked. He felt it would be an appropriately decadent end to a decidedly decadent day.

As he entered the bar, he saw Chef Lydon nursing a brandy at the corner of the bar. He waved and the chef raised his glass in a little salute. John asked the barman for a cigar and a book of matches. He was just about to leave when he heard the Chef call

"Hey! Yank, come over here." he sounded well on his way to being hammered but John welcomed the chance to speak with the famous, infamous chef.

"How's it going?" John asked while shaking Lydon's hand.

"Grand, yea, good," the chef responded. "you seem like the serious one in the group, I mean, you look like you give a shit about this business."

John was shocked at the chef's intuitiveness. He didn't think he made a connection with the chef before, at least not one he could perceive.

"Well, my family has been in the bar and restaurant trade for a long time, ever since my great grandfather who emigrated from Ireland opened his first saloon over a hundred years ago." John said proudly.

"So, it's in yer blood. Might as well not fight it. You're screwed." Chef Lydon said.

"Well, screwed or not, I'm into it. I want to learn as much as I can before taking over the family business."

"Do," Lydon said. "work on someone else's time until you know the business inside and out. Work every position. Don't go on the piss every night." he said raising his brandy a little for emphasis.

"Do you still like the business?" John asked worried he might be getting too personal.

"More than ever. I bitch for effect. Too many people watching Iron Chef or some *shite* thinking they want to be famous. It's bloody hard work, not a fecking game. I try to put off the ones who don't have the passion." Lydon said.

After a short pause, Chef Lydon invited John for one quick nightcap. This would be John's third or fourth nightcap of the night and he knew when the Irish say one, it often extends to several.

"Sure, sounds good." John accepted.

"Kenny," Chef Lydon called the barman over. "get this man whatever he wants."

Kenny, the barman, smiled and asked if he should bring a wine list. The chef looked at him with a menacing smile "Feck off with that, you'll have him ordering a bottle of Dom."

"I'll have a Jameson with a little ice, please." John said interrupting the contest.

"Good choice." the chef said.

The two talked for an hour. As John predicted, this nightcap turned into three. The chef gave him his advice, insight, and the benefit of his experience. However, he never tried to discourage John from staying in the field. If anything, he treated him as a mentor. John felt blessed to have an audience with such a high profile professional even if some of the advice was now coming slightly slurred.

John finally made it to his room, abandoning the idea of a walk and the smoke. It was now two in the morning and he was ready for bed. Thankfully, no one was in the room when he got there and he was able to get right to sleep.

Chapter 41

The next morning, the group was free to go to breakfast whenever they wanted. There were no scheduled appointments, tours, or required events until dinner. Dr. Carney had given the students the day to experience the property as guests. They were free to use the amenities, so long as they paid for them, wander the grounds, go into town, or do whatever they might do if they were their on holiday. At the end of the day, they would meet for dinner, which was scheduled for a little local restaurant, in the next village over.

John was happy to finally have time alone to sort out his thoughts. He made it to breakfast but found none of the others in the dining room. He overheard two servers gossiping about a couple of American girls who were caught asleep under a dining room table with two guys in the morning when the breakfast crew was setting up. Unfortunately, they moved out of earshot when they were detailing what happened, but John knew he could probably fill in the blanks.

After taking a long walk where he finally was able to smoke his cigar from last night, John got the urge to call home. His thoughts were still a jumble but it had been nearly two weeks since he had spoken to his folks or Old Joe at the Hound. He went to his room and pulled out a long distance calling card that he had bought in Dublin a week earlier. He picked up the phone and dialed his parents first. After a short pause, the phone began to ring. On the third ring, he finally got an answer.

"Hello, Frawley residence?" his sister's voice answered.

"What's up, Erin?"

"Well, if it's not the world traveler. We thought you lost our number."

"Things have been busy. Sorry it's been a while. What's going on there?"

"Not a thing. Getting hot. Shane and I are going to the shore for the weekend."

"Sounds fun. Its nice here but still chilly at night." After a little more small talk, John asked for his parents.

"They're not here. They were going to the club for lunch and won't be back for a while."

"Tell them I called. I'll try them again in a few days."

"You got it. Take care of yourself." Erin said and hung up the phone.

John decided to try his Grandfather at the Hound. The phone rang twice before a familiar voice ran through a familiar answer.

"Flying Hound, this is Patrick, how can I help you?"

"You can stop screwing my wife you rat bastard." John said on impulse.

"Which one is your wife?" Pat responded without hesitation.

"I don't think you're kidding." John replied.

"What's up John? Where the hell are ya?"

"I'm in County Mayo right now but the group is leaving for Galway tomorrow."

"Must be nice. Meeting any fine lasses?"

"I am strictly here for educational purposes."

"Bullshit. I won't keep you, though. I am sure you are looking for Joe."

"Thanks Pat. Talk to you soon."

A minute later, Old Joe made it to the phone. "This call is costing you a fortune I bet."

"Not too bad if you use a calling card." John said trying to keep Old Joe from worrying. "How are things at the Hound?" John asked before realizing he should have asked how his Grandfather was first.

"Just great. Summer business is as good as ever. I hope you're still planning to work the end of summer for me. I need a vacation."

John knew Old Joe did not take vacations. He was just trying to make sure he was still coming home.

"I'll be there for the Fourth of July weekend and will stay until the fall semester starts. I'm sure looking forward to the rest of the summer back home."

"Aren't you enjoying Ireland?" Old Joe asked.

"I' m having a great time. I've learned so much and there's a ton of things I can't wait to try out at the Hound. This place is truly magical."

"My father, your Great Grandfather always spoke of Ireland as heaven on earth. I only wish I could have made it there myself. Anyway, I'm glad you're there and experiencing it for the both of us."

John started to miss home badly. Up until then, he had been too distracted to actually miss home. But now, after talking to his family, he was looking forward to getting back.

The day went by quickly. John explored every part of the property including a trip to Cong to check out a few local pubs. Dr. Carney gave instructions to meet at 6:00 in the front lounge and John was surprised when he looked at his watch and realized he was going to be late if he didn't get a move on. The plan was to go to a local seafood restaurant in a neighboring town that also featured live Irish music and dancing. John was looking forward to a more casual setting where he could relax.

The group convened in the front lounge of the hotel at 6:00. Dr. Carney prepped them about the evening plans and told them to be on the bus by 6:30. Dermot was already on the bus waiting for them. The drive would only be a few minutes down the road.

Chapter 42

The group enjoyed the evening, but John could not help but notice the group's dynamics beginning to change.

Tony and Rachel were now fully established as a couple. Jeff and Carol, who sat next to each other at dinner, were also becoming openly comfortable with each other. Now, Charley and Becky, who also were side-by-side at dinner, were giving off a "new couple" vibe. The dark, intimate atmosphere of the pub combined with music and dancing made the night feel like they were out for a Broadway show, perfect for a date.

Unfortunately, John did not see himself hooking up with Nancy or Emily, who were too busy chasing local boys anyway. He decided just to enjoy the atmosphere and be happy he was not responsible for anyone but himself. Still, he wondered if it was the surreal circumstances of this kind of trip that led to these couples finding each other, and if they would hold up once back in the real world.

When they got back to the hotel, there was no talk of nightcaps or the Dungeon bar. The gang was tired and looking forward to their next stop. John said goodnight to everyone as they parted ways.

Dr. Carney gave final instructions for the next day, which had the group leaving for Galway by 10:00 in the morning. This was met with a collective moan from the students who acted like he had announced pre-dawn calisthenics.

"You'll want to have breakfast before we go because there are no lunch plans for tomorrow. We are meeting with the Galway Chamber of Commerce president at 11:00 AM, followed by a tour of University College Galway. We will check into the hotel by 3 in the afternoon and will meet for dinner at 6:30. Please dress business casual for tomorrow and, once again; please try to come up with something important or intelligent to ask." Carney said with his usual delivery.

Chapter 43

The next two days were a blur. It seemed that the pace had picked up considerably with the students having much less time to themselves than at the start of the trip. John was absorbing all of the information that was coming his way but most of the rest of the group were showing signs of strain. Dr. Carney announced on a regular basis at this point, that this was an academic class and not a tourist outing all in an attempt to keep the group on task.

The students found Galway to be fantastic. It was a vibrant young city with much more of an artsy feel than Dublin. The students enjoyed themselves thoroughly, despite an aggressive schedule. Nancy picked out several pubs and late night clubs she was planning on visiting after dinner while the three new couples soaked up the charm of the place like newlyweds on their honeymoons. John was particularly drawn to the famous pubs that had recently morphed from small intimate places to a new breed of super pub. These places retained much of their history and character but, despite quaint shop-front entrances, their interiors were super-sized. The King's Head looked like a friendly little pub from the outside but once inside, it seemed to go on forever. John had mixed feelings about this evolution of the traditional pub but once they filled, the atmosphere was much like the cramped and lively pubs in Dublin.

"We will reconvene this afternoon at 6:00 in the lobby." Dr. Carney announced once the group checked-in and got their rooming assignments for The Great Southern Galway. This beautiful Victorian Hotel sat in the city center right in the middle of the action. The students were happy for a little city life after several days in the country.

Nancy and Emily decided to go shopping. Mike tagged along saying he needed new sweat pants for working out. The happy couples all went their separate ways. John decided to try to call his parents again. He went to a convenience store and bought another calling card for the Unites States. He found a pay phone near the bus station and dialed his parent's number. After two rings, the answering machine picked up. John was depressed a little and was looking forward to talking to his parents. He left a short message saying he would try again in a day or so.

He then considered calling Old Joe again but decided not to since they had just spoken. Instead, he decided to walk around the city, explore some of the pub life, and just relax.

The next morning, the group met in the lobby as instructed by Dr. Carney. Dermot was standing outside with the bus ready to load up for the next leg of the trip.

"What did you think of dinner last night?" John asked Nancy.

"Great. It was a cool little place." she answered. "It reminded me of a little place in Soho or the Village. Hard to believe it's in Ireland." Emily added.

"It was very trendy and cosmopolitan. Not at all what I expected for the West of Ireland." John said. They were talking about the meal, the wine, and the pubs and clubs when Dr. Carney instructed them to load up. They would make one stop on their way to County Clare and they needed to get going to stay on schedule.

Just outside of Galway city, Dermot pulled the bus onto a narrow side road the paralleled a small river. The group looked at each other wondering if he made a wrong turn. After about a mile down the road, Dermot pulled the bus up along side a thatched roof cottage that looked like someone's home.

Dr. Carney stood up to brief the students. "As many of you know, Galway is famous for oysters. Even though this stop is not on the official itinerary, I thought it was important for you to visit one of Galway's most famous oyster houses, Moran's-on-the-Weir. We have a reservation for lunch and I want you all to at least try one oyster."

"I ain't touching one of those slimy fuckers." Tony said half under his breath.

"Me neither." Nancy agreed.

John, on the other hand, was thrilled with the opportunity to visit this famous spot, home of Galway's famous oyster festival.

Moran's looked tiny when you first walked in, with a small bar and a couple of little snugs. However, like many of the new super-pubs, Moran's opened into a very large dining room in the back with long pine tables and chairs. Obviously, Moran's was used to handling busloads of tourists who also want to try Galway's finest.

The students were shown to a table that could accommodate the entire group. Dr. Carney sat at the head. "I will order a few dozen oysters for the table. You can order whatever else you want from the menu but remember, at least one oyster for each of you. I will be taking pictures." he said as Tony and Nancy made faces like they already had an oyster in their mouths.

A few minutes after the waitress brought their drinks; large oval platters arrived and were placed down the center of the table. Dozens of freshly shucked pearly oysters lying on top of a seaweed bed faced the students. Charley wasted no time and grabbed a large juicy specimen and sucked it right off the shell.

"Awesome, just awesome." he announced.

Nancy gasped.

Tony looked in disbelief. "You are sick, dude. That's just disgusting."

"I'm telling you, these are the best. Where I come from, we eat a lot of oysters and these are some of the best I've had."

Slowly, the students dug in. Dr. Carney was busy clicking away with his camera as each student picked up their oyster and gulped them down.

Mike and Jeff liked oysters and had them many times before. Becky tried oysters but was not a big fan. John loved oysters having been introduced to the fried variety by his grandfather at a very young age. He chose a smaller one to begin with. He squeezed a lemon wedge on the oyster and a drop of Tabasco sauce. The texture was perfect. The flesh was firm and meaty and not at all slimy. The slight brininess gave it a fresh, clean taste without any trace of fishiness. Tony was not convinced. He protested and even said he was allergic. Dr. Carney was not buying it though and Tony finally capitulated. He drowned his oyster in lemon juice and gulped it down without chewing. He grabbed his Club Orange and chased the oyster with a full glass of soda. Dr. Carney got his photographic proof but did not convert Tony to become an oyster lover.

Finally. It was Nancy's turn. She was out most of the night drinking hard and not sleeping much. As pretty as she was, this afternoon, she looked rough. As she stared down at her oyster, she turned a slight shade of green. Slowly, she brought the fork to her mouth and slid the oyster between her quivering lips. Unlike Tony, she did not attempt a quick chewless swallow. Instead, she held it in her mouth and chewed it a little. He face contorted and her cheeks puffed out a little. She looked around as if she might get sick.

"I've seen that look before." Tony said pointing and laughing.

Carney took a quick shot anticipating the moment coming to a quick end. Suddenly, Nancy swallowed with great effort and grabbed the glass of Guinness to wash it down. She coughed after the drink and put her head down on the wooden table. The students laughed and offered another.

"It wasn't that bad. I just feel like shite." Nancy said raising her head as she spoke. "If I wasn't so hung, I might even try another. For now, I'm done though."

After lunch, the group boarded the bus and settled in for the two-hour drive to Ennis in County Clare. John was pleasantly full with that little high that comes from eating extraordinary food without over doing it. He rested his head against the window in the back of the bus and enjoyed the ride.

Chapter 44

Ennis was a busy country town that was not generally a big stop for tourists. Dr. Carney liked to use Ennis as a base for a few day trips that he usually included on the tour. He also liked the Old Ground Hotel as an example of a traditional Irish independent hotel. This was also the point in the trip where Dr. Carney kept the hard-core academics to a minimum and let the students really experience Ireland.

Dermot parked the bus just outside of the Old Ground. The students got off of the bus, got their luggage together, and joined Dr. Carney in the well-worn lobby to get their room assignments.

Carney had briefed the group just before they got to town telling the students the day's itinerary. They would have the balance of the afternoon to themselves and would then meet back at the hotel by 6:30 to go to dinner. John was delighted to have some free time and a schedule that only required enough energy to make it to dinner.

Dr. Carney gave out the keys and turned the students loose. John asked if anyone was interested in taking a walk around town.

Jeff and Carol said it sounded like a good idea and Mike also decided to tag along.

Tony and Rachel were already in the bar of the hotel. Emily decided to join them once Nancy announced she was going up for a nap. Charley and Becky were still feeling out their relationship and decided to go off on their own using the excuse that Becky needed to find some famous book store that the others doubted even existed.

John's group left the hotel and started up one on the narrow main streets that crisscrossed Ennis. The little shop fronts were colorful and very traditional. John thought they all looked like pub fronts even though they were bakeries, butchers, photo shops etc. Jeff and Mike spotted a sports shop and went in to have a look. Carol stayed outside with John.

"Nice town, huh?" John said trying to make small talk.

"I like it. It's more what I thought Ireland would be like." Carol answered.

John could not think of much else to say and busied himself looking up and down the busy street. Mike came out first carrying a plastic bag.

"What did you get?" Carol asked.

"Just some work-out clothes. I wanted sweat pants to go jogging in. I only brought shorts but the mornings are so damned cold."

"I know! It's hard to believe it is summer." Carol said.

Jeff walked out carrying his own bag. He lifted the bag saying "souvenirs for the family."

After some more window-shopping and a quick tour of a ruined abbey, the group came upon an ancient looking pub called Cruise's. The stone and pine interior almost made it look medieval. The place was not too busy but had the feel of a real locals place. John loved the place as soon as he set foot in the door. It had charm, a feel of history, and, unlike some of the Galway pubs, it felt completely genuine.

"Let's get a pint." he declared to the group.

"Sounds like a plan." Carol said making John like her a little more.

They found a little snug in the corner and settled in. John got up to get the first round. Everyone but Mike ordered a beer. Mike said he still had to work out and would wait until later that night to have anything. John brought the drinks over putting their glasses down on the heavy wooden table. The atmosphere was comfortable and the conversation effortless. The Guinness was going down way too easy. Before they knew it, it was 5:45 and time to go. As they adjourned, John took a final look around trying to make mental notes of what he liked so much about the place. Even through the buzz of a few pints, John recognized the things that made the pub special. It was friendly, cozy, genuine and unobtrusive. There was no loud music to drown out your conversation. Televisions were not in your face distracting you and breaking up your attention. It was quiet but not dead. There was a balance that couldn't be designed, it had just happened. They all felt it but none of them could really describe it. They walked home having enjoyed the craic.

Chapter 45

Nightcaps in the Old Ground Bar followed another excellent dinner. Every one of the students were there, even Nancy, who revived herself having slept right up until the bus took them to dinner. They talked about goat's cheese and black sole. They discussed the merits of Doolin lobster and what made the Kerry Gold butter so good. John enjoyed the fact that after only a few days, this group of free elective students was turning into dedicated foodies.

The next morning, the students were scheduled to take a day trip to see some local sights, tour the Shannon Hotel College, and visit a local farm for a demonstration. Dr. Carney gave instructions the night before to meet in the lobby by 9 AM. Their first scheduled stop was the hotel college and the professor wanted everyone to be on time. By ten after 9, all of the students were in the lobby along with Dermot. The strange thing was Dr. Carney was nowhere to be found.

"Where is the good doctor?" John wondered out loud.

"Maybe he had a few too many last night." Mike said.

"He went up right after we got back from dinner. I saw him on the steps and he said good night to me." Becky said.

By 9:20, Dermot decided to phone Dr. Carney's room. The college was expecting them at 10:00 and it would take at least fifteen minutes to drive. Dermot went to the front desk and asked for a house phone. He dialed Dr. Carney's room but the line was busy. A few minutes later, he tried again and this time Dr. Carney answered.

"Will you be joining us this morning, sir?" Dermot said teasing the professor. "Oh, I see. So sorry to hear. Right. Ok then." Dermot's voice grew serious.

The students could tell something was up by the way Dermot was responding to whatever Dr. Carney was saying.

When he hung up, Jeff spoke up. "What's the deal? Is he sick or something?"

Dermot, looking concerned said Dr. Carney would be right down and he asked us to wait for him on the bus.

"I need everyone on board right away, please." The tone of Dermot's voice was not playful. Everyone turned and went to the bus without saying a word.

The students waited patiently for a few minutes. Jeff and Carol were whispering different theories about what was going on. John was looking out the window wondering if there was an issue with the hotel college. The rest of the group just sat. Finally, Dr. Carney climbed up onto the bus. He looked pale and distracted. His goofy expressions were gone and he made no attempt to joke or rattle off one of his pseudo-Irish sayings. He asked for everyone's attention, he had an announcement to make.

"Unfortunately, I will be leaving for the States this afternoon. There has been an emergency back home and I'm afraid I will be unable to complete my part of the tour. I am indeed sorry. The institute will be sending Katy Welsh out to take over and finish the tour for me. She was due to take over in a couple of days anyway so she will just start a little earlier than planned. I am sorry but you will not miss out on anything scheduled over the last half of the trip. You have been a great group and I regret not being able to complete my part of the trip with you. Please make sure you continue to conduct yourself appropriately with Ms. Welsh. Again, I apologize for the inconvenience."

"Is there anything we can do doc?" Nancy asked showing genuine concern.

"No, nothing, thanks. I will be leaving from Shannon a little later but for now, just go with Dermot and follow the schedule. Thanks for the concern." He stepped down with a little wave, a salute really, and walked back towards the hotel.

A murmur started as soon as Dr. Carney left the bus.

"What do you think is up with him?" Becky asked.

"Must be some kind of family emergency. The Institute wouldn't make him come back if it was business related." Charley said.

John listened to the different possible explanations. He felt bad for Dr. Carney, even though he was a little goofy, he ran a tight ship and knew what he was doing. However, John suddenly felt something else aside from the concern he had for Dr. Carney. He felt a rush of full-on panic. He had given Katy little thought since the trip began but now he was realizing that she would be with them starting now. He knew she was due to take over for Carney in a few days but was not yet mentally ready for her imminent arrival.

A minute later, Dermot fired up the bus. Dermot was a good driver and a competent assistant but he was not really qualified to lead the trip. Today, however, it was up to him to complete the agenda.

"OK, listen up." Dermot said trying to emulate Dr. Carney. "I know there is some confusion but we will carry on with today's plans. By the time we get back, it should be sorted." With that, he put the bus in gear as they headed off for the hotel college.

The students arrived a little past 10:00. Mr. Tierney, program director for the Hotel College was waiting at the reception for the group. Before welcoming the Americans, Mr. Tierney had a brief exchange with Dermot. Their heads shook as they seemed to acknowledge the circumstances relating to the now missing group leader. When they finished, Mr. Tierney smiled and approached the students.

"You are all very welcome to the Shannon College of Hotel Management. We have a little tour set up for you followed by a reception with some of our students and faculty. I am sorry to hear about Dr. Carney's circumstances but we will do our best to carry on."

The students were still a bit in shock but listened politely. John was excited to see the facilities and looked forward to meeting some of the students. He could tell that the nature of this college was much more hands-on than Cornell. Just the same, he wanted to know how Ireland educated its future hospitality professionals.

Mr. Tierney led the students through the campus. They toured lecture halls, test kitchens, laboratories, computer labs, dining halls and the small hotel the students operated. It was all very professional and state of the art. The College was well funded and the students, all dressed in business suits, certainly looked professional. John was impressed. This little college had facilities that rivaled Cornell. The students were focused and committed unlike some of his friends back home.

"These guys are serious about their profession." John said to Tony.

"Yea, I'd hate to wear a suit and tie to school though. It must be a pain in the ass."

"I guess they are preparing them for life in a suit." John relied.

The tour ended in a small meeting room in the hotel, set up with refreshments and cookies. Three students from the college were standing behind the refreshment table poised to serve their guests. Two guys and one girl stood at attention waiting patiently to meet the American students and answer any questions.

"Please relax and have a coffee and a sweet." Mr. Tierney said. "Say hello to three of our best, Aileen, Paul and Angus. If you have any questions, feel free to ask."

The Americans mobbed the table. Nancy had her eyes on the boys from the college.

"What's there to do for fun?" she asked Angus who smiled and said they often go to Ennis or down to Lahinch or Doolin if the weather was nice.

"We're staying in Ennis if you want to come by later."

The boys blushed. Irish girls were a bit more reserved but Nancy didn't care.

"What's the name of our hotel, the Old House or something?" she asked Emily.

"The Old Ground." Angus answered before Emily could respond.

"The Old Ground, right. We should be back after dinner some time. Maybe you can show us what you do for a good time." Nancy said sending the boys blushing all over again.

After a half hour or so, Dermot announced that they needed to get to the next meeting. Mr. Tierney said goodbye and wished them luck. He handed out brochures from the college in case any of them knew a prospective student. The group made their way to the bus and took off for Inagh, a tiny village near the coast in County Clare.

Chapter 46

The ride from the hotel college was quiet. The students were subdued still contemplating Dr. Carney's departure from the tour.

"Do you think he left yet?" John asked Tony.

"I dunno, how hard is it to get a last minute flight?"

"Something pretty bad must of happened." Rachel said.

"He wouldn't just bail if it was minor. Someone must have died or something."

"Maybe." John said turning his gaze back to the countryside.

Dermot pulled the bus off of the main road and onto a small side dirt road. He told the students to hold on, as the road was pretty bad. The students knew from their itinerary that they were visiting a goat's cheese farm where the cheese they had had the previous night was produced. John thought it was a fantastic use of local ingredients and swore he would find these types of suppliers when he ran his own place.

The bus struggled over a steep hill leading down to a covered pen filled with goats and an industrial looking building that appeared to be new. Dermot stopped the bus in front of the building and asked the students to wait until he found the owners.

"Wow, this place is so cool!" John said looking out the bus window. "The source of the food is so close to the people who use it. Back home, it seems everything comes from California or Mexico. Can you believe we were eating cheese from this farm?"

"I've never seen someone so geeked over cheese before." Tony said with a sneer.

"It's not about cheese, it's about local small farmers providing ingredients to local shops and restaurants. It's so old school. It's like it was in the States fifty or sixty years ago." John's excitement was largely lost on the group.

Dermot came out of the little building and climbed onto the bus. "Right, we're in the right place." he announced. "Everyone please get off of the bus and wait by the door." "The cheese maker will be here soon. He is making a delivery back in town."

Nancy and Emily walked over to the pen holding the goats.

"Look how cute." Nancy squealed.

"Man, they stink." Emily replied. Soon, most of the others gathered around the barn looking at the wooly goats with their sharp little horns.

"Please, leave them be." Dermot called over. "I'm not sure you are allowed near them."

"They're grand." a voice said from behind Dermot. A rugged middle-aged man appeared from the building holding a set of car keys in his hand. "Goats won't hurt you."

Dermot turned and extended his hand. "Mr. Jenkins I presume."

"That's me." The man replied. "Please call me Mathew.

"Mathew, it's a pleasure. Please meet the students from the American Institute."

"You are all very welcome. I am surprised so many Yanks would have an interest in goat's cheese." he said with a smile.

"Most of them are studying the food industry and catering." Dermot lied.

"Oh, very good." Mathew said waiting for someone to elaborate.

"Can we pet them?" Nancy asked gesturing towards the goats.

"Of course, just be careful they don't chew on your clothes." Mathew said as he walked towards the pen. He unlatched the gate and walked in. He herded the goats back from the gate and invited everyone to come in.

For the next half hour, the students became kids again. They played with the animals, snapped pictures and generally enjoyed themselves. Even Tony relaxed a little and made Rachel take a picture with him pretending to mount a goat.

Mathew Jenkins was also enjoying himself. He had other school groups visit his operation but those students were usually pre-teen. He got a huge kick out of seeing these young adults enjoying themselves like little kids.

"Ok, time to head inside to see the rest of the operation." he announced and waved the students towards the building.

Inside, Mathew's daughter, Maura, had a table set up with different cheeses, Kerry sparkling water, and a couple bottles of South African white wines. Mathew introduced his daughter to the students.

Maura was in her early thirties but had a more youthful appearance. She smiled as her father introduced her and then launched into a well-rehearsed presentation of how cheese is made and what the different varieties were available. She talked about aging, storing, and distribution.

John was amazed that the cheese makers had to limit how much cheese each client could be sold in an effort to ration the limited amount of cheese available. He thought that in the States, it would all simply go to the highest bidder.

Finally, Maura invited the students to try the cheese and help themselves to the wine. The students didn't need any additional prodding.

After the presentation, tasting and a brief tour of the remaining facilities, the group was ready to go. Dermot corralled them onto the bus after thanking Mathew and Maura.

"So, where to next?" Maura asked Dermot once the group was on the bus.

"Down to Lahinch for the afternoon. We are visiting a youth hostel there and the local golf course. They are trying to see a variety of accommodations here in Ireland as well as other food and beverage operations. Unfortunately, their professor has been called home due to a family illness." Dermot said catching the attention of several of the students who were in earshot.

"So, Carney has a family illness. That's why he is leaving." Carol said listening for more details.

"Oh, that's awful." Maura said looking up at the bus. "Will the tour be cut short?" she asked.

"Not at all." Dermot replied. "The institute is sending a replacement as we speak. She should be here late tonight. I'm meant to collect her at the Ennis train station at half eight. Of course, that's if it leaves Dublin on time and doesn't get held up in Limerick."

Carol turned to the students sitting behind her. "So, Katy will be here tonight I guess."

Dermot finished his conversation and got on the bus. As he pulled back onto the main road Carol decided to press him for more details.

"So, Dr. Carney has a family problem, huh." Dermot looked straight ahead. He glanced at her before talking trying to decide if there was a need to keep the details from the group.

"Well, as far as I know, his father has taken ill. I can't say that I know more than that."

"You're picking up Katy Welsh tonight?" Carol asked.

"That's the plan. She will be in just after dinner if the train from Dublin is on time. She will be your new leader starting tomorrow." Dermot said with some relief in his voice.

John was only half listening until Katy's name came up. His stomach instantly jumped as if he had taken a cheap shot to the gut. He wondered if he heard correctly.

Nancy quickly confirmed. "Oooh, your girlfriend is on her way. How interesting." she said smiling back at John.

"Whatever." John said trying to remain cool. He was nervous and excited. He knew Katy was not the love of his life and mostly what he felt was extreme attraction. Despite this and the fact that she was spoken for, he was secretly thrilled by the news.

Chapter 47

The bus rolled west towards the Atlantic coast. They passed through the tiny village of Ennistymon when the bus finally reached the sandy strand of Lahinch. Dermot asked for everyone's attention again mimicking Dr. Carney's routine of quickly briefing the group a few minutes prior to their arrival.

"We are going to stop in Lahinch on the way back from the cliffs. When we get to the cliffs, you can walk up to the tower for the best view. Please stay back from the edge. Every year or so, we get some eegit angling for a photo who falls off the cliff. I do not want any casualties."

The bus passed by Lahinch and rumbled through Liscannor on its way to the Cliffs of Moher.

The bus arrived pulling into the half full parking lot. There were a variety of rental cars, cars with foreign plates, tour busses, and campers. People were making their way up both sides of the cliffs. To the left, one could walk for miles along that face of the cliff. To the right, steep steps made of Liscannor flag stone ascended to O'Brien's Tower that looked like a miniature castle tower. People were on top of the tower looking out to the vast Atlantic Ocean. Next stop, Boston or New York.

"Please, everyone back on the bus in forty minutes." Dermot said as the group got off of the bus.

"What the fuck, dude? Can you believe that Katy chick will be here tonight?" Tony said as he walked towards the cliffs with John and Mike.

"Well, I guess they needed someone who knew their way around a little and since she was taking over soon anyway, why send someone else? I heard her talk about leading weekend excursions with some of the visiting students." John said.

"Yea, plus she knows us well enough. I guess the institute figured she could handle it." Mike added.

All of the students made it to the tower overlooking the cliffs and the ocean. Waves broke on the rocky shore below with sea mist sweeping up the cliff face reaching the students as a cool mist on their faces. The view was stunning. They had a clear day letting them see as far as one could. The fresh air and the sea mist made the setting even more magical.

The bus backtracked towards Lahinch.

Dermot told the students that they would be touring a local youth hostel as part of their program to visit and experience different types of accommodations during the tour. After the tour, they would have a couple of hours of free time to relax and enjoy this beachside village. Later, they would meet for dinner in Brown's Hotel, a small locally owned hotel.

Dermot steered the bus onto Lahinch's main street. He found parking at the top of the street next to the Catholic Church.

"OK. We made it. Just wait here for a moment while I find Paddy Coyne, the man who operates the hostel." Dermot got off the bus and walked towards the top of Lahinch's promenade, which hugged the town's sandy coastline.

"This looks nice." John said to Mike.

"It's more what I expected Ireland to look like." Mike answered.

The village was comprised of one main street that gradually inclined from the bottom of the street to the top where it veered right towards the sea and then up out of town. The shops and houses on the main drag looked as if they could have been there for a hundred years. Many of the buildings actually would have been there for that long. People scurried around the street, surfers carried surfboards and others ocean kayaks towards the beach.

"I counted at least seven pubs in this town." Charley said.

"And I'm looking forward to visiting most of them." Nancy added.

Dermot returned to the bus followed by a short white haired man who looked to be in his early fifties. Dermot asked the students to come off of the bus and meet Paddy Coyne.

Paddy said hello and asked the group to follow him up the street to the youth hostel's entrance. The group gathered in the small reception area clogged with bikes, backpacks, surfboards and various other implements of youthful travel.

"Man, I guess this is an entirely different way to experience Ireland." John said to Mike looking around the room.

Paddy gave the students a brief overview of the operation, its rules and regulations, and a little of his own personal history. He was born in Lahinch but immigrated to New York when he was younger. He worked in the banking and finance industry making enough money to retire by the time he was fifty, move home, and open his own little business. As he put it, he's " lived the American dream and woke up in Ireland."

After a brief tour, Paddy wished the group well and got back to running his hostel. Dermot turned the students loose on the town telling them to meet back at the church at 7pm to go to dinner.

Chapter 48

John was preoccupied. He had enjoyed the tour and meeting Paddy, Mr. Tierney, Mathew Jenkins, and his daughter Maura, but his thoughts kept returning to the fact that Katy would join the group tonight and take over the tour. He thought things might be awkward. Then he thought he might be imagining things and maybe there never was anything between them. Even though it had been only ten days or so since they were in Murphy's together back in Dublin, he was no longer totally clear on what had transpired.

"Dude, are you in there?" Tony said snapping John out of his daze. "Let's check this place out. I want to see how they surf in Ireland and maybe hit some of these pubs while we have time before dinner."

"Sounds good." John said without enthusiasm.

Mike, Rachel, Nancy and Emily joined them while the rest of the group went their own way.

"Why don't we walk down the beach and then come back up the main street?" Nancy suggested pointing to the promenade.

The afternoon was perfect. It was warm by Irish standards especially for that time of year and the sun was high in the summer sky. John took in a breath of fresh sea air as he gazed out into Liscannor Bay. Waves crashed and seagulls screeched. He had forgotten about Katy for the time being and just enjoyed the scenery.

"Wow, look at all of these dudes surfing. It's so cold they're all in wet suits. The water must be freezing." Nancy pointed out to the surf. "Let's go down to the beach so we can see if these jackasses are even cute."

"I'm game." Emily said as the two of them started down the steps towards the beach. Mike joined them saying he needed the exercise.

John, Tony, and Rachel stayed on the promenade electing to wait for them to return at the other end of the strand.

"Those girls are like dogs in heat." Tony said prompting a punch in the arm from Rachel.

"That's not nice. Just because you got lucky by finding me, don't be ragging on them." she said.

"It looks like there have been a few more happy couples coming out of the wood work." John added. "I mean, where are the new lovebirds?" he said referring to Charley and Becky and Jeff and Carol.

"I don't get it. I wouldn't have put any of them together." Tony said.

"Well, I wouldn't have put you two together." John said. "I mean, a classy girl like Rachel with a thug like you?"

Rachel pointed and laughed. Tony took off after her as she turned and ran down the prom squealing with delight.

John watched amused but that punch in the gut came racing back. The talk of couples redirected John's attention to the imminent arrival of Katy Welsh.

Chapter 49

As the returned to the promenade, Nancy yelled out, "Some decent talent. They were definitely cuter up close. We met a couple of guys staying in that youth hostel that we saw earlier. They said there was a good band on tonight at one of the pubs. I think it was called Flannigan's or something like that."

"Let's go into town and check things out." Emily added.

Back at the bottom of the street, they passed the types of stores you'd expect at a seaside village. There were ice cream and candy shops, souvenir stands selling everything from kites to postcards, and real estate agents in case you wanted your very own holiday home. They came to their first pub that would not have necessarily been of interest to the group if not for the name above the weather worn door.

"I can't believe it." John said as he read 'Frawley's Pub' half out loud.

"It's a sign." Nancy said. "Let's go in."

"It looks a little scary." Rachel said noting the lace curtain across the shop front window. There didn't appear to be a light on but half of the two-part door was slightly ajar indicating Frawley's was open for business.

John pushed open the old faded door that led to a little inner hallway with another door. Along the coast in Ireland, such designs were needed to keep the wind from whipping into your house when one opened the door. Today, though, there was no wind blasting in from the north.

John turned the knob to the inner door beginning to doubt this was a public bar at all. The door pushed open exposing a tiny, four stool bar that resembled a counter in a corner store more than a bar. There were no lights on and the only light came from the lace-fronted window.

"Is anyone home?" Tony asked coming in behind John.

"Wow, spooky." Nancy said making her way inside.

John peered through the little door behind the bar and saw a little old man sitting in front of a television in what appeared to be his living room.

"Hello." John called through the door. "Are you open?"

The man rose out of his chair without looking and turned the television off. He came through the door linking the bar to his house. He smiled at the group and said hello.

"Can we get a drink?" John asked cautiously, not sure this man even ran a bar.

"Of course you can." the man said.

"I'll have a Guinness." John answered.

"Make it two." Tony said.

Mike ordered a Harp and the girls each had a Bulmers.

He put the drinks on the counter. "16 Euro." he said.

They all pulled their money together putting it on the counter. The man picked up the cash and put it in a cigar box under the back bar. He didn't even count it.

"My name is Frawley." John said suddenly trying to engage the man.

"Oh, I see. That's a fine Irish name." he said adding nothing more.

John had planned to ask him about his family to see if there was any connection but the old man acted like he didn't even understand the connection, so John left it at that. The man returned to his television.

"Very odd." Nancy said sipping her cider.

"Its still a cool old place. By the looks of it, nothing has changed here for a long time. He has corn flakes and flour for sale behind the bar." John noted. "In the old days, a lot of country pubs were also grocers. I didn't know they actually still existed"

"Makes sense." Tony said. "I mean, if your going out, make it a one stop shop. You could get shitfaced at night and bring your corn flakes home with you for breakfast the next day."

"I say we finish these bad boys and hit the bricks." Nancy said. "Your dad doesn't seem to be too interested in exploring the old family tree with you anyway."

John had to admit, he was a little disappointed. Frawley was not too common of a name and it would be cool to find some long lost cousin. But as he looked out the front window watching the village streets getting busy as the evening approached, he agreed with Nancy.

The friends finished their drinks and decided to explore the other pubs in the village. Their first stop was the Atlantic, aptly named considering its proximity to the ocean. This pub had a nautical flair with ship's wheels and knotted ropes adorning the walls. The wood was highly polished and the whole place was reminiscent of a seafood restaurant down the Jersey shore. Again, the place didn't hold the group's interest very long and they decided to move on again after one round.

Their next stop looked promising. Combers, an ancient looking place that looked like it was a haunt for Lahinch's younger set. As soon as they opened the doors, they could see a sizable crowd of younger people gathered around the bar and booths. Towards the back, near a roaring wood burning stove, John spotted Jeff, Carol, Becky and Charley hovering around a small table.

"Well-well, look who it is." John pointed to the couples.

"How cozy." Rachel said just as the others noticed them. Jeff waved and started pulling some stools together.

"Where have you guys been?" Jeff asked when they all sat down.

"Looking for cute boys." Nancy answered.

"Yea, but we couldn't find any." Tony replied sarcastically.

Everyone was relaxed and having fun. Nancy and Emily were happily chatting with a few surfers they had met earlier. The three couples were enjoying their own company.

John was deep in thought. He replayed the last couple of weeks in his head. He wondered again about Katy and their encounters. He wondered if Liam would come along to keep her company. He tried to play out in his mind different scenarios that could evolve over the last days of the trip. He was excited and terrified about the possibilities. Just as he was about to become completely lost in thought, a fiddler started to play. John snapped back to the pub, as did all of the others. Soon, a tin whistle joined in followed by an old-fashioned squeezebox. The trio looked to all be in their seventies and could easily be on a postcard for Irish tourism. The reel was enchanting. For the next half hour, no one spoke as the old boys played traditional jigs and reels.

Finally, while the musicians took a Guinness break, Becky realized they were late for dinner. Quickly, the students grabbed their things leaving the pub in a rush.

Dermot stood at the top of the street waiting patiently. "Its easy to loose track of time in the pubs." he said beckoning them to get on the bus.

After another spectacular dinner in one of Lahinch's finest local restaurants, Dermot loaded the students on the bus. He was happy to be turning the reigns over to Katy when they got back. It was one thing driving a bus of high-energy students around the country but it was another thing all together directing the operation. Soon, he would be back to his old role as driver and baggage handler and that suited him just fine.

John found himself increasingly nervous on the quiet ride back to Ennis. The sun was about down and the rolling green hills and ancient stonewalls faded to shadows. He tried to shake himself out of the nervousness, reminding himself that nothing really happened with Katy and nothing was likely to. He vacillated between hoping Liam was with her and wishing he wasn't.

Chapter 50

The streets of Ennis were still busy even though it was well past 11 in the evening. None of the students mentioned a nightcap or pubs when they arrived. After such a long day and the shock of Dr. Carney's sudden departure, most of the group thought only of getting some sleep.

John, however, knew he was too wired to just hit the sack. After a few feeble attempts to rally some of the troops, he made up his mind to stop in the hotel bar by himself for a whiskey. He needed to take the edge off before he could think of sleep.

The bar at the Old Ground was fairly busy. The semi-circular bar was full except for one stool at the very end. John made a beeline for the stool, preferring to have a seat at the bar than a table where he might have to share space with someone and end up being sucked into a conversation. All he wanted now was a place to sit and think without interruption.

John secured the seat and settled in. The highly polished pine gave the space a brighter feel than a typical pub. A few American tourists occupied a large table on the other side of the room. They were talking loudly discussing their dinner earlier at

Bunratty Castle, which, according to their comments, featured an "authentic" medieval feast.

John was a little embarrassed by his countrymen and was hoping not to have to talk. Their cable knit sweaters and Irish caps looked like they had recently been bought in some local shop. Only American tourists dressed that way to try to "fit in." Their outfits reminded him of a Clancy Brothers album cover that he seemed to remember from Old Joe's record collection.

Next to him at the bar were two women dressed in business suits drinking brandy. An older gentleman wearing more of a country suit was standing behind them occasionally interrupting their talk. John overheard something to the effect that they were in town from Dublin for a conference. He guessed the old timer was just trying to chat up the city women.

The rest of the place was dotted with other foreign tourists, locals, and a few other business types. John felt he slotted into the background well enough to be unnoticed.

He called the bar man over and ordered a Powers with ice. Now, after a couple of sips, he began to relax. The soft burn of the whiskey warmed and mellowed him at the same time. He began to tune out the background noise and started to think more about Katy. Would she walk into the bar? Was she even there yet? How would this play out? If something did happen, what would the last two weeks in Dublin be like? John thought of these things with increasing anxiety. He realized he was making little headway when a figure he recognized appeared in the lobby just outside the bar. Katy Welsh was checking in.

John's heart raced. He didn't want her to see him but, at the same time, he could not take his eyes off of her. She carried a duffle bag and a large purse while pulling a large roller bag. She had on a dark blue long jacket cinched at her waist. Her long hair was down softly caressing her face. She looked radiant. John was so transfixed; he didn't even realize at first that she was alone. No sign of Liam anywhere. Dermot helped her with her suitcase but no one else appeared. Once again, John was thrilled and terrified all at once.

Katy stood at the front desk checking in for some time. John thought of going over to her to say hello. Innocent enough, he thought. He decided against it realizing it was getting very late and he was in the bar drinking whiskey alone. What would she think?

Finally, the desk clerk handed her the keys to her room pointing to the stairs behind her. As she turned, John quickly turned away, hoping she didn't see him. When he looked again, she was gone. Relief. Now he could relax a little, have one more drink, and try to go to bed.

When John was half way through his second Powers and was feeling calm and mellow, he felt a tap on his shoulder. He thought it was someone trying to move him over so they could order a drink. When he turned, he saw Katy smiling behind him. His heart began to race but the whiskey kept him in check enough to at least appear to be calm.

"Drinking with all of your friends I see." Katy said looking around the bar.

"I am the last one standing, well, actually, I just couldn't sleep." John answered sounding cool and collected.

"How's it going here now that Carney had to go?"

John caught her up on the details. The technical nature of the conversation helped to soothe John's nerves.

"I'm sorry, here I am going on about things and I haven't even offered you a drink." John said noting the formal tone of his own voice.

"OK, but just one. The train ride in was brutal. We were due in hours ago but there was some problem in Limerick. Anyway, I'll have a gin and tonic please." John ordered the drink and decided he would have another himself. After all, it would be rude to make Katy drink alone.

They continued to catch up. Katy was finishing her drink and John was about to ask if she'd like another when a familiar voice coming from the bar entrance interrupted them.

"Let the party begin." Tony announced drawing a little cheer from the American contingency across the bar. John couldn't help but feel a little resentment for the intrusion. At the same time, he was relieved to have some support.

"Welcome to Ennis." Tony said to Katy.

"Thanks. Good to be here."

The three made small talk for a few more minutes before Katy said she was tired and needed to get to bed. John tried to convince her to have one more but didn't press her. She said good night and reminded them they had an early start tomorrow.

"There's a new sheriff in town." she said blowing fake smoke from her fingertip.

"Well, I hope she brought her hand cuffs." Tony said with a smart-assed look on his face.

Katy shot him an amused look and said goodnight. John watched her as she walked towards the steps. He tried to stop looking but couldn't stop looking. He knew Tony was aware of his preoccupation with Katy's exit.

"How long before you hit that?" he said with a twisted smile.

"Oh please, what are you talking about?" John protested. "I'm not getting involved while I am here. Strictly business." he said raising the Powers as if making a toast. "Join me for another night cap."

Tony rolled his eyes. "I guess I can. Rachel is done with me for the time being anyway."

"You fighting?" John asked.

"No, I just got laid and she's asleep. Now, set me up dude." The night grew later. Before they knew it, it was past three and the barman was making last call. John knew tomorrow would be rough but at least he had made it through tonight. The real action would begin in the morning.

Chapter 51

"Pick up that fuckin' phone." Tony moaned in John's general direction.

"What?" John responded half in a daze.

"The phone, man, pick it up. It's on your side."

John rolled over and stared for a second at the phone that was ringing incessantly. Adrenalin suddenly kicked in as John realized they might have overslept.

"Hello?" he answered. "Uh, ok, we'll be right down." He hung up the receiver. "Shit, fuck, fuck."

"What's the deal?' Tony asked.

"They're waiting for us on the bus. If we're not down in five minutes, we will have to find our own way to Killarney. Fuckin' hell."

They both jumped out of their beds and immediately started throwing their things into their luggage. Two minutes later, they were on the steps leading to the lobby. John knew he looked bad, smelled bad, and generally was not off to a good start to impress Katy.

"What a start."

"Don't worry. They won't go anywhere without us." Tony said sounding less than confident.

They ran through the lobby and out to the curb.

"Shit, where are they?"

"No fucking way did they go without us." Tony said.

"Looks like they did. Shit!"

"You just made it," a voice said from behind them. Katy was standing in the doorway of the hotel. She was smiling but looked a little annoyed. "is this what I'm to expect for the rest of the trip?"

"No! No, I mean, we're never late." John stammered. "Where's the bus?" Just as the words came out of his mouth, Dermot rounded the corner with the bus and all of the other students.

"They went for petrol. If it weren't because the bus needed gas, you'd be walking."

Everyone clapped when they got on the bus. Nancy openly laughed reminding them how rough they looked.

John went to the back of the bus while Tony nudged Rachel over. "Thanks for waking me."

Rachel glared at him. "Well, if you hadn't run out on me maybe I would have."

"Run out? What are you talking about? We were done and I wanted to find my boy."

"I hope you did. You can sleep with him for now on I guess."

Tony worked on Rachel for the first full hour of the long drive south. Eventually, John saw Tony put his arm around her and watched as she snuggled into his shoulder.

I guess he's worked his magic again, John thought to himself.

John was suffering. The adrenalin from the morning panic wore off and now he was concentrating on not getting sick. He needed to brush his teeth and take a shower. He could not wait to get to Killarney where he could get off the bus and get some fresh air.

The bus traveled south along the Atlantic coast. They stopped in Killimer to catch the ferry to Tarbert over the mouth of the Shannon River. John was thrilled to get off of the bus. He decided to stay outside on the ferry and enjoy the view and the fresh air. As the ferry began to cross, he noticed a little bar and concession stand selling snacks. He bought a Flake bar and bag of salt and vinegar Tayto's. Junk food usually takes care of a hangover and John was buying some of the best.

The bus rolled off of the ferry making its way south through Listowel and down the N69 to Tralee. The group was subdued for the most part after their busy two-day stop in Clare. John slept part of the way, as did most of the others. Katy sat in the front and mostly chatted with Dermot. She was also busy reviewing the remaining itinerary making sure she mapped out the details.

Finally, the bus made it to the outskirts of Killarney. The students were booked into a small family owned luxury property in the town center.

Katy, following Dr. Carney's recommendations, asked for everyone's attention. "We are in Killarney for tonight only. After we check in, we will meet in the lobby to review the plans for this afternoon and tonight. We will also go over tomorrow's plans including our strict departure time." she was making sure to make eye contact with John and Tony.

The bus pulled up in front of a small hotel, The Strand, on Killarney's very busy main street. The town was charming and filled with tourists. John noted how many American accents he heard. He figured Killarney was one of those places in Irish-

American lore that was special. "Christmas in Killarney" drummed up those sappy feeling about Ireland that Irish-Americans get even if they've never been there.

Once the group checked in, they met in the little lobby next to reception. Katy waited with a clipboard in hand and a large file folder next to her. She looked professional and was trying to take her role seriously. Upon seeing her, John felt like any kind of hook-up now was very far-fetched.

"OK, listen up. We have a few things to get done this afternoon and I want to go over them." Katy said as she began to go over the day's itinerary, which included tours, meetings and official visits. To John and the others, the trip was following a predictable pattern regardless of who its leader happened to be.

After the official program ended for the day, John found himself wandering the vast Mucross House in the Killarney National Park. Earlier, the group had the opportunity to tour the house with one of the last people to live there when it was a private residence.

The man, Tony Vincent, was a child when his family gave the house and all of its land to Irish government creating a National Park. His recollections of the house and the high society of that era were remarkable. Listening to him was truly like listening to living history. John imagined what it was like when Ireland was still part of Great Britain and places like Mucross House, Ashford Castle, and others were the bastions of British gentry.

Walking back towards town, past the 15th century Mucross Friary, John heard someone call his name.

"John, hold up!"

He turned to see Katy from behind one of the Friaries ruined walls.

"Where're you heading?" she asked.

"Back to town, the hotel. I need a shower to revive myself a bit before dinner."

"How's the head?" she asked using an Irish expression.

"Getting better. The exercise and fresh air helps a lot."

"Mind if I walk back with you? I need to get back to the hotel and make a few calls."

"No, no problem at all." John said happy to have the company. He wasn't nervous or anxious. Perhaps a combination of his mild hangover and the fact that he had not expected to see her mitigated his feelings.

He was casual and loose and Katy was equally at ease. Her business demeanor from earlier was now more relaxed and she was more like she had been when they were back in Dublin.

"How are you enjoying the trip so far?" she asked filling the long walk back to town with small talk.

"I'm having a blast. Dr. Carney did a good job and we've seen some cool stuff. A lot of what I've experienced will stay with me forever."

"That's great." Katy said. "This kind of trip should have life long memories."

John's nervousness suddenly reappeared. Katy had a way of saying things that were open to interpretation. John couldn't help but wonder what kind of memories she had in mind.
They walked slowly out of the park and onto the main road leading to town. They passed a line of horse drawn carriages, handsome cabs that gave tours of the park.

"How 'bout a tour for you and your lady?" One of the drivers asked. John could feel himself blush a little but, on another level, he enjoyed the assumption.

Back in the hotel, Charley and Becky were sitting in the lobby looking at pictures from earlier in the trip. They both looked up when Katy and John walked in together but made no comments or funny faces. John was relieved it wasn't Nancy or Tony. They would surely have made a spectacle.

"What are you two up to?" Katy asked Charley and Becky.

“She just got some of the film developed from the first part of the tour.” Charley answered.

“It seems so long ago that we were at Ashford.” Becky added.

John considered her comment. So much of the group dynamic has changed in a little over a week. The group had gelled into one group of friends and, in a couple cases, more than friends. Now, with Carney gone, Dermot back to his role as bus driver, and Katy joining the tour, the dynamic was changing again.

Chapter 52

John sat in one of the overstuffed high-backed chairs just off of the main lobby. Katy had asked the group to meet in the lobby at 7:00 so they could walk to dinner, which was booked for 7:30 at a nearby local restaurant known for their fine steaks. John was the first one to get downstairs and considered having a beer in the bar while he waited, but then decided it would be safer to wait in the lobby. He watched as people walked by the pane-glassed windows across from where he was sitting. The new luxury chairs, marble floors, and gold leafed crown molding gave this small hotel a luxurious feel. Clearly, the Irish economy launched this formerly modest place to the ranks of boutique luxury property.

Ireland had emerged from one of the poorest economies in Europe a dozen or so years ago to one of the strongest and fastest growing. Almost overnight, the Irish went from having no phones in their houses to having the latest cell technology. Cars were rare a decade ago and those who had them usually drove old tired bangers. Now, Mercedes and BMW's ruled the roads and only the latest models would do.

John wondered about this newly found prosperity and what it might do to the Irish psyche. He thought it would be a shame if the Irish got spoiled and lost their humble nature. However, after thinking about this for a few moments, he realized his thinking was seriously flawed.

Wasn't it about time the Irish enjoyed the good life? How anyone could resent the success of a country that had for so long been badly oppressed was beyond him. He thought prosperity would be a good thing for the Irish and doubted anything could change the fundamental nature of a civilization that had endured so much trouble and difficulty for a thousand years.

"Snap out of it, yo. Your in one of your now famous trances." Tony said bringing John back to earth.

"I'm still a little hung and out of it." John said as Tony sat in the big chair next to him.

"Hair o' the dog time." Tony suggested.

"No chance. I am trying to be on my best behavior for now. I mean, after this morning's debacle…"

"I know, trying to impress the teacher, maybe earn a good grade." Tony teased.

"Cut me a break, man, I'm too out of it to deal with your shit." John snapped.

"Easy big guy. Just a little joke. I don't care if you tap that or not."

"There's no tapping in my plans. Fuck it, let's get a beer."

"Now you're thinking clearly." Tony said as the two got up and made their way to the little lobby bar across the hall.

By 7 PM, everyone was in the lobby including Katy. Mike saw Tony and John in the bar and called them to the lobby. Katy shot John and Tony a look that suggested she was less than pleased to see them coming from the bar.

"We are going to be dining at Foley's tonight which is just down the road." Katy said. She went on to describe the place as an old-style local hotel restaurant that was known for its use of local ingredients and innovative recipes. It all sounded good to John who was living off of a candy bar and bag of crisps.

"Man, I'm starving. The beer cleared my head but it woke my appetite."

"I'm glad this place is more casual. The big dining rooms and fancy joints are great but sometimes you want to relax." Tony added.

The students walked in behind their new leader up the street to the little hotel that housed the restaurant. Upon entering, John immediately picked up the vibe in the restaurant. The place was old but neat and well maintained. Long tables of tourists and locals talked loudly in the long narrow dining room. A group of American golfers were the loudest by far talking endlessly about this shot and that green and who got "up and down." The place had energy and John welcomed the buzz. A quiet dinner in some formal restaurant would have knocked him out but this place, even with the Yanks, was just what he needed.

The manager at the door welcomed Katy and the group of students. She was clearly expecting the group and immediately picked up a stack of leather-jacketed menus and led the way to the table. The manager placed the menus in front of each seat at the long rectangular table. Katy asked the students to sit where they liked creating a mad scramble by the couples to sit next to each other. John sat at the end seat at the top of the table. Everyone else found their seat and began to review the menus.

"John." Katy called from the other end of the table. "Could you switch with Mike? He's left handed and needs an end seat."

Everyone turned to look at John. Mike happened to be sitting next to Katy who was on the end of the table across from them.

"Sure, no problem." John answered trying hard to sound casual.

No one said a word but John had no doubt that some of them, Nancy and Emily in particular, were drawing certain conclusions.

"Thanks, man." Mike said passing John. "I can't stand bumping people the entire meal."

John thought this could not be a set up. How would Katy know about Mike if he didn't say something? It was just a coincidence that he was next to Katy to begin with. Now, he was next to her. He could smell her perfume. His appetite was fading a little as the sense of excitement began to overtake him.

Suddenly, Katy's leg pressed against his. Was he really feeling this? He thought to himself, his heart starting to jump in his chest. Then, suddenly, her leg moved back. Again, thinking to himself he wondered, was that a signal, a sign, or just an accident. He could not be sure, but he sure liked it while it lasted.

The meal was superb. The food was so simple but fresh and bursting with flavor. John could not get over how simple things, like butter, tasted so good. Something as simple as the baked chicken with bacon was so flavorful. In the States, chicken tastes like the sauce you put on it, in Ireland chicken tastes like chicken. John couldn't tell if the others shared his enthusiasm for the food, but they were all eating like it was their last meal.

The dinner ended and there were no more under the table leg calisthenics between John and Katy. Over coffee, Katy briefed the group on tomorrow's itinerary.

"We leave tomorrow at 10AM sharp. We will be making two stops on the way to Midleton where we are booked to stay tomorrow night. Please do not stay out all night raising hell. We have a busy day tomorrow." Katy said looking directly at John and Tony.

With that, she excused the group who slowly began to trickle out onto the streets of Killarney.

“What are your plans?” Katy asked John as he got up from the table.

“I don’t really know. Most of the others are going to some pub they found near the hotel. I’m trying to take it easy tonight after last night’s fiasco.”

“Sounds like a plan. Do you want to walk me back to the hotel?” she asked.

John gulped. He thought he gulped so hard, she could hear it. “Sure, yea, no problem. I’m going that way anyway.” His attempts to sound casual and dismissive were transparent enough, but Katy didn’t let on she suspected anything. Perhaps, she really didn’t.

The two walked side by side down the busy main street. The pubs were packed with Yanks and other tourists singing pub sing-alongs. John felt no desire to join in and was concentrating in not over-thinking his walk home with Katy.

“I never really liked Killarney.” she said looking over to him.

“No? Why not?”

“It’s contrived. I mean, it is lovely and in the winter its grand but now with the pre-planned sing-along and the other trappings of fake Irishness, it bugs me.”

“I know what you mean but at the same time there are some tourists that want this, particularly the Yanks.” John said, trying to sound informed.

“It’s too bad, though. The real Ireland is so much better.” Katy replied.

“Yeah, you’re right, but don’t forget, a lot of Americans prefer the Epcot version of Europe rather than enduring the reality of a place.”

“That’s what’s so pathetic. We want the sanitized version of things that robs us of the real experience.” Katy said looking genuinely sad about this.

Suddenly, they were in front of the hotel. John was so absorbed with Katy that the ten-minute walk seemed more like ten seconds.

"Well, here we are." Katy said.

"Yep, I guess we're here." John said instantly recognizing the stupidity of his reply.

"See you tomorrow. I have some work to get done." Katy said putting her hand on his shoulder. John felt a little twinge of panic or desperation.

"Do you want a nightcap?" he blurted out as she turned to go in.

"No, not tonight, I just need to get some paperwork done and turn in. It was a busy day."

"Oh, come on" he started to say but cut himself off. He heard neediness in his voice that he knew was not attractive, "Maybe tomorrow." he said instead.

"Maybe tomorrow." she repeated and went inside.

John stood at the door staring into the hotel lobby. He was a little in shock. It's not that he expected a homerun but he felt he was cut way short. Again, he started wondering if it was all in head. Finally, he shook his head and began to walk down the street not sure where he was going.

John passed a few crowded pubs trying to decide if he wanted to venture in or just go home. His confusion about Katy was turning a little sour and was likely to become outright anger if he was not careful. He peered in the front window of a pub called Butler's.

The place was teeming with revelers of every type. The Americans he saw at dinner, the golfers, were there chatting up some local girls. Then, he spotted some familiar faces. Nancy and Emily were on a stage towards the back of the pub singing karaoke. Mike was sitting at the table in front of them shaking his head and looking embarrassed. After taking a moment to consider his options, drinking alone in the lobby bar or going to bed, John pulled open the door and went to join his friends.

"Where's your lovah?" Nancy teased as she finished a rousing version of Hotel California.

"Tony's with Rachel, you know that." John fired back suddenly in a lighter mood.

Mike, drinking for one of the rare times on this trip, suggested John get on stage and sing a song.

"I will if you will." John joked.

The girls tried to egg them on but there was no way they would budge.

After a few rounds and enduring decent to downright awful attempts at *Hot Legs*, *Nothing Compares to You*, and *Mustang Sally*, John began to fade. The booze from the night before failed to reignite and he needed to get to bed. The warm stagnant air in the pub was making him sleepy. Just as he was about to tell the group he was off, he saw out of the corner of his eye a woman in a blue jacket much like the one Katy had on earlier. He only saw her from the side but he could swear it was her.

"I'm off!" he announced to his startled friends.

"Are you ok?" Emily asked out of concern.

"Yea, just tired, see you later."

Mike looked at him and then at the girls. "What the fuck? Do we offend?".

"Really, I'm beat. Too much partying. I need some air." John said making a gesture that indicated he might throw up. This seemed to get him off of the hook as the three nodded in unison indicating they understood.

John flew out the front door of the pub. He ran into a couple strolling down the street. "Sorry, my bad." John said looking past them in the direction the woman in the blue jacket went.

"Fecking tourist." The man he bumped into muttered as he walked on.

John did not pay any attention to the insult as he looked intently for the woman. By now she was over a hundred yards in front of him. He began to walk fast and even jogged a little slipping by people while keeping an eye on the woman. As he closed in on her, he saw she was on a cell phone.

"Probably talking to that tool Liam." he said out load. She turned the corner and went into an alley. By the time he reached the turn, she was out of sight. He walked quickly through the alley reaching another road. He looked up and down the back road but saw no one. The only thing that caught his attention was a neon sign in the window of a small pub across the street. The sign advertised Miller Genuine Draft, which John thought was odd. There were no tourists, no loud music, no karaoke blaring bad tunes. The place reminded him of the local taprooms back home.

John slowly walked across the street. He hesitated when he got to the door of the pub. If she were inside, would she think he was following her? The fact that he actually was following her made it worse. He decided to have a peek in the window. There were lace curtains that were half drawn up blocking most of the view inside. John could make out a few guys sitting at the bar. There appeared to be a few tables scattered around towards the back but only one had people sitting at it. The man looked to be about thirty or so and wore wire-rimmed glasses with a burgundy scarf around his neck. The woman he was with looked to be about the same age and was wearing jeans and a light blue sweater. No one else was visible. John thought he lost her.

Then, coming out of a small hallway that led to the toilets, Katy emerged. He couldn't believe it. She wasn't wearing her blue jacket, which John suddenly noticed on the chair next to the woman with the blue sweater. When he turned back, Katy was looking right at him. His heart literally felt like it stopped. He ducked and ran back across the street to the alley. He felt like a complete jackass. He prayed she did not see him looking in the window. If she did, she would surely think he was a creep or just plain crazy. He walked back to the main street and headed straight for the hotel.

Along the way, John began to think about what had just happened. Did she blow him off knowing she had plans? Was she just trying to get rid of him? Why did she ask him to walk he home if she had plans? Who were those people she was with? The questions kept coming. The answers did not. John was perplexed and humiliated. She was a young professional and he was a student following her around like a lost puppy. He felt like a sap and decided then and there he was out of the game. Katy was the professor and he would only think of her as such for now on.

Chapter 53

John was up early the next morning. He skulked home after seeing Katy the night before and went right to bed. He considered hitting the lobby bar, but in the end, he was just too mentally fatigued. Thanks to this decision, he was out of bed and in the breakfast room of the hotel bright and early. His head was clear and for the first morning in a while, he felt good. He was a little embarrassed about the night before with Katy but aside from that, he was actually in a very positive mood. Perhaps, the pressure of knowing Katy was coming, and knowing something might happen between them, had been too much for him. Knowing now that all bets were off seemed to lighten his spirits and relieve the pressure.

John ordered the full Irish breakfast. It was 7:30 in the morning and most of the breakfast room was still empty. The only other two parties eating were a group of Asian men dressed in business suits reading over legal looking papers and an older American couple bickering over plans to see the Ring of Kerry. John considered what it must be like to be married to someone for so long. Watching the two senior citizens argue over whether to take a tour bus or hire a private car for the tour was a little disheartening.

"Why pay for a private car when there is a perfectly good bus taking the same tour?" the woman said.

Her husband shook his head. "I didn't come all the way to Ireland to sit on a damned bus with a bunch of tourists snapping pictures out the window!"

John could see they were well dressed and appeared to have the means to hire a private car. He could not help but wonder if this is how all marriages eventually end up.

Between bites of his rashers and eggs, he watched the drama play out. The man dressed in a polo golf shirt and pressed khaki pants with a white knit sweater draped around his shoulders looked like a dude. He would be dressed the same in the grillroom of his local country club. His white hair was thin but well groomed. He wore glasses but did not look the seventy plus years he likely was. His wife, also in a golf style shirt wore designer jeans and carried an expensive Chanel purse. Neither said much for a few minutes.

John figured they were stewing and he waited for an eruption. Instead, he witnessed something remarkable which restored his faith in the idea of a long and happy marriage. The man looked up from his bowl of porridge and gazed at his wife. She focused on her toast but clearly was listening.

"Why would I want to share you with a bus load of other people when we could have a romantic drive by ourselves?"

The wife looked up with a smile. The smile was not exactly innocent. She knew she was being buttered up but still had enjoyed the effort. Without any more discussion, she conceded.

"Fine" was all she needed to say and the fight was over and no hard feelings were left.

John smiled and realized married life was work but, if you loved the person, it was really a labor of love.

As if on cue, Katy walked into the breakfast room, just as John had started to feel better about male-female relations. She looked around and seemed pleased, no one else was there yet. She walked over to John's table.

"Mind if I join you?"

"Not at all."

"You're up early"

"Yea, I had an early night. You can't hoot with the owls and soar with the eagles you know."

"I guess I just figured you hooted most nights." she said joking with him.

"No, hardly ever. Mostly what I do is research for my business. When I'm out on the town, it's pure research."

She laughed but said nothing.

John waited for her to say something about the previous evening but the subject never came up. He was beginning to see a pattern with Katy. She preferred to leave certain things unsaid, adding to her mystery. John was actually relieved and happy enough to just shoot the breeze.

After breakfast, the group met in the lobby, dragging their luggage down from their rooms. Dermot was waiting outside with the bus. Katy called everyone to attention.

"Today, we will be doing some sight-seeing on our way to Midleton. The drive should take about three hours but there are some planned stops to break things up. Please get your bags to Dermot and load up. I want to be on the road in fifteen minutes."

"Yes sir." Tony mumbled under his breath.

"What a drill sergeant. I wonder if she's that strict in bed."

"Shut up, would ya?" John said rolling his eyes for effect.

"A little touchy, are we?"

"No, not at all. I have a healthy respect for Ms. Welsh." John replied with mock respect. "Our relationship is purely professional" he said to Tony who gave John a sideways glare.

"What's up with that?" Tony asked.

"Nothing, literally." John answered. "Nothing's going to be up either, apparently."

"Bummer, dude." Tony said letting the conversation drop.

Rachel walked over. "Are we packed sweetie?"

"All set, babe."

John saw the other happy couples helping each other with their bags. He remembered the older couple from breakfast and suddenly realized he was envious of it all. Why should Tony and Rachel, Charley and Becky and Jeff and Carol be so lucky? Even the single ones did not seem as lonely as he was feeling today.

Chapter 54

Dermot drove the bus down the N22 towards Cork City. Everyone was well rested and lively. The happy couples, as John now referred to the six in question, were grouped together while the remaining singles spread out throughout the bus. Katy was up front chatting with Dermot confirming the details of the drive. John, sitting towards the back of the bus was reading a book and mostly keeping to himself.

"Whatcha reading?" John looked up and saw Katy looking at him smiling. She was standing in the isle holding onto the back of the seat in front of him for balance.

"Just something I picked up in Killarney, it's called *The Van* by Roddy Doyle. It's really funny." John said without much enthusiasm.

"Yea, I like Roddy Doyle but not all of his books are that funny. I just finished *The Woman Who Walks into Doors* and found it very good but very depressing."

"Remind me to skip that one, I don't need more depressing things in my life."

Katy looked at him trying to decipher his cryptic response. "What do you have to be depressed about? You're out here in the beautiful countryside with your mates having a grand old time. What do you have to worry about?"

"Nothing. Just something a guy says. Everything's just great."

Katy shrugged and turned to go back up front. Suddenly, the bus hit a bump sending Katy careening backwards. She started to fall when John grabbed her and pulled her towards him. For a very brief second, she was laying in his arms. He felt and enjoyed her closeness in that little second.

"Are you alright?"

Katy giggled and stood up. "Good catch. I'd have been on my arse if you didn't catch me." she said as she got up off his lap.

"Anytime." he said looking back to his book.

"Nice catch, indeed." Nancy said from behind John. "What a gent."

"Just a coincidence." he replied.

"Sure, whatever you say sport."

Dermot pulled the bus off of the highway just before Cork City. He took a couple of shockingly small back roads leading to one of Ireland's biggest tourist draws, the Blarney Stone. Dermot negotiated the narrow road leading to a small square just next to Blarney Castle.

"OK, everyone look alive. This is our first stop of the day. I will pay your admission into the castle but it's up to you to pay the extra fee if you want to climb to the top and kiss the Blarney Stone. We will meet back here in 1 hour. Remember to be careful. This is not like Disneyland."

The group climbed off the bus. Katy walked with them to the old Victorian looking gatehouse that led to the castle and the Blarney Stone. The sun was shining and the grounds behind the gate reminded John of a park or the lawn of a great mansion house back home. Katy signed the slip for the tickets and came out of the little gatehouse.

"Here are your tickets." she said handing everyone their tickets. "They are good for admission to the castle and grounds. You can explore anything you want and can kiss the stone but just make sure you're back in an hour."

The group walked through the gatehouse pushing the ancient turnstile one at a time. Inside, the grounds were even more beautiful. The park-like setting was lush with the greenest lawn you could imagine. A little brook bisected the lawn leading from the castle.

"Man, look at that." John said pointing to the castle ruins off in the distance. "It definitely is not Cinderella's castle."

The ruins were impressive. The ancient tower house stood with its floors and roof long since gone. A round tower flanked one side of the castle. Dungeons and caves ran beneath it. John was amazed. The Blarney Stone was a classic tourist trap but this trap was magnificent.

John crossed a little footbridge leading up to the castle itself. The group had splintered once again into couples and singles. John walked with Mike and Nancy who were both busy snapping pictures of the ruin. John couldn't help but feel bad for them knowing many of their pictures and subsequent memories would be based on postcard snapshots void of actual people. As he thought of this, he realized his own photos would be similar. This realization added to his growing feeling of loneliness.

Alone now, John decided to climb the narrow winding stairs to the top of the castle. There were people both in front of him and behind him eliminating the chance to change his mind and return to the park outside the castle. He listened as people spoke to each other in different accents and in different languages, eagerly anticipating the encounter with the Blarney stone. Originally, he'd had no intention to kiss the stone but once he saw the hundreds of people making what looked like a pilgrimage up the narrow stairs, he decided he may only be here once and shouldn't miss the chance.

The top of the castle was much higher than it looked from the ground. John, after being encased in the narrow stairwell for twenty minutes or so, had trouble adjusting to the sudden sunlight. There was also enough wind to make him nervous. He could not imagine what it must be like for some of the senior citizens that walked up the stairs with him. Certainly, perched on this narrow walkway atop this roofless ruin with the wind whipping around them must be daunting. However, it was not until John edged closer to the two older gentlemen sitting with their legs hanging over the side of the castle wall with thick wool blankets over their laps that he really started to worry.

As they got to the front of the line, each person was instructed to sit and lean backwards over the wall with their faces facing the stonewall. The old man sitting on the edge of the castle wall held their legs to keep them steady. The drop was at least five or six stories. These people were risking life and limb to hang upside down over a 100-foot high wall to kiss a stone, and the only thing keeping them from falling was an older Irish man who looked like he may have had a few pints the night before.

Before he knew it, John was himself hanging upside down facing the cold Blarney Stone. His hair fell around his face as he puckered up and kissed the stone. The older Irish man hoisted him back up and sent him on his way. The entire thing took only a few seconds and John was on his way down a second set of stairs before he even knew what had happened.

Chapter 55

An hour or so later, everyone was back on the bus. Katy took a quick head count and said something to Dermot. The bus roared to life and pulled out of the Blarney parking lot and back towards the highway.

"Did you kiss it?" Nancy asked John.

"Damn right I did! What the hell, I may never be back. Plus, I could use a better rap." John answered.

"Do you know what the locals do to that stone after the tourists are gone? It's disgusting. How many nasty lips smack that thing everyday? Gross!" Tony said making a face like he just ate something rotten.

"I choose not to think about it." John said. "Anyway, it was an experience."

As it turned out, only two others, Carol and Jeff actually went up and kissed the stone. The others mostly milled around the grounds and eventually went for ice cream at the snack shop near the entrance. Some of them said they didn't like the height, while others just followed Tony's lead and claimed they heard the local kids peed on the stone at night. In any event, John was happy he had done it. At the very least, it seemed to elevate his mood and dispel some of his looming loneliness.

Katy stood up once the bus reached the dual carriageway. John looked at her and was once again struck by her beauty. The sun caught the back of her hair giving her radiance. The light coming through the bus' windshield also enhanced her figure. John could not take his eyes off her as she briefed the crew about the next stop. He convinced himself back in Killarney that their relationship, or lack thereof, was to be professional. Nothing would happen, but now, as she stood in the front of the bus facing the students balancing on the seat backs, John knew he wanted her. He knew he needed her. He also knew that nothing had changed to give him any hope of attaining his goal.

After only a few miles, the bus exited the dual carriageway. Dermot drove the bus into the large town of Midleton. John had read about this whiskey Mecca where all of the primary Irish whiskey brands were distilled. Bushmills in the North was the only real exception. The group was scheduled to tour the Jameson Heritage Centre on the grounds of the old Midleton Distillery. John was excited to see the distillery even though they had already visited Kilbeggan earlier in the trip. Midleton was the real deal and the home to so many great whiskies like Jameson, Paddy, and Powers among many others.

The bus made its way down the town center before pulling into the car park next to the old distillery. The new distillery was directly behind the old one with its high smoke stacks billowing plumes of white smoke or steam. John immediately took note of the juxtaposition between the old stone distillery with its graceful copper pot stills, elegant water wheels, and 19th century industrial architecture as compared to the new steel and glass distillery currently turning out Ireland's "water of life."

Inside the welcome center, the group gathered around Katy for their tickets to the tour.

"We will be going into the distillery in a few moments. Please stay in the lobby until our guide calls us"

John was still focused on her, and more than ever, found himself extremely attracted to her. He found himself drawn to her with increasing intensity, and as much as he tried to blame it on loneliness, he couldn't deny it, it was her causing these feelings.

The lobby had filled with other tour groups. One bus was filled with French speaking tourists, while another group seemed to be comprised of Germans. All of these groups from different places drawn by the allure of Irish whiskey.

"The English speaking tour will start in three minutes. Anyone for the English tour will please assemble at the entrance to the theatre." a voice from a loud speaker announced.

Katy got them all together and moved them towards the theatre, where two British couples, three back-packers from New Zealand, and a family of four from the States had already gathered for the whiskey tour.

John followed the guide with sincere interest. He thought about the whiskey they served at the Hound and realized what a waste it was when his customers simply did a shot of Jameson or worse, dropped it in a pint of beer. He found the history of Irish whiskey along with the production to be very interesting and when the tour finally ended, he found himself excited by the prospect of trying the whiskey at the tasting following the tour. It was like the time his parents took him to the Hershey factory tour when he was a kid and he was dying for chocolate after the tour was over.

The group gathered samples and sat down to enjoy them. John was at a table with Jeff, Carol and Mike while the others were at adjoining tables. Much to John's surprise and delight, Katy walked over and sat next to him with a bottle of mineral water.

"No whiskey for the boss?" Mike asked.

"Nope, not yet anyway. I have to at least pretend to be responsible." she said with a sigh.

"It is part of the educational experience, you know." Carol added.

"That's a reach. Anyway, I'm saving myself for when we get to the hotel. Today, I feel like having a glass of wine or two."

John suddenly felt a pang of excitement. Katy was ready to party, he thought. Maybe that would create an opportunity. He immediately caught himself and decided he needed to move away from her. As he started to get up, Katy grabbed his arm and pulled him back to his seat. He looked around but no one seemed to notice. Katy said nothing but smiled at him when he looked at her with a surprised expression. What the fuck is this about? He thought. The pang of excitement began to grow and, much to John's chagrin began to manifest itself physically. Now he couldn't get up even if he wanted to. Panicked, he grabbed Carol's glass, which was still half full and shot down.

"Help yourself." Carol said.

"Oh, sorry, I thought you were done." he looked around to the other tables to see if anyone else had some leftovers. Mike had finished his but offered John a voucher he found on the floor for another.

"Could you get it for me? I have a strange cramp I can't get rid of."

"Um, Sure." Mike said a little puzzled and got up to go to the bar.

Katy shot John a smile that made John feel like she knew what was lurking below the table.

"Belly up." Mike said, dropping the shot glass down in front of John. John grabbed the glass trying to act casual and shot the whiskey back.

"Take it easy, we still have to get through dinner." Katy said grinning at John. John felt the whiskey beginning to work. He started to calm down, and by the time Katy said it was time to go, he was able to get up from the table without embarrassment.

Chapter 56

The whiskey had mellowed the group as they headed out of Midleton, towards the Ballymaloe House, their next stop. Dermot had informed Katy that it would be a short ride, so she decided to make her announcements as soon as they got started.

"We will have dinner in the hotel tonight at seven. Ballymaloe is an old manor house set in its own grounds and it has a famous cooking school associated with it, which we will visit tomorrow. I want us all to meet in the lobby at 6:00 to review tomorrow's itinerary before dinner." with that, Katy sat back down.

John did not dare to think about her or he might be stuck on the bus for hours. Instead, he thought of the Hound and Old Joe. He had been out of touch for a few days now and wondered how things were going. He had learned and experienced so much on this trip that he wanted to apply to the Hound. He was becoming a different person and saw his business in a different way. He was not looking forward to his last year at Cornell. He was too anxious to get on with his career. He knew, however, that he had not only to finish this tour and then two more weeks in Dublin, but also a full year back in college before he could really get started. It all seemed so far away at this point. John thought about Katy some more to take his mind off of the future. She was a nice distraction even if only for the moment.

Dermot drove the bus over a tangle of back roads past large country estates and farms. Eventually, he came to the top of a small hill where the road bisected another road, running parallel to the hill. Where the roads met, an old iron gate marked the entrance of Ballymaloe House. The old gate was more run down looking than fancy and stood just in front of a cattle grate indicating a working farm. Most of the group was looking out the windows wondering what they were in store for. John looked out his window but the excitement of the new stop on the tour was momentarily lost. He did not know exactly why he was less interested in the trip at this point but figured it had something to do with Katy and his desire to get back home. The two sensations conflicted a little and cancelled out his enthusiasm for much else.

Dermot angled the bus through the old iron gates and over the rollers in the ground designed to keep cattle or other farm animals from escaping. The winding narrow drive followed a sheep's pasture on one side and some open fields that had recently been tilled on the other. The driveway meandered through a small wooded area that eventually opened up to the lawn in front of the main house. The gracious ivy clad country house encompassed an ancient Norman Castle giving the whole place an exotic but familiar feel. John could feel the excitement begin to return to his senses. He was anxious to get on with his life but he knew the rest of this trip and all of the adventures yet to come should not be missed.

The bus came to a stop just in front of the old house. The group got off the bus and looked around. Next to the main house, a series of smaller utilitarian looking buildings hinted at the real business of the place, farming. An old stable area had been converted into guest rooms, but all of the remaining buildings still looked like they were part of a real working farm. Next to the house, a small pool was one of the few hints that the place was open to the public at all.

"What do you think?" Tony asked John as they looked around.

"Looks cool. A real farm. The place is known for the food. I read somewhere that the lady who opened this as a hotel was responsible for Ireland's culinary awakening and her daughter in law is some kind of Irish Martha Stewart."

"I just hope they have a bar." Nancy chimed in.

Chapter 57

Katy had gone into the main house to check on the rooms. A few minutes later, she emerged with two young men, boys actually, and a middle aged women dressed in a frumpy old-style uniform. They all looked very serious as they approached giving some members of the group the feeling something might be wrong. However, once Ms. Murray was close enough to make eye contact, she smiled and waved with genuine affection.

"You are all very welcome."

She started with a greeting that was becoming very common to John and his fellow travelers. The nice thing, though, was that no matter how often they heard it, it always sounded authentic and heart-felt. Ms. Murray did appear to be genuinely happy to see them as did her smiling young sidekicks.

"I have all of your room assignments in the house. Some of you will be in the main house while a few are over here in the gatehouse. Tommy and Jim will help you with your bags once you get your keys."

The two young lads were dressed in black pants and white buttoned down dress shirts with thin black ties around their necks.

They resembled prep school boys wearing slightly rumpled uniforms. They smiled at the group and said quiet "hellos." After they got their keys, she thanked Ms. Murray and asked the students to meet her back in the lobby after checking out their rooms.

John was assigned a room with Tony. They were one of the groups to be housed in the newly renovated gatehouse. Tony thought this might be a bad break but John was excited knowing he would be able to see the inner workings of the farm. They elected to leave the bag boys, Jim and Tommy, to help the girls, electing to drag their own bags from the bus to the courtyard of the gatehouse.

"I can smell the cows." Tony announced as they began towards the door leading to their room.

"It's fresh." John said using a phrase he had heard a local guy use to describe the extremely harsh odor emanating from fields that had been recently sprayed with manure.

"Fresh, my ass."

"Whatever you say."

They made it up the stairs and into their room, the Red Room. All of the rooms, even the ones in the main house, had names instead of numbers. The names corresponded roughly to some attribute of the room. The Castle Room was partially housed in the old castle part of the house. The Ivy Room had windows that were encased in thick ivy. The Red Room, as in Tony and John's, had a red bedspread and a single red wall. Tony said the red gave him a headache but John was happy with the color saying it was warm.

"Well, you can have it to yourself, Rachel got a single so I'll be shacking up there tonight. Who knows, maybe tonight will be 'Hot for Teacher' night."

"No chance. I have moved on and now I'm just thinking about enjoying the trip with no complicating factors. We only have tonight and then we're back to Dublin." John said suddenly realizing that this would be the last night on the road. Tomorrow, they had a few stops on the way back to Dublin but they would all be sleeping in their own rooms at the end of the day. The thought bothered him a little as he realized that nothing was going to happen with Katy. Once they were back in Dublin, he would probably only see her in passing and then, after that, he would be back in Lawrenceville and she would be in Ireland.

John found himself becoming angry. The excitement and anticipation of having Katy on the trip was turning into bitter disappointment. Even though he had convinced himself he had given up on the idea of the two of them getting together back in Killarney, he secretly held out the hope that something may actually happen. Now, John started to realize that the trip was down to one last night, anticipation and excitement were now gone and disappointment and anger began to ebb in.

Chapter 58

Katy called the crew to order.

"As you know, tonight is our last dinner together. Ballymaloe is famous for their food and cookery school. Tonight, we will experience the food and tomorrow, we will visit the school. I want everyone to meet in the bar by 6. Dinner is at 9 sharp. Please dress nicely and be on time. For the rest of the afternoon, feel free to enjoy the grounds and relax. We have a busy drive back tomorrow so rest up today."

John was transfixed. Katy looked beautiful addressing the group and John could hardly concentrate one what she was saying. He felt drawn to her and felt the bitterness of their lost opportunity. He considered the fact that there may not have been an opportunity to begin with. Maybe she was looking forward to returning to Liam in a passion filled reunion upon their return. The thought sickened him and he put it out of his head. For now, she was here with him. They still had tonight.

Tony grabbed John's arm as the meeting broke up. "So, what's the plan, Stan?"

"Dunno. What are you going to do?"

"Well, it is the last day on the road so, might as well drink."

"Capital idea. Let's get some beers and drink out on the back porch. The sun is still out and we can catch a late afternoon buzz."

Tony smiled at the idea. "Rachel" he called over to his now established girlfriend.

"Drinks on the veranda?" he asked with his best snooty accent.

"Sounds like a plan." she replied.

"Hey, what about us?" Nancy whined.

"It's a public place. Join in if you dare."

Tony, Rachel, Nancy, Emily and John made their way to the little bar just off of the living room in the main house. The others said they were going to join in later. Mike said he needed to work out before dinner, would meet them at 7. Jeff, Carol, Charley and Becky wanted to go for a walk but said they would return in an hour or so. Katy was off to her room as soon as her meeting ended.

There was no bartender when the drinkers arrived in the little bar room.

"Are they closed?" Nancy asked.

"I'll ask the receptionist." John said as he poked his head around the corner.

The receptionist was on the phone but smiled politely acknowledging John. After answering a question about horse riding, she hung up and turned to John. The young lady, maybe seventeen, looked very much like Jim and Tommy, the bag boys. John was sure they were siblings or close cousins. He loved the idea of a family enterprise. He found himself missing Old Joe and the Hound, yet again.

"Can I help you?"

"Yes, thanks. Is the bar open?"

"Always. Just a sec." she replied, as she picked up the phone. "Roger, there are guests waiting in the bar." "He'll be right with you. He's just finishing stocking the cooler."

"No rush. Thanks a lot." John said returning to his friends.

A minute later, Roger, a taller and slightly older version of the bag boys and receptionist appeared.

"The bar is open." Roger announced as he smiled at the group of friends. "What's your poison?"

Tony and Rachel ordered light beers. Nancy decided on a cider while Emily had a gin and tonic. John ordered a Jameson with ice inspired by their earlier visit to Midleton.

"Would you like me to bring your drinks to the parlor?"

"Can we have them out on the porch?" Nancy asked flashing Roger a flirty smile.

"Of course you can. Anywhere you like. It's a lovely day anyway." Roger said picking up the tray leading the group outside.

The air was warm and fresh. The farm smells were completely absent around the back of the house. The porch overlooked a stream and little wooded area with a garden next to that. The bucolic scene made John feel relaxed and at ease. The others also seemed to settle in with their drinks comfortably enjoying the view and the company.

"I can't believe this trip is almost over. In a way, it feels like we just left Dublin." Emily said as she sipped her G&T.

"It has seemed short but at the same time, we all got to know each other so well in a short period of time." Nancy said.

"It's a road trip thing. Throw a bunch of strangers in a bus for a couple of weeks, add copious amounts of liquor and shake. Presto, new best friends." John said.

"Or, more than friends." Rachel added smiling at Tony.

"Gross." Nancy rolled her eyes.

Roger kept the drinks coming. The sun was fading and shade now spread over the entire porch. Carol and Jeff arrived ordering hot whiskies to stave off the chill. The conversation took on a reminiscent tone as the friends were recalling the trip and even some of their time in Dublin before the trip started. John, with the aid of three Jameson's, began to zone out a little. He thought of home and the bar, his parents and family in general including those he was supposed to look up over here and never did.

"Surprise, surprise, fancy meeting you all here." Katy's voice broke the trance and made John's heart begin to race.

"It's almost six, shouldn't you all be getting ready for our farewell dinner?"

John winced at the thought of a farewell anything with Katy. He decided then and there he would put in one last effort if the chance arose this evening. His determination, fueled by the knowledge that his opportunities were ending along with his trip, made him energized and more excited then ever, never mind the courage the whiskey provided.

The group began to break up heading off to their individual rooms to shower and change for the closing dinner. Tony asked for the room key saying he needed to get some things to take to Rachel's room. John felt a little envy as the two of them left together sensing that Tony and Rachel were going to make the most of her private room.

Nancy and Emily asked Roger for one for the road.

"And two for the ditch." he added.

Carol left with the girls.

Jeff asked John if he wanted to stay for one more.

"Sure, we've got a little time." John said as the two made their way into the little bar.

"Don't be late." Katy warned as she made her way inside. She smiled warmly at John as she made her way down the steps to her room of the bottom floor.

John and Jeff took their drinks outside to the front of the main house to catch the last of the setting sun's rays. They sat on a wooden bench overlooking the little par three golf course, and the helicopter pad that whisks in big shots from Dublin who want to try Darina Allen's famed cooking.

"Some place, huh?" Jeff said.

"It's awesome. Hard to believe we are on this working farm drinking cocktails on the last night of the trip. It has truly been a blast. I wish we had a few more days." his own words surprised him a little considering earlier that day he yearned for the trip to be over so he could get on with his life.

"So, you and Carol really hit it off." John continued.

"She's great. If it weren't for this trip, I would have never met her. I believe the same would be true for Becky and Charley. It's funny how this trip has changed us all so much in such a short period of time."

"It has in so many ways. New friends, new opinions, new experience, it all has been profound." John took a deep sip of his whiskey.

"What about your girl, Katy? Any thing going on there?"

"Nope. Not a thing as a matter of fact. I guess it wasn't meant to be. Anyway, it would be awkward back in Dublin, so I'm glad nothing came of it." John lied trying to convince himself.

"There's still tonight." Jeff pointed out. "You never know how these things are going to go."

"I'm pretty sure on this one but, you're right, who knows, you never know."

After polishing off one more round, Jeff said he needed to get to his room to get dressed. John knew he had to go but was enjoying the sunset and the fresh farm air. He wanted the experience to last a bit longer but once Jeff left, he decided he probably should go back to his room and get ready for dinner and anything else their final night on the tour might hold for him.

Chapter 59

The Red Room was completely dark when John returned. Tony was staying with Rachel so he was likely to have the room all to himself until they checked out in the morning. He switched on a light switch bringing low light into the room. The bright and cheery red from earlier in the day now appeared more ominous.

From his window, John could see the kitchen entrance towards the back of the house. Cooks dressed in black and white striped shirts hustled in and out carrying various provisions for the evening's meal. The scene combined with the atmosphere in the room and several Jameson's on the rocks made John melancholic. He once again yearned to be back home. This time though, the feeling was more of the homesick variety and not the desire to tuck into his career. John watched as the young cooks laughed with each other over a smoke at the back door. He thought of Clem and Alex and the waitresses back at the Hound. He thought of Old Joe sitting at his designated table drinking a coffee and bullshitting with some salesman.

The loud ringing of the phone by his bed brought John back to reality. He looked over at it and, at first, was startled and confused. Who's calling me? He thought. He picked up the phone after the third ring.

"Hello?"

"Get down here, boy, we're all waiting for you." The familiar sound of Tony's voice focused John.

"Shit, what time is it?"

"6:30, you were supposed to be here a half hour ago. Hop to."

"I'll be right down. Save me a seat at the bar."

"Will do. Oh, your professor looks particularly hot this fine evening. You better get down here before someone else starts cracking on her."

John hung up and raced to the bathroom. His heart was pumping fast as the adrenaline set in. He showered and changed in minutes. The thought of Katy waiting in the bar drove him. He flew down the steps and out the door leading to the courtyard of the old stables. He walked as fast as he could up to the front door of the main house. He stopped just short of the door to catch his breath and settle himself. He didn't want to look harried. He needed to play it cool, he thought to himself.

The bar and parlor were packed. There were groups of people having drinks before dinner. They were crammed into every available space in the lounge and adjacent bar. John looked around but did not see anyone from his group. A slight panic overtook him as he wondered if they had already gone into the dining room. He tried to remember what time Katy said they were eating. He glanced at his watch. It was 6:45 PM. He thought she said 7 but now couldn't remember. He began to perspire and was getting a little flustered when he spotted Mike coming through the front door. He waved him over.

"Are you just getting here?" John asked.

"Yea, I worked out and then took a disco nap. Jeff just called and woke me up."

"Tony called me too. I guess we're a little late."

"Jeff said they would be outside on the porch. I'm not sure where that is."

"Follow me, I was out there all afternoon."

The two late arrivals squeezed past the groups of people and made their way out to the porch. John took in a deep breath of fresh air and settled down again. The group was clustered around a table at the edge of the porch opposite of where they were sitting earlier. Tony spotted them first and started to clap. Soon, everyone was applauding and giving John and Mike grief for being late. John was happy to have Mike along to help deflect some of the attention directed at him for being late.

"What? Did you pass out or something?" Nancy asked John.

"No, I just lost track of time." he replied scanning the group.

"She's at the bar." Nancy said recognizing the fact that John was looking for Katy.

"Who's at the bar?" John asked feigning confusion.

"Who my ass." Nancy said. "She's well on her way too. Finally starting to loosen up a bit."

The idea of Katy loosening up gave John a little jolt of excitement. He remembered that night at Scruffy's after she had a couple. Maybe, he thought, tonight would be the night.

Katy walked through the screen door leading from the bar out to the porch. Tony had been spot on, she looked stunning. Her hair was done, and her makeup was flawless. She wore a sexy tight skirt with a silk blouse. Her shape was perfectly accentuated by her clothes. She was elegant, professional, and sexy as hell all at once. John tried not to stare but he couldn't take his eyes off of her.

"Well, look who finally made it." Katy said carrying a glass of red wine from the bar. "I would have bought you a drink if I knew you were going to show up."

"No problem, I'll get the next round." John said trying to sound casual. "What will you have Mike?"

"A Kettle One and soda. Thanks."

"Anyone else ready?" John turned and looked at the group.

"Great timing, we all just got a new one." Tony said.

"Great timing, indeed."

Chapter 60

Everyone was having a great time relaxing and enjoying each other's company, so Katy asked the Maître D' to push the table back a while. Even Dermot, who had no driving responsibilities until the next day, was polishing off pint after pint of lager. John had recaptured his buzz from earlier and was really enjoying the moment. He knew in his heart that no matter what might happen with Katy, this trip and this experience was one of the times of his life. No matter how this all played out, he would forever remember this trip and these new friends. The thought of this made John very happy and a little sorry that it would soon come to an end.

"Well, what did you think of the trip?" Katy asked John sliding up next to him on the little garden bench he was sitting on.

"It's not over yet." John smiled. "So far, though, it's been the best experience of my life."

"I am very glad to hear that. I know I was only here for the end of the tour but I can see why so many students come back raving about the experience. Where else can you have so much fun while learning?" Katy sounded a little too much like a teacher for John to feel any encouragement in the romance department. Sure, he thought, she's sitting next to me but she's talking like she's doing an exit interview.

"Are we ever going to eat?" Mike asked to no one in general. "I am starving. Can't we move the cocktail party into the dining room?"

"Don't be a buzz-kill." Nancy yelled back.

"Yea, this is our last hurrah, let's enjoy it while the drinks are free." Emily added.

Katy heard this banter and decided she had better move on to the dining room in spite of the majority of the group protesting. Even though she had loosened up and was enjoying the drinks, she felt a pang of responsibility and didn't want word to get back to the institute that she was a teacher-gone-wild.

With some gentle prodding from Katy, the slightly to moderately buzzed group made their way into the dining room. The actual room reserved for the group was just off of the main dining room giving the group some added privacy. John figured the management at Ballymaloe planned the dining arrangements based on experience with previous tours. If the drinking kept up at the current pace, the night might get a little crazy.

The long table was set for 12 people, five on the sides and two at the heads of the table. At first, John found a seat next to Tony on one of the sides. The rest of the group started to filter in around them when Katy asked everyone to wait before sitting down.

"We have assigned seats." she announced to the slightly confused group.

She started dictating who was to sit where. She put Dermot at the one end of the table but then put Mike at the other end. Most of the students figured she would sit at the head but she chose a seat in the middle of the table and had John sit next to her. After this, she seemed to arbitrarily seat everyone else. No one thought too much of this except for John. He was thankful that no one else seemed to notice. Immediately he thought she had done this quick arrangement to put herself next to him. Maybe they were drunk enough that it didn't register. Then he thought maybe he was drunk enough to mistake what had gone on. In any event, Katy was now tight up against him at their cramped table.

The meal was spectacular. John felt it was actually one of the best meals he had ever had. Organic mushroom soup followed by locally smoked Mackerel, buttered lobster, shrimp with herbed hollandaise sauce and summer turkey with tarragon cream, all of which was just amazing. By the time the local Irish farmhouse cheese was served, John thought he would burst.

Of course, he also knew that the food was augmented by Katy's presence and her occasional accidental nudge with her foot or thigh. As was usual with Katy, John couldn't tell if she was being discreetly physical with him or if her attention was strictly inadvertent. John hoped her touches were purposeful and were a sign of things to come later that evening. At the very least, her rearrangement of the seating at the table was certainly a signal.

John considered this and kept trying to decide if there was any other way to read her. In the end, all he could do was enjoy the food and company and not take too much for granted. In the past, taking anything with Katy for granted usually resulted in frustration.

As the meal came to a close, the headwaiter came by to see if the table wanted an after dinner drink. Katy, now well lubricated after several bottles of wine with dinner, accepted. The waiter started with her, a Hennessey cognac, and worked his way around the room. John, ordering a port wine, was surprised that all of his tour mates actually ordered something. Even Becky and Mike, the least interested in drinking, ordered brandy. The mood was fantastic and everyone hoped it could last forever.

Jeff, typically quiet and reserved, took the opportunity to make a toast. "I would just like to thank Dr. Carney, Katy, and

Dermot for one of the best times of my life. I feel I have grown as a person and as an alcoholic on this trip. You have all been great and I hope to call you all my friends for the rest of my life. Thanks you all." he said, raising his glass and looking lovingly at Carol.

John, for a moment, thought a proposal might be coming but the moment passed and the next toast was starting.

Tony, standing on very shaky legs, raised his glass. "Here's to all of the new couples. This trip has brought a few people together who might not have even noticed each other back home. Congratulations and good luck."

John became very nervous during Tony's little speech of new love. He cringed at the thought of Tony mentioning Katy and him as some kind of couple in the making. He was very relieved when the speech was over and hoped no one else would feel compelled. In an effort to head off any other toasts that may prove to be embarrassing, John quickly made the suggestion to move the party back to the parlor or porch. Much to John's surprise, no one moaned or called it a night. Even Katy seemed to be enthusiastic to keep things going.

John headed to the bar to order the drinks, and suggested everyone else head straight to the parlor to get the seats.

"Do you ever get time off?" John asked Roger who was still manning the bar.

"I quit when everyone goes home. I'll be back on duty for breakfast. Its all part of the family business curse."

"I know how that is." John commiserated. "I've been in my family's bar business my whole life. Never a dull moment."

"That's for sure. In the end, though, it's grand." Roger said. John nodded in agreement as he waited for the drinks.

"Go join your friends." Roger motioned towards the parlor. "I'll drop the drinks down to you in a moment."

"Thanks, Roger. Maybe later you can join us for one or two."

"That would be grand. If things settle down, I'll take you up on that."

Nancy found a perfect seating area for the group. Two large couches and two couples, finishing off their own after dinner drinks, had just vacated four over-stuffed chairs facing the fireplace. Nancy quickly grabbed the spots telling the others to sit.

When John joined them, there was only one spot left to sit, next to Katy on one of the large couches. John looked at the others to see if there was some kind of joke being played on him. How could she have arranged having the only open place to sit next to her? Could it have simply been by chance or did she arrange it that way? It didn't really matter at this point since he was standing there looking at Katy and the space next to her. He sat, feeling a little awkward. No one was talking and the mood from the dining room had disappeared. Finally, Roger walked in carrying a huge tray of assorted drinks. He set the tray on the coffee table directly in front of the group and began dispensing the lagers, stouts, brandies, wines, and, for John, a Black Bush with a little ice. After everyone had their drink, one glass remained on the tray.

"Here's to your good health. Slainte." Roger said lifting the glass of what looked like brandy. He slugged it back in one gulp finishing with a loud "Ahhh."

The others, not expecting the barman to join them, raised their glasses and returned the salute.

Roger, got up off his knee and shook his head a little as the effect of the drink started to set in. "Nothing a shot of grandma to shake things up a little. Thanks for the drink." and he headed back to the bar.

"I asked him to join us for one but I was hardly expecting him to do a shot of Grand Marnier."

"Bartender's heroine, you know." Tony said.

"I guess it's not just an American thing." John said.

"I never even heard of that before." Katy said. "Why is it bartender's heroine?"

"Bartenders and other restaurant people seem to prefer it because it energizes you after a long shift and gives you a quick and intense buzz."

"It's one nasty hang over, though." Emily added sounding as if she was speaking from experience.

"Oooh! Let's all do one." Katy said.

The group looked at her a little shocked. Up until today, Katy had been fairly reserved. Perhaps because it was the last night, she decided to let her hair down a bit.

"You gotta be kidding." Mike said. "I haven't done shots in a long time."

"Just one, our last hurrah and all." Katy said. She showed a little devilish smile that had not previously revealed itself.

A few minutes later, Roger reappeared with a tray full of shots of Grand Marnier. The sight of the liquor-laden tray was enough to induce a collective gasp and moan from the group. Katy, still flashing her ultra sexy, ultra naughty smile, clapped in a giddy display of pleasure.

"Now." Roger announced. "This will help you sleep tonight and part of tomorrow."

"Oh God, do we have to." Becky protested.

"It's part of your grade." Katy joked.

"Who's going to make the toast?" Jeff asked. The question caused John's stomach to clench again but he was soon relieved when Katy herself stood up extending her arm with the shot clutched between her fingers.

"Here's to the American Institute, to my students, and to Ireland." Katy said proudly. Everyone picked up their glasses and replied with "cheers."

Contorted faces, smiles, giggles and assorted other responses came after the shot. Becky looked as if she might get sick as she cupped her hand over her mouth. Nancy and Emily were giving each other high-fives. Mike shook his head while Tony smiled and looked generally drunk. Carol smiled at Jeff who had a little GrandMa running down his chin. Charley patted Becky on the back. John, a veteran of bartender's heroine, sat and watched the others struggle. Katy, showing no lack of experience with the grandma herself, proposed a second shot.

"No!!!" Half of the group cried at the suggestion while a couple egged her on.

"I'm only joking. We have too much to do tomorrow to be completely wrecked." Katy said quieting the protesters.

Chapter 61

The group hung together for a while longer. John began to wish some of them would start to bail out so he could see if there was a shot with Katy. He was aware he had had a lot to drink, just like the rest of them, and he didn't want his ability to stay awake to fade.

Finally, Nancy, of all people, said she was going for a smoke and then to bed. Emily said she would join her for a smoke but might come back. The two got up and headed out of the parlor. Charley and Jeff, as if on cue, called it a night soon after. Becky and Carol followed pretending, for Katy's sake, to head off to their own rooms. Mike, Tony and Rachel stayed for one more round but, at Rachel's prompting, called it a night.

Roger came in to find his party had dwindled down to two, Katy and John. Katy ordered a glass of Pinot Grigio and John decided on one more whiskey. Katy asked Roger to bring the bill with the final round. He returned to the bar to get the drinks and tally the bill leaving the two survivors sitting next to each other on the couch. By now, there was only one other group in the parlor finishing off their coffees. Soon, they would be all alone.

Roger returned carrying three drinks. "Don't worry, this one is on me."

John was hoping Roger wasn't planning to stay long but was happy enough to have a drink with him. Instead of GrandMa, this time, Roger drank a glass of merlot. Katy invited him to sit, which, to John's chagrin, he did.

The three of them talked for a few minutes. Roger was most interested in Katy's experiences as a Yank living in Dublin. He told them about the year he lived in New York and down the Jersey shore. Just when John started to worry that Roger may want one for the road, a voice called from the reception area in front of the bar.

"Roge, are you through?. I need the bar's report."

"I'll be with you now in a minute." Roger answered and quickly got up. "I'm afraid duty calls. It was nice to meet you. I am sure I will see you at breaky, if you make it." Roger picked up the rest of his wine and returned to the bar to get his report.

John looked at Katy who still had most of her wine left.

"Walk me to my room." she said suddenly. John could not believe what he had just heard. The nerves he had kept in check all night now were sending shock waves through his entire body.

"Sure. Are you taking that with you?" he said pointing to the wine.

"Yea, I'll finish it in bed." The words sent new and more intense shock waves through him. The whiskey now seemed to have no effect on him at all.

They stood up with Katy holding onto John's arm for support. She was pretty buzzed but didn't seem out of it.

"Where's your room?" John asked.

"Downstairs." Katy replied and led him towards the back stairs. As they reached the top of the steps, Katy turned and hugged John. "Whoa, I almost lost my balance

If she had just grabbed onto John purely for support, it sure was taking her a long time to get her balance back. John was thrilled to have her warm body pressed against his but he couldn't help but be a little worried someone from the group might come by. Anyway, he wanted to get her to her room before the chance passed or something broke the spell. John was now sure tonight was his night and he did not want anything to spoil it.

John maneuvered Katy to the first step. She looked at him and smiled her newly revealed sexy smile. Before he knew it, they were kissing only having made it half way down the steps. Her lips were warm and soft but very responsive. She was pressing against him making him forget about someone walking in on them. He was now lost in the moment and was just letting things happen. Out of nowhere, a door slammed below them. They both jumped and simultaneously pushed away from each other. They looked down to the bottom of the stairwell but couldn't see anyone. A second door then slammed effectively breaking the mood on the steps.

"Let's go." John said taking Katy's arm. "We should get you to your room."

Katy looked at John and nodded. She was starting to look drunk but John convinced himself it was the effect from their embrace. They got to the bottom of the steps and started down the hallway. As they passed the exit doors leading out to the back patio, Katy spotted someone. "Shit, its Nancy and Emily," she said slurring a little "they saw me."

John couldn't believe it. They left the bar first and should have finished their smoke a half hour ago.

"We need to go say hello or it will look funny."

"Are you sure they saw us?"

"Yea."

They pushed through the glass double doors leading to the patio.

"Hey, I thought you two would be in bed." John said trying not to sound testy.

"We were but Nancy needed one more smoke." Emily said as the girls eyed Katy and him. He was now stuck. There was no way to leave with Katy without Nancy and Emily copping on to what was going on. He would have to make a little small talk and hope they left first.

"I'm going to bed." Katy suddenly said, yawning. John quickly looked over at her in utter disbelief but saw she was fading fast. Her eyes were slits. She slumped against a light post. John knew then and there it was over. He tried to convince himself that he would sneak back to her room and wake her but he knew it would never work. Once again, the excitement, the adrenalin, and the anticipation drained from his body. Katy shook herself and said goodnight.

"Can I walk you in?" Emily asked.

"No thanks. I'm fine. See you in the morning." and she was gone.

Nancy and Emily looked at John sympathetically. They knew they inadvertently interfered with John's plan but none of them could openly admit it.

"Sorry." Nancy said. Her voice was faint and far off.

"About what?" John snapped but quickly got himself together. "I'm hitting the sack too." but he decided to wait for the girls to finish their smoke and come in with him. He wasn't about to raise any eyebrows now.

Chapter 62

John climbed the back steps leading back to the main floor of the house. He briefly considered knocking on Katy's door but thought no good could come from it. He wasn't really even sure what room she was in and he worried he might be waking some other guest. In the end, he simply decided to go back to his own room.

The night air was cool and sobering. John was still in shock at his bad luck. He knew he had her, all he needed to do was get her to her room and he could close the deal. Now, he was out of time.

He surprised himself by feeling a little relieved. Certainly, he wanted Katy and was ready to take full advantage of any opportunity that arose. But, during his walk across the property, he did feel that there might be a reason the two of them should not hook-up. It wasn't Liam back in Dublin or the fact that she was technically his teacher, but something didn't fully sit well with him. By the time he got back to his room, he was numb. He crawled into bed wearing his clothes and was sound asleep within seconds.

While John did get more sleep than he would have if things turned out a little differently the night before, the alcohol's residual effects hit him hard. Countless Irish whiskies, white and red wines with dinner, brandy, several shots of GrandMa and God only knows what else, gave John a wicked hangover. Tony woke him early in the morning when he came back from Rachel's room.

"Dude, you look like hell and smell worse. What the hell happened to you last night?"

"My fucking head." John buried his head under the pillow

"How was young Katy Welsh anyway?"

"How the hell would I know? She went to bed and I got stuck with the evil step sisters." John pulled himself into a sitting position. He squinted at Tony trying to get his bearings.

"That's a bummer." Tony said without pressing John for the gory details. "I thought you had her. Anyway, we should get to breakfast. The bus leaves in an hour."

"I don't know if I can make it. Everything kills. The bartender's heroine is poison. Never again for me." John thought a little "At least not until tonight."

Tony laughed. "Come on get dressed. The food here is too good to miss. "Get in the shower. I'll meet you outside in twenty minutes."

"Fine."

Tony was sitting with Rachel on a little bench outside of the stable area. They watched John stumble out the front door still trying to get his eyes to adjust to the daylight.

"You look good." Rachel said.

"Thanks. I'm sure I do. Can we please just go eat? I am desperate for some coffee."

The three of them made their way up the path to the main house. Inside, Becky was reading some brochures in the lobby. Her bags were packed and sitting in the lobby.

"You guys better hurry if you want breakfast. Katy already told us to get our luggage ready for Dermot."

"Shit, I need food and caffeine." John panicked.

"I am sure we have time for something quick." Tony said as they went into the dining room.

Ms. Murray greeted them warmly. She, like so many of the other workers at Ballymaloe, had several jobs. This morning, she was in charge of the dining room for breakfast.

"I have a nice table for you by the window. By the looks of your man here, you might want some fresh air." she said motioning towards John as she led them to their table.

By he time they had their breakfast, and went out to the van, Dermot was just about finished loading the luggage, which happened to be when Katy finally arrived. She looked surprisingly good given the fact that she was fairly hammered the night before. John saw her walking across the lawn in front of the house towards them and was again relieved that there would be no real awkward moments this morning. Katy made it to the bus smiling at Dermot.

"Is everyone ready?" she asked.

"Everyone is accounted for. A few of the girls went over to the gift shop but their gear is on board. We are ready to get going."

"Good, we have a lot to do on our way home."

Katy wasn't lying. On the way back to Dublin, the group had several stops. The first was just a few miles down the road from Ballymaloe House. The students were to tour the Ballymaloe Cookery School located at a farm nearby. Darina Allen gave them a private tour of her school and demonstration kitchen where she filmed her weekly television show. She lectured the students on the evils of margarine and synthetic sweeteners. She pontificated on the benefits of local produce and other ingredients. She spoke of simple preparations and quality. Darina was well ahead of her time in her attitudes about food. John was impressed and affected by her attitude and passion for the best the good Earth could provide. He knew he could embrace her attitude and make it part of his own. After the tour, he bought one of Darina's cookbooks and spent he next two hours on the bus studying it.

The next stop was Waterford Crystal. This was not exactly part of the official academic itinerary but Carney included it as one of the stops because students enjoyed the experience. Carney also knew that every now and then, the students would get him a memento in crystal as a sign of their appreciation.

Finally, Dermot followed the N25 to the N11 on the final stretch home. Dusk was setting in while the mood on the bus began to sink. Some of the group was looking forward to getting back but others, particularly the couples, knew that their return could end the fantasy that had taken root on the tour. Charley was scheduled to return to the States in two days. Carol and Jeff worried about what might become of their relationship when they get back. Only Tony and Rachel were together when the trip had started, and now, they were stronger than ever.

John fell asleep just outside of Dublin. It had been a long couple of days and he was feeling it. He was looking forward to a quiet night in his dorm room by himself. He vowed not to drink for a few days. He called it a health break.

A mile or so from the Institute, John woke up to the sound of young boys selling the "Evening Herald" on the street corners. He looked up and saw they were now in the centre city.

"Home sweet home." he mumbled to himself and stretched.

He looked around and noticed several others still sleeping. Katy was talking with someone on her cell phone. John figured it was Liam lining up their reunion plans. John just groaned.

Dermot pulled the bus into the alley behind the student's residence. The electric gate opened and Dermot pulled in. By now, everyone was awake but a little bleary. The sun was now gone but there was still a little light in the sky. Katy stood up once Dermot pulled the parking brake and opened the door.

"Before you all go, I just want to thank you for being so delightful. I really enjoyed the trip and I hope I was an adequate fill-in for Dr. Carney."

Tony started to clap. Soon, a generous round of applause rose up in the bus.

"Thank you Katy and Dermot for a wonderful trip." Tony said with another burst of applause.

Katy teared up a little and quickly got off of the bus. Dermot smiled and waved and got off to help with the bags.

The students dispersed quickly. A few quick hugs went around but there was no real feeling like the trip had ended. Most of the group would be together for the next two weeks anyway so there were no long goodbyes outside of the residence that evening. John grabbed his bag from the bus and went inside. He caught a quick glimpse of Katy inside the residence office talking with the residence manager. He decided to leave well enough alone and went upstairs to his room.

Chapter 63

Maybe it was his body beginning to detox or maybe it was just his need to unwind, but John's health night did not last long. After he went up to his room to unpack, he laid in his bed and tried to relax. All of the thoughts and fresh memories of the trip were flooding into his head. He thought of the places they visited and the people he met. He tried to absorb the information he picked up and considered how he would use it back home. Inevitably, his thoughts turned to Katy Welsh with her long brown hair, dark eyes and those legs that went on forever. After a half hour of this line of thought, John realized he might want to go for a walk or a cold shower.

Finally, he decided on both. He would take a shower and wash the road off of his body and then go for a walk to clear his head. He was pleased with the plan and began to collect his shower gear from his bag when someone knocked on his door. Immediately, he thought of Katy. Maybe it was her trying to recapture the mood from the night before. He went to the door and cautiously opened it.

"What are you doing in there?" the female visitor said.

"Nancy, what's up?"
"We are taking Charley out for dinner and drinks. He is leaving the day after tomorrow."

"Why not take him tomorrow then?"

"Duh, certainly he's got plans with Becky. It's their last night together before he goes home."

"Fine, let me get a quick shower. Where are you taking him and when?"

"We are meeting at Scruffy's in an hour and then we were going to take him to the Bad Ass Café for pizza."

"Sounds good. I'll meet you in the lobby in an hour." he attempted to sound enthusiastic but it came out as forced. Nancy started to leave but turned just before John shut the door.

"Don't worry about Katy. There are other fish in the sea."

She sounded genuinely sympathetic. John smiled and closed the door with a genuine "thanks." He was touched by Nancy's sincerity. Even though she was usually a smart-ass party girl, she must have sensed John disappointment that his plans for Katy would not materialize.
John wished he hadn't answered the door. He was tired and mostly felt like some peace and quiet. He had spent the last week and a half constantly with his fellow students and now just wanted to decompress and be alone. He realized, however, that it would be rude to blow Charley off especially if everyone else was going.

The shower did John a world of good. The restlessness he felt earlier when he was laying in bed had now turned into energy and excitement. Suddenly, he felt refreshed and ready to go out on the town. The hangover haze had lifted and he now felt strangely invigorated. He dressed quickly and made it downstairs a full twenty minutes before Nancy said the others would meet him. Instead of waiting, John decided to go down the street to the Spar market and buy a calling card for the USA. He wanted to call home and tell his parents he was back in Dublin. He also wanted to call the Hound to check in and talk with his grandfather.

"Hello?" his dad's voice came after the first ring.

"Dad?"

"Yes Johnny boy! How's the trip?"

"Amazing, really amazing. I am having one of the best times of my life."

"I hope you're learning something as well." his dad answered in a light, joking voice.

"Oh yea, it's been very informative. I can't wait to put some of what I learned into practice. It's really been an eye-opener."

"Glad to hear it. All is well here. Your mother is out to the mall with your sister, surprise-surprise. They are doing well. The bar is busy for this time of year. Your grandfather has been working more than he likes. He says when you get home he's going to Atlantic City for a weeks vacation."

"Sounds good to me." he chatted a while longer with his dad, filling him in on most of his travels but leaving out anything to do with Katy.

After a few more minutes, John hung up telling his dad he would call him again before coming home. He considered calling Old Joe, then eventually deciding against it, based on the fact that it was a Friday night and everyone was going to be busy. He decided to wait until tomorrow morning when it would be a quiet Saturday afternoon at the Hound and his grandfather would have time to talk.

John walked back towards the residence. Nancy and Emily were on the front steps smoking as usual. Tony and Rachel were sitting next to each other on the bottom step. John was happy to see them. He felt genuine affection for his friends and was even starting to sense that he was really going to miss them when they all went back to their real lives.

"Where's the guest of honor?" John asked when he was within earshot.

"He is taking a walk with Becky." Nancy answered.

"Maybe they want to be alone. Has anyone asked them?" John asked.

"Yea, they were all good with going out for a drink and maybe a quick bite. I think they will exit right after dinner though." Nancy said.

A few minutes later, Mike, Jeff and Carol joined them on the steps. It felt a little funny to John to be amongst close friends when, on this same spot just two weeks before, most of them were no more than acquaintances. Now, the group hung together like friends that knew each other for life. John wondered if their friendships would fade as fast as they came.

Finally, Becky and Charley came around the corner. Becky looked like she had been crying. Charley put on a smile but you could tell he was also suffering.

"Well, where to?" Charley asked.

"Maybe we could stop at the Stag's Head instead of Scruffy's for a quick one before going over to the Bad Ass." John suggested.

"Sounds like a plan." Tony said as they all set off for the pub.

The walk was far enough to build up a thirst. The Stag's Head was a well-preserved Victorian palace with a long narrow bar and stained glass windows giving it a chapel-like feeling and it was packed. Students, businessmen and women, and all other walks of Dublin life were jammed into the place.

John made his way to the bar and ordered a round for the crew. They decided to take advantage of the warm evening and had their pints out in the alley on the side of the pub. There were others outside with the same idea but at least there was room to breathe.

"So, you leave tomorrow?" John asked Charley once they settled into their ad-hoc beer garden.

"Yea, 'fraid so. I only wish I had known this was going to be such a blast. I might have been able to stay the rest of the time. Now, my dad says he needs me back at work."

Becky's eyes filled with tears as Charley talked making John wish he had been more sensitive.

"Of course, I also had no idea I would meet someone like Becky."

The tears in her eyes now raced down her cheeks. Charley put his arm around her and tried to comfort her.

"You'll visit before the summer is over." he told her quietly.

John wanted to slip away but found himself with nowhere to hide. Eventually Jeff and Carol came over giving John an out.

"I need to hit the jacks before we go." he announced and slipped into the pub's side door leading down to the toilets.

Chapter 64

Throughout dinner, John found his thoughts wandering. He wanted to be there for Charley and Becky but kept thinking about the Hound, home, and about Katy. He was relaxed enough with his friends to not feel overly compelled to be part of the conversation. His friends, likewise, did not really notice that he didn't have much to say. The mutual comfort level was unique considering what little time they've known each other. Now, the time passed and the talk turned to drinks.

"We're not at freakin' Ashford Castle anymore." Tony joked when Rachel suggested an after dinner drink.

"No but we can still pretend we are civilized."

"I think we are heading out." Charley interrupted. "I have to get my things together and stuff."

"Oh, you can't crap out early on your last night." Nancy said.

"Give them a break. They want some time alone." Emily said.

"Whatever." Nancy huffed.

The group left the Bad Ass and walked up towards Trinity College on Dame Street. Tony suggested they stop in the Old Bank pub for a drink. Nancy and Emily agreed on the spot. After some prodding by Tony, Mike, Jeff and Carol also agreed. John, feeling a little buzzed but still good, agreed to one. Becky and Charley resisted the plan and decided to just go back to the residence. Everyone gave Charley a hug knowing they wouldn't see him tomorrow before he left.

"You guys have been great. Keep in touch." he said before turning with Becky to leave. The remaining punters turned into the entrance of the pub and continued their night.

"So much for my health night." John said as the bartender put a Black Bush and ice in front of him.

"There will be plenty of health nights back home. For now, let's enjoy ourselves." Tony said making perfect sense.

"Yeah, you're right. You only go around once and who knows if I will ever be back."

The session turned out to be one of their longer ones. Everyone drank heavily, even Mike who usually never got caught up in the endless rounds. Before they knew it, it was 2 AM and the pub was closing. Nancy suggested one last stop at one of the after hour clubs but, after multiple rounds, no one else seemed too enthusiastic.

"I'm calling it a night." Jeff said while Carol nodded her head in agreement. Mike also finally called it quits. Rachel and Tony bowed out next.

"What about you. John? Are you game for a quick one?" Emily said.

"Sure, why no?" John slurred.

The three survivors soldiered on to Lillie's Bordello, a well known after hour's club. The line was starting to get long as the regular pubs closed. However, John, being in the company of two attractive young women, found himself passing by the velvet rope as a large bouncer ushered them in. Nancy and Emily squealed in delight as they made their way into the club. The last thing John remembered was the girls giggling and taking one sip of Irish whiskey. After that, the night became a fuzzy blur. He woke up early the next morning still fully dressed, lying in his bed on top of the covers, as the sun streamed through his open window.

Chapter 65

John's aching head, bloodshot eyes and nauseated stomach were becoming an all too common morning condition. He was starting to worry a little that he was becoming affected by Ireland, and not in a good way. Back home, people partied a lot and sometimes even did so to excess but in Ireland, however, the party never stopped, at least not for him. After Charley's going home send off, John resolved to really try to take it easy on the drinking and finish the summer program off strong. He knew he would be going back to reality soon so he better start getting himself prepared.

The new classes were scheduled to start in two days. John had enrolled in an organizational behavior class that he wanted to use as a psychology elective back at Cornell. Only Jeff had enrolled in the same class with the remaining others divided up between an art appreciation elective and an international marketing class. This separation helped John stick to a healthier lifestyle in the coming weeks avoiding the impromptu "wanna go for a pint?" question after each class. Instead, John spent his time studying and exploring Dublin. He was happy for the milder times but occasionally missed the party.

The group had fractured somewhat once they got back to Dublin. Even those who hung out together before the tour spent less time together for several reasons. The couples, Tony and Rachel, and Jeff and Carol spent time together or just as couples. Mike was spending more time studying and working out while Nancy and Emily took Becky into their little sisterhood once Charley left. The three of them still partied and went out a lot but the novelty had worn off. Occasionally, several of them would go out on the piss together but Charley's farewell was the last night they would all be together until the night before they all went home.

The final two weeks flew by. John enjoyed the organizational behavior class finding the material engaging. He was relieved that the class managed to stimulate his intellect. If the class was a blow-off, he might be more tempted to indulge in the pub life more often. However, in this case, his class kept him focused and the lack of temptation worked to his advantage.

On the Wednesday of the final week of class, Nancy stopped by to organize one last night out for the group. She wanted to do something Friday night because some people were leaving Saturday and others were going Sunday. John suggested doing something nice and fairly tame. Surprisingly, Nancy agreed. The party was starting to wear her out and a quiet meal with friends suited her just fine.

Eventually, the plan had come together with all of the friends deciding to meet for a drink at Scruffy's and then go for dinner at Captain America's on Grafton Street. The American style bar and grill seemed appropriate for the Yank's last meal in Ireland. After dinner, they would hit McDaid's Pub for a few before calling it a night. The plan was not overly ambitious and, by the group's standards, relatively tame. Of course, John and the others never discounted what might happen on any given night out.

John's flight was on Sunday, which he considered trying to switch to Saturday but quickly changed his mind due to the Friday night plan. He figured he give himself the extra day to relax and, if need be, recuperate.

He spent Thursday getting ready for his final on Friday morning. He managed to avoid a Thursday night session that Nancy tried to talk him into. He needed a good grade and was saving himself for Friday. When he woke Friday morning, he was very happy and relieved that his head was clear and his mind sharp. He felt ready to take on the world, or, at the very least, his organizational behavior final.

John left the residence walking towards the classroom building. He saw a few other students also heading in the same direction but none of them were his crew. He wondered if last night got out of hand. He thought maybe he should have knocked on their doors to see if they got out of bed. His fears were alleviated when he spotted Nancy and Becky having coffee in one of the café's on the way to class.

"I see you made it out of bed." John said to both of them.

"Let's just say, we haven't yet made it to bed." Nancy said with a sly smile. Becky waved as if to acknowledge her role in last night's events.

"Everyone else up?" John asked.

This time Becky answered. "Emily and Rachel are already down there." she motioned towards the classroom building. "We haven't seen anyone else yet but I am sure if the girls are up, their boys must be as well."

"Good luck with the exams. I guess I'll see you later today. All the plans still on for tonight?" John asked.

"If we can rally ourselves. I'm going to need a disco nap." Nancy said. She looked tired and a little pale but she smiled just the same. John knew she would be ready.

The exam turned out to be a breeze. John remembered that school, even college, was not so hard if you went to class, did your assignments, and paid attention. Drinking, chasing girls all-night and sleepwalking through lectures just made something that was actually very simple, very complex. He was glad he wouldn't happen but he still considered it.

John made it back to the residence by 1 p.m.. He figured he would grab a bite to eat from one of the newsagents and start getting his stuff together for the trip home. He had Saturday but he didn't want to spend his last day in Dublin just packing.

Just outside of the residence hall, there was a newsagent and small deli that John had been frequenting. The ladies, sisters actually, that ran the place got to know him by name.

"Will you be having your regular then John?" Siobhan asked him.

"You know it."

Siobhan got right to making John his tuna salad with sweet corn and mayo on white.

Siobhan's sister, Attracta, finished with a customer who was buying the paper and looked over at John, "So, when does the term end?"

"It's over today."

"Oh, I see. So you'll be leaving us soon then?"

"Unfortunately. I leave Sunday."

"Ay sure, we'll miss you. All of the Yanks this summer were so nice. It's not always the way you know." Siobhan said.

"There are no bad Yanks." John said. "They must have been Canadians."

The sisters laughed. "This one's on the house, John. Come back to see us when you come back home again." Attracta said.

John blushed and thanked them. He didn't want to take the free sandwich but knew there would be no use arguing. As he left, he felt sad that he would most likely never see the sisters again. All of these new relationships were so fleeting. He was starting to finally feel like a local, and not a tourist, and now his time here was just about up.

John took his sandwich and Club Lemon soda and went up to his room. He sat in front of the large window looking out onto the busy street below and found himself reflecting on his time here. It did, in many ways, feel like he had just arrived. Then again, the thought of his first Irish breakfast down in the dining hall felt like a lifetime ago. His reflections eventually turned to Katy. He had hardly seen her since the tour ended. He spotted her once in Merrion Park holding hands with Liam but they were in front of him and hadn't seen him. One other time, she passed him in the hall of the classroom building and smiled but only said "hey" and kept walking. Whatever magic might have been present on the tour was surely lost when Dermot brought the bus into Dublin city.

Once the sandwich was finished and John gulped the last of the Club Lemon, he began to turn his thoughts to packing. He pulled out his luggage, one bag still half full of clothes from the tour, and began to put his clothes, souvenirs and other things in the bags. He kept enough stuff out for the next day and a half but had most of the job done before 3 in the afternoon. His friends wouldn't be meeting until later so he had to decide what he wanted to do for the next couple of hours.

John considered his options. He considered showering and getting dressed for the evening's festivities early so he could head down to the pub for a few cocktails. The thought was appealing enough but the idea of a few beers alone and the subsequent drink fest that would likely follow was too contrary to his recent healthier lifestyle. He thought of going for a jog. Again, he liked the idea but lacked the sheer motivation to act on it. Sleeping was out of the question since he was the most well rested he had been in weeks.

Suddenly, as if out of nowhere, John decided to try to outline, with pen and paper, his future. Somehow, John felt it would be the perfect time to put together a plan for his life, or at least for the next few years. He had had such inclinations before but never had the clarity of purpose to really chart things out. He always felt there were too many potential variables that might cause his course to change. Today though, standing in his empty room on the third floor of the American Institute's residence hall, John felt ready. Perhaps it was this experience that acted as a catalyst for this endeavor. Perhaps it was the fact that his college life would soon be ending and he knew what his life's work was meant to be. Of course, there was always the chance that his healthy lifestyle combined with the relief of finishing his summer abroad academic requirements was enough to prompt such a plan. John didn't care that much about why he suddenly had this strong urge, he only knew that it was there, and he wanted to act on it.

The two hours went by like two minutes. John outlined, in a stream of conscience, what he thought he wanted his future to be for the next five years. He wrote at a frantic pace not wanting to break the spell. He worried that if he stopped to think too much, he would get bogged down or lose his train of thought. For almost two solid hours, John wrote and outlined until his hand hurt too much to continue. Thankfully, John got his thoughts down on paper before his hand gave out or his time to be alone ran out.

Chapter 66

John's game plan, as he began to think of it, was pragmatic and ambitious at the same time. He had goals, such as finishing Cornell on the Dean's list, that were not necessarily beyond his reach. He had other ideas like expanding his grandfather's business to become one of the top grossing independent restaurants in the country in the next five years, that were far more challenging. However, after reviewing what he had written, John felt the program was do-able.

This exercise marked a significant growth as a person and an adult for John. He felt it, and, deep inside he knew it too. He now had a specific direction, with clear progress markers and exact goals. He knew things could still change and were even likely to do so, but he sensed that his plan was flexible enough to bend, yet strong enough to keep him focused and on track. He was proud of what he had done. He was also a little tired and realized he needed to get a move on or he would be late for the night out. He grabbed the clothes he had left out for that night and hit the shower.

As John had sort of suspected, the night was fun but somewhat anticlimactic. Perhaps the hype and pressure to have one last hurrah doomed the spontaneity that was often the key catalyst of a big session. John had learned one major factor of a good time in Ireland, and it had more to do with less planning.

By no means was the night a disaster though. Nancy, Rachel, and the other girls were dressed to kill. The guys were all in fine form. The problem, as best as John could tell, was a certain level of distraction. At dinner, the conversations were a little forced and the joking often missed the mark. Later, McDaid's was great, but so crowded with American tourists that no one could really get into a good conversation. Tony suggested a change of venue at one point but Mike decided to call it a night since he was on an early flight the next day. Jeff followed suit saying he wanted to spend time with Carol. Finally, Becky said she needed to pack and wanted to call Charley, who was home by now. Soon, most of the others were making plans to call it a night. Finally, Nancy said her and Emily were going to Scruffy's for a nightcap. Tony and Rachel agreed to go as well.

"What about you?" Tony asked John. "Surely you can't make the last night such a dud?"

"Sure, I'll go, why not?"

The remaining group left McDaid's and headed to Scruffy's. They cut along Stephen's Green passing throngs of people from all walks of life. In front of the Shelbourne, Tony shouted that he saw Bono inside and suggested a detour inside the hotel. Nancy said he was crazy and refused to be taken in by one of Tony's practical jokes. Tony insisted he was telling the truth but didn't put up much resistance.

It was nearing 10 PM when they got to Scruffy's. The place was crowded but not as bad as McDaid's. The group found a snug that had just been vacated by a group of young businessmen that had likely been there since happy hour. "I'll buy the first round since I'm only planning on staying for one." John said.

"Don't make any grand predictions." Nancy said.

"We'll see… Now, what's everyone having?"

Three rounds later, John was ready to call it quits. The smaller group had more fun than the earlier attempts at revelry but as the alcohol started working it's magic, John began to sense the night could turn out to be a massive session, which did not really interest him. He was committed to a healthier lifestyle by now and did not want to backslide to the point he would feel like hell all the next day.

"I'm off." John announced.

"Sit the fuck down." Tony protested but John had made up his mind.

"Busy day tomorrow. I'm sure I'll see you all before you go." he said and hurried towards the door. He didn't want to argue with the group and be talked into staying.

As he reached the door of Scruffy's, he could still hear Nancy and Tony giving him grief.

"Come on back you wuss." Tony's distant voice said.

"Wimp." Nancy chided.

John was happy to be going. He pulled on the door yanking the person on the other side towards him. He bumped into the other person with a strong thud.

"I'm so sorry!"

The other person giggled a little and looked up at him.

"Katy! What are you?" he was shocked and embarrassed a little.

"Hi John. Hurrying off?" Katy said smiling at him.

"Well yea, I was going to leave but…" John was stammering. He was trying to quickly figure out how to go back into the pub without making it a scene. He could invite her over to the others and ask her to join them. She had just spent over six weeks with these people and had been drinking with them on more than one occasion. It shouldn't be too weird. But it was. John stalled. Finally, the trance was broken when a male's voice called from the other end of the bar.

"Over here love." Liam called.

Katy's smile dwindled to a frown and she pushed by John. John came back to reality quickly understanding that he didn't have to worry, her boyfriend was there.

"I'll see you later."

"Do you really have to go?" Katy asked tempting John to backtrack.

"Yea, lots to do. I'm leaving Sunday and I haven't even started to pack." he lied.

"Oh. Well, maybe I'll see you around tomorrow."

"Yea, for sure." John said and walked back out the door.

John smiled to himself as he walked back to the residence. An encounter with Katy like the one that just happened would have normally sent him into a tailspin. This time, however, he was cool and calm. Maybe it was the fact that he was leaving town in less than 48 hours or maybe he really had moved on. Whatever it was, John was happy to be on his way to the residence with a decent but not crazy buzz that would hardly even register the next morning.

Chapter 67

The residence was very quiet when John got back. Many of the students had already left for home. Many others were still out celebrating the end of term. A few were making last minute preparations to leave in the next day or two. In any event, the place was quiet, which John felt made the atmosphere a little creepy.

No one was left on John's floor. The hall lights were out with the dim glow from the transom over John's door. He unlocked the door and went inside. It was now nearing mid-night. John brushed his teeth, got out of his clothes and climbed into bed. He thought about what he still needed to get done tomorrow before leaving. He replayed the encounter with Katy in his head, but this time, he only did it once instead of over and over. He smiled again at the thought of the encounter.

Soon, he was sound asleep.

Sometime later, after John had fallen into a deep sleep, a sound entered his consciousness. He recognized the noise his doorknob made as it turned past the latch. At first, he couldn't clear his head enough to put the noise together with the reality that he was in bed and it was still dark out. He wondered if he had remembered to lock his door. About half the time, he simply left it unlocked anyway. This time, he couldn't recall. Before he had time to consider it further, someone had come inside and closed the door. John wondered in that moment if someone was drunk and stumbled into his room by mistake. He briefly considered the possibility that it might be a prowler but who would rob a student room in a secured residence hall. Maybe it was Tony playing some half-assed joke. As all of these things raced through his mind, he also considered the idea that he was dreaming, or hallucinating, or both. He hadn't drank that much earlier but maybe there was some kind of detox going on in his body that was playing tricks on his mind.

He didn't have time to sort out the right answer. Even though his room was mostly dark, there was enough light coming in from the hall for John to make out a silhouette. The form was definitely female. The shape was perfect with the light highlighting curly long hair, round, full breasts and sensual curvy hips. The legs were mostly in shadow but they appeared to go on for a long way.

The figure approached and was now standing over John at the side of the bed. The light now shone in such a way that John could just see the chin and full red lips of the person who had snuck into his unlocked room. The intruder put her index finger up to her pursed lips indicating her desire for John to be quiet. John, now fully awake and becoming aroused by the thought of what might be coming, just stared and kept quiet as demanded, he watched as the figure slowly undid the buttons on her blouse revealing a dark lacy bra. Next, the person unbuckled her pants and unzipped the fly of what appeared to be jeans. With a wiggle of her hips, her pants fell around her ankles leaving just her g-string panties and lacy bra. Finally, her bra was gone with a quick one-handed twist of her hand. The dim light sensually outlined her perfect natural breasts. John could not take his eyes off of her. He was now fully aroused and while he was thoroughly enjoying the little strip tease; he now needed her to get into the bed. He didn't have to wait long, the g-string came off as quickly as the bra and soon the figure was on top of John straddling him with her naked, perfect body.

"Ka…" John started to say but was cut off with a sharp

"Shhhh. No talking, no names, just tonight." The girl whispered.

John listened, trying for that second to confirm that it was her. He was not exactly sure but the passion overtook him and for the next two hours, he just went with it.

The sun was up and broke through the cracks above and below the shades covering John's windows. He lay naked under his sheet with his pillow over his head. As soon as he became aware of the sunlight, he shot up and out of bed. He was alone. He looked around for clues to confirm what happened last night was real. There was virtually no sign of Katy or anyone else for that matter. John began to wonder if he had been dreaming. He was in a state of shock but he knew, in his heart, that what he experienced was completely real. After all of the anticipation, frustration, and disappointments over lost opportunities, he had finally been with Katy. It was well worth the wait for John. He couldn't claim to be the most experienced guy of his age group but he was no slouch either. What he experienced last night, however, was like no other time he had ever had.

For what felt like a long time, John sat on the side of his bed looking out the window to the street below. Saturday traffic was light and few people were walking down Merrion Row. The sun was bright and warm, giving John a sense of well-being. He wasn't hung over but was still a bit tired from his middle of the night encounter. While he sat, he contemplated his future. He even reviewed the life outline he had made the day before, and tried to determine if last night's experience changed anything. Eventually, he decided it had not. He wouldn't pursue Katy and would not even try to see her again before leaving the next day.

Eventually, he got showered and dressed. He walked down the steps and into the front hall of the residence. The place was still fairly quiet in spite of the fact that it was a moving out day for most of the residents. John stepped through the old wooden doors in the front of the residence and out onto the cobble stone steps.

"Hey stranger."

It was Emily smiling and waving. Her dark brown curly hair framed her pretty face. John noticed how good she looked and for the first time, appreciated her tight body and long legs. John smiled back but could not hide the look of confusion that started to overtake his face. He felt his lips form the words "fuck me" but did not say it out loud. Emily walked over to him looking almost through him.

"Nancy said she thought she heard noises coming from your room last night. Everything ok?" John couldn't speak for a minute. He had not clearly seen who was in the room with him last night but thought for sure it was Katy. Now, something or someone was trying to play tricks on him. Could it have been Emily? Or Nancy? It couldn't have been, they were all friends but he never noticed chemistry.

"Everything is fine, great. I guess I was just restless."

"Well, hopefully tonight will be more peaceful. After all, us girls are flying out later this afternoon so we won't be around to bug you."

John smiled. He decided then and there that it did not matter if it was Katy, Emily, or Nancy, or even someone else. This part of his life was over and he was anxious for the next part to begin.

John's experience in Ireland had changed him even more profoundly than his overall experience at Cornell. The people, pubs, culture and pure history made John truly know and understand that there was a very real world outside of his own. He had never felt more at home and more alone at the same time. The six weeks in Dublin strengthened John's resolve to follow his heart and realize his destiny.

Chapter 68

John sat in the Clock Tower Pub just outside of Duty-Free in Dublin International Airport. He checked in, checked his bags, several more now than when he arrived, and made his way through security. He wondered if having a drink so early in the day with several hours of travel ahead of him was a good, idea but after six weeks of near alcoholic level drinking, he didn't have to think about it for too long.

He found a high top towards the end of the bar that two women drinking tea had just vacated. He pushed their cups and pots to the side and made a little room in front of where he sat. Looking around, he was amazed at the number of people drinking pints and glasses of wine this early. He figured it was just part of traveling and the fact that when people traveled, they didn't follow the same rules as when they are at home.

After a few minutes, a bartender came out from behind the bar and walked over to John. The young man looked haggard. His eyes were bloodshot and glazed. His skin looked almost the shade of skim milk. His clothes looked as if he'd slept in them the night before. That is, of course, if he made it to bed at all.

John gave the approaching bartender a knowing look. John had been in the same condition more often over the past weeks than he'd care to remember. The thought brought a smile to John's lips, which he tried to stifle. He didn't want the unfortunate bartender to think he was laughing at him or his apparent hung-over condition.

"What can I getcha?" the barman managed without sounding the least bit hospitable.

"Pint of Guinness." John answered sounding very comfortable with the delivery of his order. He must have said that phrase a thousand times since he arrived and heard it said many more. The words sounded good coming out of his mouth. At first, he was not sure why but then it struck him that he felt at home. For the first time since he left the States, he felt perfectly comfortable in Ireland. His comfort resulted from confidence along with familiarity. Most importantly, and to John, most surprisingly, was a real feeling of growth, or accomplishment, or something he couldn't easily define.

The bartender made his way back to the table with John's pint. The dark black stout with the creamy white head looked like a work of art in its tulip glass. John actually felt his mouth begin to water.

"Now" the bartender said putting the pint down on the beer mat he had left when he first took the order.

"Cheers."

The barman nodded and trod away.

John contemplated the pint in front of him. He lifted the glass and breathed in the unmistakable aroma of the stout. This was an aroma John could smell in Dublin, particularly when near

St. James' Gate, whenever the wind was blowing in the right direction. Nostalgia suddenly overtook John who found himself already missing Dublin and his friends. He also revisited Katy in his mind and his feelings for her were shifting from lust to something else. Again, John struggled with the right description of the way he felt sitting in that airport bar on the day of his departure.

The pint was quickly gone. John savored every sip imagining the pints back home surely wouldn't be the same. He let the stout settle in his stomach leaving a warm and soothing feeling. As John waited for the bartender to bring him another, he tried to figure out his emotions and sensations. The noise and chatter of the pub insulated him and his thoughts. He considered the scenario back in the Newark airport drinking light beer in the Garden State Diner. How he had changed since then. It actually felt like he was remembering a different person.

In his recollections, he saw himself as someone less mature, less worldly, and a lot more ignorant to the ways of the world. Now, with his second pint nearly gone, the word to describe how he felt suddenly came to him.

"I feel clear." he said to himself.

Clear was the right word to summarize the effect his time in Ireland made him feel. His thoughts of his previous self conjured up a guy who was confused and conflicted. Now, he was clear and confident to move forward. In a way, the feeling was a little disconcerting. He became used to living in a semi state of confusion. Now, he felt he knew the way forward in his personal and professional life. As he finished off the pint and began to contemplate a third, he realized that Ireland, and the people he got to know there, really did give him the clarity that he was missing from his life. Of course, it was not until he started to become removed from the experience that he could start to feel the effects.

He only hoped the effects he was now coming to grips with would continue and not fade away. Something told him, however, that the change was not fleeting and he was now a different person.

Chapter 69

"Continental flight CO25 is now boarding. All passengers should proceed to US Customs located at Gate 4. Boarding will begin soon. Thank you." the robot-sounding voice announced through the public address system.

John heard it but did not make any movement to indicate he understood the message. In reality, John was fully aware the announcement was for his flight but he was resisting the idea. He was contemplating his time in Ireland and found himself tempted to turn away from the departure gates, run back through the terminal and jump on the 61A bus back to Dublin City Center. The impulse, while in no way plausible, was very strong. John forced himself out of his fantasy and began to collect his carry-on bags. While he wanted to stay, he knew it was time for him to get on with his life, his real life.

Chapter 70

It was two full days back in the States before John made his way down to the Hound. It wasn't that he didn't want to stop by, but ever since landing in Newark, he had found himself in a little bit of a funk. On one level, John was energized and enthusiastic about his future. He would finish the summer working with Old Joe and then return to his last year of college. After that, he would go to work full time in the Hound and begin the new era as John Frawley, proprietor. There were no doubts in his mind about this plan. Yet, he couldn't shake the feeling of being down or dull. He missed his new friends. He was surprised how much he wanted to see them. He even found himself thinking of Katy. He desperately wanted to call her. However, for the life of him, he could not fathom exactly why he wanted to get in touch. Most of the time he knew her, he felt he had a crush or infatuation. Now, it felt more like love. But how could he be in love with her. Hell, he wasn't even sure if his encounter on the last night in Dublin was actually with her. Regardless, John was out of sorts and having trouble leaving the past behind.

Finally, after sitting around moping for a couple of days, John decided to stop into the Flying Hound and visit Old Joe. Even Mack Sr. encouraged him to get out of the house and do something. His father and mother noticed something was a little off with John from the time they picked him up from the airport.

At first, they had just assumed it was jetlag or something, but their concern grew when John made no effort to visit his grandfather or even leave the house. John's mother tried to ask him once what the matter was but John just brushed off the questions and claimed he was just tired. How could he answer when he himself didn't know what was wrong with him?

John walked into the Hound expecting to see Old Joe sitting at his usual table. Instead, he ran right into Pat standing at the bar polishing glasses.

"Well fuck me, look what the cat dragged in. I heard you were back but when you didn't stop by, I just figured you gave up the booze." Pat said putting his bar towel down and extending his hand to John.

"I'm just settling in a little, trying to get back on US time." John said trying to reduce the chance for speculation. "How are thing here?"

"Good. Good. You know, the summer is just OK but everything is fine. Old Joe is around here somewhere. I just saw him a minute ago." Pat responded. "So how was it? Did you get any Irish pussy?"

John tried hard not to blush. It is hard to bullshit a seasoned bartender. After all, they've heard enough to know when it's true and when isn't.

"I don't know," John started, "you know, I mean, it was a lot of fun."

"You dog. You so got laid! Who was the lucky lass?"

"I actually don't know."

"Awesome!" Pat interrupted, assuming John was sleeping around with one-nighters. John decided not to refute Pat's assumption and played it off as naturally as he could. In truth, John was not actually embarrassed about his mystery night before leaving Dublin but was actually a little protective of Katy. He didn't want her to be just someone he banged (if he had banged her) and talk about it in a bar.

John's reaction to his own protectiveness caught him by surprise. All along, he told himself Katy was just an innocent distraction, that she wasn't an obsession, and that he certainly was not in love with her. However, the more he tried to tell himself this, the more he found they didn't feel genuine. As much as he wanted to deny it, there was something more to Katy and him than he wanted to admit and now that he was away from her, he started to recognize this fact.

Chapter 71

Old Joe wasn't in the bar. John looked around after speaking with Pat for a while but his grandfather was out of sight. He made the rounds and said hello to everyone recounting his time in Ireland at least ten times. Finally, John spotted Old Joe coming out of the storage closet in the back of the dining room.

Old Joe had aged. John was immediately struck by how his grandfather had changed in the month and a half since he last saw him. For the first time, John recognized that his grandfather was nearing the end of his life. In that moment, John's resolve to take over the business was suddenly strengthened. He immediately found the inspiration to get to work and start making the transition to the Hound's new leader.

Chapter 72

A year later, after graduation, John went to work full time for his grandfather in the Hound. His grandfather gave him the slightly archaic title of Duty Manager that basically meant he was in charge of the place whenever he wasn't there. While John had worked every job in the bar, he had never really had, or cared for, an official title. However, Old Joe wanted to make this appointment official and even told his grandson to get business cards made up.

Mack Sr. was less enthusiastic. He was at least, supportive enough not to object for the time being. John remembered his Dad's words, "Outside of getting someone knocked up, you really can't make a mistake at this point in your career." this was said with the understanding that it could not go on indefinitely.

John took his new job seriously. He knew the Hound might someday be his so he put all of his education and experience into making it the best place possible. To Old Joe's credit, he let John run the business. Of course, Joe would provide experience and insight but he knew it was time to start handing off the reigns and let the new generation find their way.

The first six months as duty manager flew by. John was busy trying to apply what he learned at Cornell and what he experienced in Ireland to the Hound. Old Joe guided him, but generally let him find his own way. Even though John was not new to the Hound, he was new at being in charge. During those first six months, John was very appreciative to have Old Joe there to catch him if he fell.

John's six month on-the-job training came to an abrupt end early one morning in mid November. John had arrived at the Hound by 10 AM as he was in the habit of doing. The phone in his basement office was already ringing when he made it to the bottom of the stairs and unlocked his office door. John rushed to the phone and grabbed it off its cradle.

"Hello?"

"John, it's me."

John heard and instantly recognized Mack Sr.'s voice. He also recognized that there was something wrong by the way his father was speaking.

"Old Joe is gone. He died early this morning. Your mother and I are just leaving the emergency room but he died before we ever got here. He called us from his house saying he didn't feel well. He said he was going to the hospital. We called an ambulance for him and went to the hospital to meet him but…" Mack Sr.'s voice cracked a little and trailed off.

John was in shock. Old Joe was fine when he went home yesterday evening. John said goodnight as he had most nights not considering these would be his last words to his grandfather, mentor and idol.

After his dad hung up, John sat at his desk and stared at his blank computer screen. He didn't cry or even get choked up. He knew Old Joe would be happy that he didn't endure a long illness or become a burden to anyone. Still, John could not believe he was gone.

The next six months went by as quickly as the previous six. Following Old Joe's funeral, John got right back to work. This time, he was solely in charge. He took on the role with a renewed commitment to run the Hound and make Old Joe proud. He was now free to use his own experience and expertise to make his mark on the Hound, just as his ancestors had done before him.

Epilogue

"Hey John!" Clem yelled from the top of the steps "Can you bring up a bottle of sherry when you come up? I want to do Steak Dianne as a special tonight."

"Be right up" John croaked, his voice clammy after sitting quiet for so long.

It had been over three years since Old Joe died and left the Hound to John. As he sat thinking about what his dad had said he started to think back over the last three years. He thought of Ireland and the experience that profoundly changed him. He thought of those friends from the tour. Tony was in touch and kept him up to date on all of the gossip and happenings from the group. Tony and Rachel had their second child last month.

Charley and Becky never got back together. Charley was running the family business and Becky was working on her PhD.

Mike was coaching hockey back at his old high school.

Jeff was still with Carol but they hadn't yet made it official.

Emily and Nancy ended up moving into an apartment together in Los Angeles. Nancy makes a living doing infomercials while Emily runs a bookstore and coffee shop.

Outside of Tony and Rachel, John didn't keep in touch directly with the rest of the crew. However, in a way, he still felt as close to them as he had the day he left Dublin. They were part of the past that made him who he is today.

John thought of Katy and that last night in Dublin. After all of this time, he still wasn't sure what really happened. At times, he thought he had figured it out, but eventually he always came to the realization that he'd never really know.

Reflecting on his time in Dublin, his six months with Old Joe after college, and his life at the Flying Hound, John knew he was where he was supposed to be. He had no real doubts that the Hound was his fate.

John climbed the stairs from his basement lair. He remembered the sherry but forgot the doubt his dad had put in his head a while before. While John could occasionally think about other jobs or another life, he rarely considered it for long. After Old Joe and Ireland, he felt right about running the Hound. He had no worry about the future or his aging college degree. He was happy and focused.

Acknowledgments

To all of my former students, colleagues, faculty members and business associates, thank you for serving as the primary inspiration for this story.

To all my family members, thank you for always believing and supporting me.

To Kelly, thank you for pushing, prodding, reading and editing. You encouraged me to do it, and you didn't stop until it was finished.

To Mom, Suzanne and Joanne, thanks for combing through the raw manuscript and providing all your feedback.

To Stephen King. Without "On Writing" I would have never gotten going.

To Ireland, you were the greatest influence of all.

Finally to my dog Cheeca, the original Flying Hound.

Made in the USA
Charleston, SC
10 February 2012